WILLIAM SHAKESPEARE was born in Stratford-upon-Avon in April, 1564, and his birth is traditionally celebrated on April 23. The facts of his life, known from surviving documents, are sparse. He was one of eight children born to John Shakespeare, a merchant of some standing in his community. William probably went to the King's New School in Stratford, but he had no university education. In November 1582, at the age of eighteen, he married Anne Hathaway, eight years his senior, who was pregnant with their first child, Susanna. She was born on May 26, 1583. Twins, a boy, Hamnet (who would die at age eleven), and a girl, Judith, were born in 1585. By 1592 Shakespeare had gone to London, working as an actor and already known as a playwright. A rival dramatist, Robert Greene, referred to him as "an upstart crow, beautified with our feathers." Shakespeare became a principal shareholder and playwright of the successful acting troupe the Lord Chamberlain's men (later, under James I, called the King's men). In 1599 the Lord Chamberlain's men built and occupied the Globe Theatre in Southwark near the Thames River. Here many of Shakespeare's plays were performed by the most famous actors of his time, including Richard Burbage, Will Kempe, and Robert Armin. In addition to his 37 plays, Shakespeare had a hand in others, including *Sir Thomas More* and *The Two Noble Kinsmen*, and he wrote poems, including *Venus and Adonis* and *The Rape of Lucrece*. His 154 sonnets were published, probably without his authorization, in 1609. In 1611 or 1612 he gave up his lodgings in London and devoted more and more of his time to retirement in Stratford, though he continued writing such plays as *The Tempest* and *Henry VIII* until about 1613. He died on April 23, 1616, and was buried in Holy Trinity Church, Stratford. No collected edition of his plays was published during his lifetime, but in 1623 two members of his acting company, John Heminges and Henry Condell, published the great collection now called the First Folio.

**Bantam Shakespeare
The Complete Works—29 Volumes
Edited by David Bevington
With forewords by Joseph Papp on the plays**

The Poems: Venus and Adonis, The Rape of Lucrece, The
Phoenix and Turtle, A Lover's Complaint,
the Sonnets

Antony and Cleopatra	*The Merchant of Venice*
As You Like It	*A Midsummer Night's Dream*
The Comedy of Errors	*Much Ado about Nothing*
Hamlet	*Othello*
Henry IV, Part One	*Richard II*
Henry IV, Part Two	*Richard III*
Henry V	*Romeo and Juliet*
Julius Caesar	*The Taming of the Shrew*
King Lear	*The Tempest*
Macbeth	*Twelfth Night*

Together in one volume:

Henry VI, Parts One, Two, and Three
King John and Henry VIII
*Measure for Measure, All's Well that Ends Well, and
    Troilus and Cressida*
Three Early Comedies: Love's Labor's Lost, The Two
                        Gentlemen of Verona, The Merry
                        Wives of Windsor
Three Classical Tragedies: Titus Andronicus, Timon
                        of Athens, Coriolanus
The Late Romances: Pericles, Cymbeline, The Winter's
                        Tale, The Tempest

Two collections:

Four Comedies: The Taming of the Shrew, A Midsummer
                Night's Dream, The Merchant of Venice,
                Twelfth Night
Four Tragedies: Hamlet, Othello, King Lear, Macbeth

William Shakespeare

ANTONY AND CLEOPATRA

Edited by
David Bevington

David Scott Kastan,
James Hammersmith,
and Robert Kean Turner,
Associate Editors

With a Foreword by
Joseph Papp

BANTAM BOOKS

NEW YORK · TORONTO · LONDON · SYDNEY · AUCKLAND

ANTONY AND CLEOPATRA

*A Bantam Book / published by arrangement
with Scott, Foresman and Company*

PUBLISHING HISTORY

*Scott, Foresman edition published : January 1980
Bantam edition, with newly edited text and substantially revised,
edited, and amplified notes, introductions, and other
materials, published / February 1988
Valuable advice on staging matters has been
provided by Richard Hosley.
Collations checked by Eric Rasmussen.
Additional editorial assistance by Claire McEachern.*

ISBN 0-553-21289-3

Published simultaneously in the United States and Canada

PRINTED IN THE UNITED STATES OF AMERICA

O   0 9 8 7 6

Contents

Foreword

It's hard to imagine, but Shakespeare wrote all of his plays with a quill pen, a goose feather whose hard end had to be sharpened frequently. How many times did he scrape the dull end to a point with his knife, dip it into the inkwell, and bring up, dripping wet, those wonderful words and ideas that are known all over the world?

In the age of word processors, typewriters, and ballpoint pens, we have almost forgotten the meaning of the word "blot." Yet when I went to school, in the 1930s, my classmates and I knew all too well what an inkblot from the metal-tipped pens we used would do to a nice clean page of a test paper, and we groaned whenever a splotch fell across the sheet. Most of us finished the school day with ink-stained fingers; those who were less careful also went home with ink-stained shirts, which were almost impossible to get clean.

When I think about how long it took me to write the simplest composition with a metal-tipped pen and ink, I can only marvel at how many plays Shakespeare scratched out with his goose-feather quill pen, year after year. Imagine him walking down one of the narrow cobblestoned streets of London, or perhaps drinking a pint of beer in his local alehouse. Suddenly his mind catches fire with an idea, or a sentence, or a previously elusive phrase. He is burning with impatience to write it down—but because he doesn't have a ballpoint pen or even a pencil in his pocket, he has to keep the idea in his head until he can get to his quill and parchment.

He rushes back to his lodgings on Silver Street, ignoring the vendors hawking brooms, the coaches clattering by, the piteous wails of beggars and prisoners. Bounding up the stairs, he snatches his quill and starts to write furiously, not even bothering to light a candle against the dusk. "To be, or not to be," he scrawls, "that is the—." But the quill point has gone dull, the letters have fattened out illegibly, and in the middle of writing one of the most famous passages in the history of dramatic literature, Shakespeare has to stop to sharpen his pen.

Taking a deep breath, he lights a candle now that it's dark, sits down, and begins again. By the time the candle has burned out and the noisy apprentices of his French Huguenot landlord have quieted down, Shakespeare has finished Act 3 of *Hamlet* with scarcely a blot.

Early the next morning, he hurries through the fog of a London summer morning to the rooms of his colleague Richard Burbage, the actor for whom the role of Hamlet is being written. He finds Burbage asleep and snoring loudly, sprawled across his straw mattress. Not only had the actor performed in *Henry V* the previous afternoon, but he had then gone out carousing all night with some friends who had come to the performance.

Shakespeare shakes his friend awake, until, bleary-eyed, Burbage sits up in his bed. "Dammit, Will," he grumbles, "can't you let an honest man sleep?" But the playwright, his eyes shining and the words tumbling out of his mouth, says, "Shut up and listen—tell me what you think of *this*!"

He begins to read to the still half-asleep Burbage, pacing around the room as he speaks. ". . . Whether 'tis nobler in the mind to suffer the slings and arrows of outrageous fortune—"

Burbage interrupts, suddenly wide awake, "That's excellent, very good, 'the slings and arrows of outrageous fortune,' yes, I think it will work quite well. . . ." He takes the parchment from Shakespeare and murmurs the lines to himself, slowly at first but with growing excitement.

The sun is just coming up, and the words of one of Shakespeare's most famous soliloquies are being uttered for the first time by the first actor ever to bring Hamlet to life. It must have been an exhilarating moment.

Shakespeare wrote most of his plays to be performed live by the actor Richard Burbage and the rest of the Lord Chamberlain's men (later the King's men). Today, however, our first encounter with the plays is usually in the form of the printed word. And there is no question that reading Shakespeare for the first time isn't easy. His plays aren't comic books or magazines or the dime-store detective novels I read when I was young. A lot of his sentences are complex. Many of his words are no longer used in our everyday speech. His profound thoughts are often condensed into poetry, which is not as straightforward as prose.

Yet when you hear the words spoken aloud, a lot of the language may strike you as unexpectedly modern. For Shakespeare's plays, like any dramatic work, weren't really meant to be read; they were meant to be spoken, seen, and performed. It's amazing how lines that are so troublesome in print can flow so naturally and easily when spoken.

I think it was precisely this music that first fascinated me. When I was growing up, Shakespeare was a stranger to me. I had no particular interest in him, for I was from a different cultural tradition. It never occurred to me that his plays might be more than just something to "get through" in school, like science or math or the physical education requirement we had to fulfill. My passions then were movies, radio, and vaudeville—certainly not Elizabethan drama.

I was, however, fascinated by words and language. Because I grew up in a home where Yiddish was spoken, and English was only a second language, I was acutely sensitive to the musical sounds of different languages and had an ear for lilt and cadence and rhythm in the spoken word. And so I loved reciting poems and speeches even as a very young child. In first grade I learned lots of short nature verses—"Who has seen the wind?," one of them began. My first foray into drama was playing the role of Scrooge in Charles Dickens's *A Christmas Carol* when I was eight years old. I liked summoning all the scorn and coldness I possessed and putting them into the words, "Bah, humbug!"

From there I moved on to longer and more famous poems and other works by writers of the 1930s. Then, in junior high school, I made my first acquaintance with Shakespeare through his play *Julius Caesar*. Our teacher, Miss McKay, assigned the class a passage to memorize from the opening scene of the play, the one that begins "Wherefore rejoice? What conquest brings he home?" The passage seemed so wonderfully theatrical and alive to me, and the experience of memorizing and reciting it was so much fun, that I went on to memorize another speech from the play on my own.

I chose Mark Antony's address to the crowd in Act 3,

scene 2, which struck me then as incredibly high drama. Even today, when I speak the words, I feel the same thrill I did that first time. There is the strong and athletic Antony descending from the raised pulpit where he has been speaking, right into the midst of a crowded Roman square. Holding the torn and bloody cloak of the murdered Julius Caesar in his hand, he begins to speak to the people of Rome:

> If you have tears, prepare to shed them now.
> You all do know this mantle. I remember
> The first time ever Caesar put it on;
> 'Twas on a summer's evening in his tent,
> That day he overcame the Nervii.
> Look, in this place ran Cassius' dagger through.
> See what a rent the envious Casca made.
> Through this the well-belovèd Brutus stabbed,
> And as he plucked his cursèd steel away,
> Mark how the blood of Caesar followed it,
> As rushing out of doors to be resolved
> If Brutus so unkindly knocked or no;
> For Brutus, as you know, was Caesar's angel.
> Judge, O you gods, how dearly Caesar loved him!
> This was the most unkindest cut of all . . .

I'm not sure now that I even knew Shakespeare had written a lot of other plays, or that he was considered "timeless," "universal," or "classic"—but I knew a good speech when I heard one, and I found the splendid rhythms of Antony's rhetoric as exciting as anything I'd ever come across.

Fifty years later, I still feel that way. Hearing good actors speak Shakespeare gracefully and naturally is a wonderful experience, unlike any other I know. There's a satisfying fullness to the spoken word that the printed page just can't convey. This is why seeing the plays of Shakespeare performed live in a theater is the best way to appreciate them. If you can't do that, listening to sound recordings or watching film versions of the plays is the next best thing.

But if you do start with the printed word, use the play as a script. Be an actor yourself and say the lines out loud. Don't worry too much at first about words you don't immediately understand. Look them up in the footnotes or a dictionary, but don't spend too much time on this. It is more profitable (and fun) to get the sense of a passage and sing it out. Speak naturally, almost as if you were talking to a friend, but be sure to enunciate the words properly. You'll be surprised at how much you understand simply by speaking the speech "trippingly on the tongue," as Hamlet advises the Players.

You might start, as I once did, with a speech from *Julius Caesar*, in which the tribune (city official) Marullus scolds the commoners for transferring their loyalties so quickly from the defeated and murdered general Pompey to the newly victorious Julius Caesar:

> Wherefore rejoice? What conquest brings he home?
> What tributaries follow him to Rome
> To grace in captive bonds his chariot wheels?
> You blocks, you stones, you worse than senseless
>   things!
> O you hard hearts, you cruel men of Rome,
> Knew you not Pompey? Many a time and oft
> Have you climbed up to walls and battlements,
> To towers and windows, yea, to chimney tops,
> Your infants in your arms, and there have sat
> The livelong day, with patient expectation,
> To see great Pompey pass the streets of Rome.

With the exception of one or two words like "wherefore" (which means "why," not "where"), "tributaries" (which means "captives"), and "patient expectation" (which means patient waiting), the meaning and emotions of this speech can be easily understood.

From here you can go on to dialogues or other more challenging scenes. Although you may stumble over unaccustomed phrases or unfamiliar words at first, and even fall flat when you're crossing some particularly rocky passages, pick yourself up and stay with it. Remember that it takes time to feel at home with anything new. Soon you'll come to recognize Shakespeare's unique sense of humor and way of saying things as easily as you recognize a friend's laughter.

And then it will just be a matter of choosing which one of Shakespeare's plays you want to tackle next. As a true fan of his, you'll find that you're constantly learning from his plays. It's a journey of discovery that you can continue for the rest of your life. For no matter how many times you read or see a particular play, there will always be something new there that you won't have noticed before.

Why do so many thousands of people get hooked on Shakespeare and develop a habit that lasts a lifetime? What can he really say to us today, in a world filled with inventions and problems he never could have imagined? And how do you get past his special language and difficult sentence structure to understand him?

The best way to answer these questions is to go see a live production. You might not know much about Shakespeare, or much about the theater, but when you watch actors performing one of his plays on the stage, it will soon become clear to you why people get so excited about a playwright who lived hundreds of years ago.

For the story—what's happening in the play—is the most accessible part of Shakespeare. In *A Midsummer Night's Dream*, for example, you can immediately understand the situation: a girl is chasing a guy who's chasing a girl who's chasing another guy. No wonder *A Midsummer Night's Dream* is one of the most popular of Shakespeare's plays: it's about one of the world's most popular pastimes—falling in love.

But the course of true love never did run smooth, as the young suitor Lysander says. Often in Shakespeare's comedies the girl whom the guy loves doesn't love him back, or she loves him but he loves someone else. In *The Two Gentlemen of Verona*, Julia loves Proteus, Proteus loves Sylvia, and Sylvia loves Valentine, who is Proteus's best friend. In the end, of course, true love prevails, but not without lots of complications along the way.

For in all of his plays—comedies, histories, and tragedies—Shakespeare is showing you human nature. His characters act and react in the most extraordinary ways—and sometimes in the most incomprehensible ways. People are always trying to find motivations for what a character does. They ask, "Why does Iago want to destroy Othello?"

The answer, to me, is very simple—because that's the way Iago is. That's just his nature. Shakespeare doesn't explain his characters; he sets them in motion—and away they go. He doesn't worry about whether they're likable or not. He's interested in interesting people, and his most fascinating characters are those who are unpredictable. If you lean back in your chair early on in one of his plays, thinking you've figured out what Iago or Shylock (in *The Merchant of Venice*) is up to, don't be too sure—because that great judge of human nature, Shakespeare, will surprise you every time.

He is just as wily in the way he structures a play. In *Macbeth*, a comic scene is suddenly introduced just after the bloodiest and most treacherous slaughter imaginable, of a guest and king by his host and subject, when in comes a drunk porter who has to go to the bathroom. Shakespeare is tickling your emotions by bringing a stand-up comic on-stage right on the heels of a savage murder.

It has taken me thirty years to understand even some of these things, and so I'm not suggesting that Shakespeare is immediately understandable. I've gotten to know him not through theory but through practice, the practice of the *living* Shakespeare—the playwright of the theater.

Of course the plays are a great achievement of dramatic literature, and they should be studied and analyzed in schools and universities. But you must always remember, when reading all the words *about* the playwright and his plays, that *Shakespeare's* words came first and that in the end there is nothing greater than a single actor on the stage speaking the lines of Shakespeare.

Everything important that I know about Shakespeare comes from the practical business of producing and directing his plays in the theater. The task of classifying, criticizing, and editing Shakespeare's printed works I happily leave to others. For me, his plays really do live on the stage, not on the page. That is what he wrote them for and that is how they are best appreciated.

Although Shakespeare lived and wrote hundreds of years ago, his name rolls off my tongue as if he were my brother. As a producer and director, I feel that there is a professional relationship between us that spans the centuries. As a human being, I feel that Shakespeare has enriched my understanding of life immeasurably. I hope you'll let him do the same for you.

❖

Antony and Cleopatra is unquestionably Cleopatra's play. As an original, vital character, she's the female equivalent of Falstaff, whose comic personality dominates the *Henry IV* plays. Cleopatra knows every trick in the book. She's been around in her time; one of her earliest consorts, when she was a young girl, was Julius Caesar. By the time Antony comes into her life, she has developed a repertory of tactics designed to keep a man happy and drive him crazy at the same time. She's acquired an infallible technique for moving from haughtiness and indifference to tears and sulkiness in a matter of seconds.

Many years ago, the distinguished actress Colleen Dewhurst graced our stage as Cleopatra, a role she stamped with her own sparkling personality. Cleopatra was a woman she understood thoroughly. In one scene, when she asked a trembling messenger to describe her rival Octavia, Antony's wife, a slight arch of her imperious eyebrow was enough to set the poor guy quaking. Colleen, a woman with magnetic stage presence, was perfectly suited for the Cleopatra role.

In a way, Antony is the perfect target for Cleopatra. A soldier going through the pangs of middle age, trying to hold on to his waning strength and virility, a straitlaced Roman, he becomes deeply and irrevocably attached to this warm, exotic, sexual Egyptian woman and the luxurious culture of Egypt that surrounds her.

To contrast Antony's slow decline—one of his men calls him "The triple pillar of the world transformed / Into a strumpet's fool"—Shakespeare gives us the thin, white-lipped Octavius. We understand that the cold-blooded Octavius will ultimately triumph over the vulnerably passionate Antony. Octavius is a man whose personal needs and desires—if he has any—never interfere with his political goals. When thinking of him, I can't help but hear Falstaff faulting Prince John of Lancaster in *2 Henry IV* for the same flaw: "Good faith, this same young sober-blooded boy doth not love me, nor a man cannot make him laugh. But that's no marvel; he drinks no wine."

As the play progresses, we watch the aging couple attempting to carry on like frolicking teenagers. And yet underneath this cavorting we find a desperate clinging passion—they are holding on to each other for dear life.

My favorite line in the play belongs to Cleopatra, and it goes right to the heart of her emotional seesawing about her love for Antony. In Act 3, scene 13, the two of them are having an argument, and Antony bitterly accuses her of selling herself like a whore. "You have been a boggler ever," he cries at one point. Her simple yet ambiguous rejoinder later in the scene, "Not know me yet?" is a masterpiece of double entendre.

There's a lot of pain in this play; Antony suffers terribly as he helplessly watches himself slip away from everything that was once important in his life. And when his closest friend, Enobarbus, defects to the camp of Octavius, in Act 4, scene 6, Antony's remorse is great, but he is powerless to change his downhill course. The departure of Enobarbus is reminiscent of the departure of Lear's Fool, who also disappears halfway through the play, in the face of inevitable disaster. Though we never learn what happens to the Fool, in this play we watch Enobarbus die of a broken heart in the camp of Antony's greatest enemy.

Antony and Cleopatra, this tragic story of aging lovers, is a complex play to produce, because it jumps around so much between Egypt, Rome, Syria, Athens, sea battles, shipboards, military camps, and Cleopatra's monument. There have been periods in theatrical history when productions of *Antony and Cleopatra* were overwhelmed by the heaviness of literal scenery—which encumbered the dramatic flow of the play as Shakespeare wrote it—but happily this is out of fashion. Some years ago I directed a production of the play on a bare stage, with George C. Scott and Colleen Dewhurst, which proved once again that simple staging is the best approach to *Antony and Cleopatra*.

JOSEPH PAPP

JOSEPH PAPP GRATEFULLY ACKNOWLEDGES THE HELP OF ELIZABETH KIRKLAND IN PREPARING THIS FOREWORD.

Introduction

Shakespeare probably wrote *Antony and Cleopatra* in 1606 or 1607; it was registered for publication on May 20, 1608, and apparently influenced a revision of Samuel Daniel's *Cleopatra* that was published "newly altered" in 1607. *Antony and Cleopatra* was thus roughly contemporary with *King Lear* and *Macbeth*. Yet the contrast between those dark tragedies of evil and this Roman tragedy of love and political struggle is immense. Unlike *Macbeth*, with its taut focus on a murderer and his wife, *Antony and Cleopatra* moves back and forth across the Mediterranean in its epic survey of characters and events, bringing together the fates of Pompey, Octavius Caesar, Octavia, and Lepidus with those of the protagonists. *King Lear* gives proper names to fourteen characters, *Macbeth* to eighteen, *Antony and Cleopatra* to thirty-one. The Roman play requires no less than forty-two separate scenes, of which most occur in what modern editors label Acts 3 and 4—although no play is less suited to the classical rigors of five-act structure, and these divisions are not found in the reliable Folio text of 1623. Indeed, it is as though Shakespeare resolved at the height of his career to show that he could dispense entirely with the classical "rules," which had never taken serious hold of the English popular stage in any case. The flouting of the unities is so extreme that John Dryden, in his *All for Love, or The World Well Lost* (1678), undertook not so much to revise Shakespeare as to start afresh on the same subject. Dryden's play is restricted to the last few hours of the protagonists' lives, at Cleopatra's tomb in Alexandria, with a severely limited cast of characters and much of the narrative revealed through recollection. Although a substantial achievement in its own right, *All for Love* surely reveals that Shakespeare knew what he was doing, for Dryden has excised a good deal of the panorama, the excitement, the "infinite variety" (2.2.246).

Shakespeare departs also from the somber tone of his tragedies of evil. He creates instead a world that bears affinities both to the other Roman plays, characterized by ambivalent political conflict, and to the comedies and late romances, characterized by imaginative reconciliation. As protagonists, Antony and Cleopatra lack tragic stature, or so it first appears: she is a tawny gypsy temptress and he a "strumpet's fool," a once-great general now bound in "strong Egyptian fetters" and lost in "dotage" (1.1.13; 1.2.122–123). Several scenes, especially those set in Egypt, are comic and delightfully bawdy: Charmian learning her fortune from the soothsayer, Cleopatra practicing her charms in vain to keep Antony from leaving Egypt or raunchily daydreaming of being Antony's horse "to bear the weight of Antony" (1.5.22), Cleopatra flying into a magnificent rage at the news of Antony's marriage to Octavia and then consoling herself with catty reflections on Octavia's reported low voice and shortness of stature ("I think so, Charmian. Dull of tongue, and dwarfish," 3.3.17). In its comic texture the play somewhat resembles *Romeo and Juliet,* an earlier play about a younger pair of lovers, although there the bawdry is used chiefly to characterize the lovers' companions and confidants, whereas in *Antony and Cleopatra* it is central to our vision of Cleopatra especially. In any case, the later play is a tragedy about lovers who, despite their quarrels and uncertainties and betrayals of self, are reconciled in a vision of the greatness of their love. In its depiction of two contrasting worlds, also, *Antony and Cleopatra* recalls the movement of several earlier comedies from the realistic world of political conniving to a dreamworld of the romantic and the unexpected. We can endorse neither world fully in *Antony and Cleopatra,* and accordingly the vision of life presented is often ambivalent and ironic as much as it is tragic. The contrast of values separating Egypt and Rome underscores the paradox of man's quest for seemingly irreconcilable goals. The ending is neither a triumph nor a defeat for the lovers, but something of both. If Antony and Cleopatra seem in one way too small to be tragic protagonists, in another they seem too large, creating imaginative visions of themselves and their union that escape the realm of tragedy altogether. Our interest is less on how the protagonists come to understand some meaningful relationship between their character and the fate required of them by a tragic universe, than on the almost comic way in which the absurdity of worldly striving, both Egyptian and Roman, is transfigured in the world of the imagination.

The Roman point of view opens the play, and never entirely loses its force. At first it may seem superior to that of Egypt. Demetrius and Philo, who invite us to view the play's first encounter between Antony and Cleopatra (1.1) from the perspective of the professional Roman soldier, lament the decline of Antony into Circean enslavement. Their tragic concept is of the Fall of Princes, all the more soberly edifying because of the height from which Antony has toppled. "You shall see in him / The triple pillar of the world transformed / Into a strumpet's fool" (1.1.11–13). Egypt is enchanting but clearly enervating—a bizarre assemblage of soothsayers, eunuchs, and waiting-gentlewomen who wish to be "married to three kings in a forenoon and widow them all" (1.2.28–29). Their mirth is all bawdry, tinged with practices such as transvestism that Roman custom views as licentious. The prevailing images are of procreation in various shapes, sleep (mandragora, Lethe), the oriental opulence of Cleopatra's barge (a golden poop, purple sails, silver oars, divers-colored fans), Epicurean feasting, and drinking. As Enobarbus says, "Mine, and most of our fortunes tonight, shall be—drunk to bed" (1.2.47–48).

Antony, for all his reckless defiance of Rome, agrees in his more reflective moments with what Demetrius and Philo have said. "A Roman thought hath struck him," Cleopatra observantly remarks, and Antony has indeed determined that "I must from this enchanting queen break off" (1.2.88, 135). His later return to Cleopatra is at least in part a surrender, a betrayal of his marriage vows to Octavia and his political assurances to Caesar. In the ensuing battles, Antony submits himself dangerously to Cleopatra's governance, and this inversion of dominance in sexual roles is emblematic of a deeper disorder within Antony. As Enobarbus concludes bitterly, Antony "would make his will / Lord of his reason," and so has subverted his "judgment" (3.13.3–4, 37) to passion.

From the beginning, Cleopatra has sought dominance over Antony in the war of the sexes. When Antony first came to her on the River Cydnus, we learn, he was so overcome in all his senses that he was "barbered ten times o'er"

(2.2.234). Cleopatra boasts that she angled for Antony on that occasion, catching him the way fishermen "betray" fish, and that when she had "drunk him to his bed" she "put my tires and mantles on him, whilst / I wore his sword Philippan" (2.5.10–23). Caesar, affronted by such transvestite debauchery, charges that Antony "is not more manlike / Than Cleopatra, nor the queen of Ptolemy / More womanly than he" (1.4.5–7). During the battle scenes, Antony's followers complain that "Photinus, an eunuch" (probably Mardian), and Cleopatra's maids manage the war: "So our leader's led, / And we are women's men" (3.7.14–15, 70–71). Antony confesses too late that they were right. He becomes a "doting mallard," one whose heart is "tied by the strings" to Cleopatra's rudder when her ships retreat in their first naval engagement (3.10.20, 3.11.56). In the mythic images used to raise their relationship to heroic proportions, Antony is like Mars to Cleopatra's Venus (1.5.19), both in a positive and negative sense. The image has positive connotations of the way in which, as Milton puts it, the "two great sexes animate the world," the masterful soldier and his attractive consort complementing each other in a right relationship of martial prowess and beauty, bravery and love, reason and will; but to the Renaissance the myth of Mars and Venus could also be read in a destructive sense as well, as an adulterous relationship in which reason is subverted to appetite. In another mythic comparison, Antony is like Hercules, not in his prime but with the shirt of Nessus on his back—a poisoned shirt given Hercules by his wife in a mistaken hope of thereby assuring his love for her (4.12.43). Antony's soldiers understandably believe that the god Hercules has deserted his reputed descendant and one-time champion (4.3.21–22).

Despite Antony's shameful violation of manhood, honor, attention to duty, self-knowledge, and all that Rome stands for, however, the end of his story is anything but a one-sided endorsement for the Roman point of view. The actual Rome, disfigured by political conniving, falls far short of the ideal. Antony has a point when he protests that "Kingdoms are clay" (1.1.37). Alliances are unstable and are governed by mere political expediency. At first, Antony's wife Fulvia and his brother Lucius have fought each other until forced to unite against the greater threat of Octavius Caesar. Similarly, Antony and Caesar come together only because Pompey has become dangerously powerful at sea and has won the favor of the fickle mob, "Our slippery people" (1.2.192). This détente is not meant to last. As Enobarbus bluntly puts it, "if you borrow one another's love for the instant, you may, when you hear no more words of Pompey, return it again" (2.2.109–111). Enobarbus is rebuked for his unstatesmanlike tone, but no one denies the validity of what he says. In this cynical negotiation, Octavia is a pawn between husband and brother, shabbily treated by both. Caesar coldly bargains away the happiness of the one person of whom he protests that "no brother / Did ever love so dearly" (2.2.159–160); Antony, although hating false promises and resolving to be loyal to Octavia, knows within himself that it won't work. To make matters worse for the fair-minded Antony, he has received great favors from Pompey that he must now uncharitably repudiate in the interests of politics. Pompey does not miss the opportunity to remind Antony of his ingratitude, but the prevailing mood is not so much of bitterness as of ironic futility. Old friendships must be sacrificed; no one seems wholly to blame, no one can stop the game. Pompey is as much in the wrong as anyone, and as powerless. Despite his idealistic hope of rescuing Rome from political infighting, he has had to ally himself with pirates who offer him sinister temptations. He could be "lord of all the world" (2.7.62) if he would only murder on occasion, but Pompey is destined to be trapped between lofty ends and ignoble means. Lepidus is still another dismaying victim of political callousness, used condescendingly by Caesar and permitted to drink himself into oblivion, until he is cashiered on a trumped-up charge and imprisoned for life.

Octavius Caesar embodies most of all the ironic limits of political ambition. He has avoided enslavement to passion at the very real cost of enslaving himself to his public career as general, triumvir, and future emperor. His ideal warrior is one who, driven by military necessity, would "drink / The stale [urine] of horses and the gilded puddle / Which beasts would cough at" (1.4.62–64). As a general he is Antony's opposite in every way. He attacks only when he has the advantage and places those who have deserted Antony in his own front lines so "That Antony may seem to

spend his fury / Upon himself" (4.6.10–11). He controls his
supplies cannily, believing it a "waste" to feast his army
(4.1.16–17). He of course declines Antony's offers of single
combat. Antony meantime recklessly accepts Caesar's challenge to fight at sea, feasts debauchingly in one "gaudy
night" after another (3.13.186), and generously refuses to
blame or penalize those who leave him. His sending Enobarbus' belongings after him into Caesar's camp convinces
that honest soldier he has made a fatal error; for, however
imprudent Antony's chivalry may be, it is unquestionably
noble and great-hearted. Caesar is a superb general and political genius, but he is also a military automaton, a logisti-
cal reckoner, a Machiavellian pragmatist. In his personal
life he is no less austere and puritanical. He deplores loos-
ening his tongue with alcohol. About women he is deeply
cynical, believing that "want will perjure / The ne'er
touched vestal" (3.12.30–31). Between him and Cleopatra
there is a profound antipathy, based in part on his revulsion
at her earlier affair with his namesake and predecessor, Julius Caesar (3.6.6). Cleopatra may entertain briefly the no-
tion of trying to seduce this new Caesar (3.13.46 ff.), for like
Charmian she loves long life "better than figs" (1.2.34), but
if so she soon discovers that she and Caesar are not compat-
ible. All that he represents she must instead grandly repudiate, choosing death and an eternity with Antony as her way
to "call great Caesar ass / Unpolicied" (5.2.307–308).

Cleopatra is a "lass unparalleled" (5.2.316) whose greatness is elusive and all the more enthralling because so mys-
terious. She rises above her counterpart in Shakespeare's
source, Plutarch's *Lives of the Noble Grecians and Romans*,
where she is an impressive queenly woman but still essentially a temptress causing the lamentable fall of the hero.
Shakespeare's Cleopatra is that, but is also something inde-
finable that can be gotten at only through paradox. Her very
character is the essence of contradiction: she knows how
"to chide, to laugh, / To weep" (1.1.51–52), to be sullen or
violent, like a skillful actor keeping Antony continually off
guard. Dispassionately examined, she is a woman no longer
young who abuses messengers like an oriental despot, who
lies about her wealth when captured by Caesar (what is she
planning to do with that wealth, anyway?), who will not risk
leaving her monument even when Antony lies outside mor-

tally wounded, and who may take her own life only when she realizes that the alternative is public shame and captivity. We cannot be sure that she would not have "Packed cards with Caesar" (4.14.19) if she had found him susceptible to her charms. Yet we are not invited to see her dispassionately. Her charm is eternal, and so are the myths surrounding that charm. Observers evoking her splendor do not describe her person directly, but rather her effects and surroundings: Enobarbus says simply that "For her own person, / It beggared all description," and goes on to catalogue her cloth-of-gold pavilion and her mermaidlike attendants. Most of all, she is paradox: she makes defect perfection, age cannot wither her, and "vilest things / Become themselves in her, that the holy priests / Bless her when she is riggish" (2.2.207–250). She is both a whore and the Lucretian Venus, both sluttish and holy.

In Cleopatra, "fancy" exceeds "nature"; the fertility of her Egypt overflows the measure, exceeding the sterility of Rome as her own imaginative fertility exceeds reality itself. When she protests that she will not go to Rome to behold herself in a wretched play and thus see "Some squeaking Cleopatra boy my greatness / I' the posture of a whore" (5.2.220–221), we realize that Shakespeare is calling attention to his own art as well, pointing out how Elizabethan boy actors on a bare stage can transform reality into a dream that we believe. Cleopatra's mystery is like that of poetry itself. The "real" world pales into insignificance of a "little O, th' earth," something "No better than a sty," full of illusory shadows that "mock our eyes with air" (5.2.80, 4.15.64, 4.14.7); and Caesar's triumph vanishes with it. In its place, Antony and Cleopatra raise up a vision of themselves as lovers who, through art, have indeed become eternal. Together they will overpicture Venus and Mars and will be so renowned that "Dido and her Aeneas shall want troops, / And all the haunt be ours" (4.14.53–54). They are virtually husband and wife—"Husband, I come!" exclaims Cleopatra just before she dies (5.2.287)—united at last in a re-creative vision almost appropriate to comedy; and in their marriage they find a kind of redemption for the defeat that history can inflict. Antony is no longer dying Hercules but the god of Cleopatra's dream whose "legs bestrid the ocean; his reared arm / Crested the world; his voice was propertied / As all the tunèd spheres" (ll. 81–83). Through Cleopatra's vision we realize how all the characteristics that made Antony at once so noble and so sure to fall before Caesar—his generosity amounting to imprudence, his spontaneity, his impatience with the ordinary, his staking his all on love when he hears of Cleopatra's supposed death—have not deserted him. His death serves to reaffirm the magnificence of the very qualities that have brought him down. His essential nobility is confirmed, even if it must be defined in non-Roman ways. He and Cleopatra share the "Immortal longings" for which she goes willingly to her death, dressed in her "best attires" like a queen (ll. 281, 228); for neither lover will accept anything less than greatness.

Antony and Cleopatra
in Performance

Antony and Cleopatra suffered virtually total neglect in the theater from the time of its first performances until the mid-nineteenth century. A record of the Lord Chamberlain's office in 1669, assigning performance rights of this and other plays to Thomas Killigrew and the King's men at the Theatre Royal, Drury Lane, describes *Antony and Cleopatra* as "formerly acted at the Blackfriars," but there is no information as to how many performances took place at this indoor theater of Shakespeare's company or whether it was also performed publicly at the Globe Theatre. (One would hope so.) Nor is there any record of Killigrew's company having played it during the Restoration. Shakespeare seems to have written a play that was so extraordinarily innovative in its disregard for the classical unities, and so candid in its presentation of Antony's conflict between love and duty, that subsequent generations turned to more classically regular and decorous treatments of the same story. Perhaps one should say they turned back to such treatments, for, in the entire history of dramatic renditions of this great love story, Shakespeare's is the grand exception rather than the norm. One way to measure the daring of his achievement is to compare it with the monotonous symmetries of Robert Garnier's *Marc-Antoine* as translated by the Countess of Pembroke (1590), Samuel Daniel's *Cleopatra* (1594, revised 1607), and Samuel Brandon's *The Virtuous Octavia* (1598).

Shakespeare's heresy was to take a great classical subject away from the practitioners of the classical school and to subject a great Roman hero to the indignities of playful seduction and risible banter as well as his own inconstancy, debilitating rage, and bungled suicide. The return to normalcy was swift. John Fletcher, Shakespeare's successor as the leading playwright for the King's men, wrote *The False One* (c. 1620), about Cleopatra's intrigue with Julius Caesar, with only a glance at Shakespeare's play. Thomas May's *Cleopatra* (1626) corresponded more nearly to Shakespeare's

subject, especially in the scene between Thidias (or Thyreus, as he is called and as he is known in history) and Cleopatra, but reduced the comic element. Sir Charles Sedley,
in a production at the Duke's Theatre in 1677 starring
Thomas Betterton and Mary Lee, further regularized the
story to accord with the requirements of the rhymed heroic
play. Sedley unified time and place by locating the action in
Egypt after the Battle of Actium, reduced the number of
characters, excised the comedy, and refined the person of
Cleopatra. The influence of heroic drama is especially evi-
dent in Sedley's symmetrical amplifications of the noble
conflict between love and honor: Maecenas is in love with
Octavia, Thyreus with Cleopatra, and the Roman Photinus
(an added character) with Iras. Photinus, in the kind of
melodramatic villainy suited to the genre (and also to the
acting style of Samuel Sandford, who played the part), con-
nives to have Antony commit suicide so that Photinus may
reign with Iras as his queen.

John Dryden's *All for Love, or The World Well Lost* (1678)
also is in the main tradition of dramatic adaptation of the
classical history. Dryden, like Sedley and others before
him, limits the action to Alexandria and to the final tragic
events of his protagonists' lives. He reduces the cast from
Shakespeare's thirty-four named roles to ten. A heroic view
of love and honor governs the conduct of the protagonists:
Cleopatra, though willing to see Antony ruined if she cannot have him, is devotedly loyal, while Antony, though torn
by his divided loyalties to Cleopatra and to Octavia, is vindi-
cated finally in his choice of love. His tragic fall is of course
great, but the compensation for this loss is plainly indicated in the play's edifying subtitle, *The World Well Lost*.
Like other adaptations of the era, Dryden's has merely a
tangential relationship to what Shakespeare wrote. Yet *All
for Love* is significant to a performance history of *Antony
and Cleopatra* in at least two ways: it defines by contrast
what it was that Shakespeare achieved, and it helps define
the taste of an age that consistently preferred Dryden to
Shakespeare.

Though not immediately a stage favorite, Dryden's play
became a great success after 1684, when Thomas Betterton
played Antony in a production at Drury Lane. Throughout the eighteenth century, *All for Love*'s eclipse of Shake-

speare's play was nearly complete. Dryden's play was regularly revived at Drury Lane and the Theatre Royal, Covent Garden. When David Garrick undertook to bring back something approaching Shakespeare's play in 1759 at Drury Lane, in a text prepared by the Shakespeare editor Edward Capell, the production failed. A new play of *Antony and Cleopatra* by Henry Brooke, published in 1778 though probably never acted, regularizes and domesticates the action in the manner of Dryden. Brooke keeps about a third to a half of Shakespeare's play but gets rid entirely of Octavius, Octavia, and some other characters, while adding Cleopatra's brother, Ptolemy, and her two children. John Philip Kemble made extensive use of Dryden in his 1813 production at Covent Garden starring Harriet Faucit, though Kemble did reintroduce some of Shakespeare's scenes before Actium. A grand sea fight at Actium added to the stage spectacle; an equally grand procession and the singing of a funeral ode concluded the performance. William Charles Macready's production in 1833 at Drury Lane, though billing itself as "Shakespeare's Historical Play of *Antony and Cleopatra*," still continued to use a good deal of Dryden's play.

Even when Samuel Phelps finally rid the text of Dryden's improvements in a production in 1849 at the Sadler's Wells Theatre, thereby staging the first successful performance of Shakespeare's play since the author's time, he was obliged to reduce considerably the number of scenes (42) in Shakespeare's original. Macready had encountered this difficulty in 1833 in his more flawed attempt to reintroduce Shakespeare's play to the stage. The nineteenth-century "picture-stage" theater, which used a curtain between each scene and a verisimilar set for each location, could not possibly do justice to Shakespeare's play. (Eighteenth-century staging had also insisted on discrete verisimilar scenes, although with its stock scenes on movable screens or shutters that easily slid onstage from the theater wings, used to represent conventional and reusable settings, it could change locations more swiftly than most nineteenth-century productions; in any case, the eighteenth century had simply evaded the problem for *Antony and Cleopatra* by relying on Dryden.) Macready's spectacle called for "a splendid hall in Cleopatra's palace," the "garden of Cleopatra's palace," a "portico attached to the house of Octavius Caesar, with the Capitol in the distance," "a hall in the house of Lepidus," a locale "near the promontory of Misenum," the "promontory of Actium with a view of the fleets of Antony and Caesar," and still more. Phelps, entertaining similar ambitions and operating under similar constraints, was also obliged to run together and transpose his scenes and to reduce their number. Phelps concentrated on the episodes where he could most authentically reproduce the ambience of ancient Rome and Egypt. The Egyptian scenes, according to the *Illustrated London News* of October 27, were "exceedingly *vraisemblable*," while those on board Pompey's galley, "with the banqueting sovereigns of the world as drunk as cobblers," were "exceedingly life-like." Phelps aided the pictorial "by his well-studied bacchanalian attitudes, some of which were exceedingly fine. The illusion was almost perfect."

The trend toward opulent and realistic detail, once begun, soon led to more drastic expedients. A revival at the Princess's Theatre in 1867 reduced the number of scenes to nineteen, leaving out entirely, for example, such episodes as that of Pompey at Messina (2.1), Octavius, Octavia, and Antony at Rome (2.3), and Ventidius in the Middle East (3.1). The banqueting scene at Misenum (2.6–2.7) was of course splendid, as it needed to be in emulation of earlier stagings. Indeed critics, while acknowledging the "witchery" of Isabella Glyn's Cleopatra, enthusiastically praised the brilliant scenery and spectacular effects provided by Thomas Grieve and Frederick Lloyds. Another revival at Drury Lane in 1873 settled on twelve scenes, sacrificing, among other matters, the death of Enobarbus and everything connected with Pompey, while providing in their stead a pictorial illustration (to the accompaniment of Enobarbus' famous words) of Cleopatra in her barge on the river Cydnus—now conveniently located in Egypt rather than Cilicia. For the marriage of Antony and Octavia, F. B. Chatterton (the manager at Drury Lane) provided a Roman festival procession of Amazons, thirty choirboys, and a ballet called the "Path of Flowers." Crowds of supernumeraries filled the stage at Actium while the crews of two contending galleys showered arrows on one another—so realistically, indeed, that Chatterton was obliged to come before the audience and assure them not to be alarmed for their own safety.

More was still to come. Lily Langtry played Cleopatra to Charles Coghlan's Antony in a sumptuous revival at the Princess's Theatre in 1890, memorable most of all for its gorgeous pageants of an "Alexandrian festival," the "triumphal reception of Antony by Cleopatra," and an allegorical ballet of "the conflict between day and night." Louis Calvert and Janet Achurch were impressive as Antony and Cleopatra in 1897 at Manchester's Queen's Theatre and later that year in London at the Olympic Theatre. The critic James Agate remembered Achurch as the finest Cleopatra he had ever seen. At Stratford-upon-Avon in 1898 Frank Benson mounted the costliest production yet seen there; and then in 1900, his costumes and properties (as well as his promptbooks) having been destroyed by fire the previous year, he nonetheless managed to put on a spectacular show at the Lyceum Theatre with the help of a wardrobe and property inventory supplied by Henry Irving's company. Herbert Beerbohm Tree summed up this tradition of massive scenes and heavy cuts in 1906 at His Majesty's Theatre when he dressed his actors (unhistorically) in the garb of the old Pharaohs and staged the first encounter of Antony and Cleopatra with an enormous cast, rather than relying on Enobarbus' description of the event.

Throughout the eighteenth and nineteenth centuries, this cutting and rearranging of scenes had also done much to enhance the prominence of lead actors at the expense of their more humble associates. Shakespeare's *Antony and Cleopatra* thus waited centuries to find a flexible open stage and a willingness on the part of directors and audiences to take the play as written. The new shape of things manifested itself at the Old Vic in 1922, when Robert Atkins, a disciple of the theater visionary William Poel, staged *Antony and Cleopatra* with no scene breaks and only one intermission. Atkins, who had played Ventidius in Tree's lavish 1906 production, knew well the limitations of depending upon scenic splendor. Harley Granville-Barker offered his enthusiastic support for Atkins's experiment in fast-paced, continuous action. A nearly uncut version followed in 1930, again at the Old Vic, directed by Harcourt Williams. Starring John Gielgud as Antony and Ralph Richardson as Enobarbus, the play, in Renaissance dress derived from paintings by Veronese and Tiepolo, was a great critical and financial success. Williams, as critic Ivor Brown noted, successfully "shaped the whole with majestic speed, force, and pertinence." A single nonrealistic set sufficed for the entire play in Glen Byam Shaw's production at the Piccadilly Theatre in 1946, with Edith Evans as Cleopatra, Godfrey Tearle as Antony, and Anthony Quayle as Enobarbus. In 1951 Michael Benthall used a revolving stage with great success at the St. James's Theatre, in a production starring Laurence Olivier and Vivien Leigh. Five stocky dark pillars served to indicate Rome, and the stage rotated to reveal an "Egyptian" set of slender Corinthian columns. The revolve permitted continuous action, creating, as theater critic J. C. Trewin has noted, a "swift glowing effect." Today one seldom sees elaborate scenery in productions of *Antony and Cleopatra*, though the recent BBC television version provided it and proved to be one of the series' more embarrassing failures.

The preeminent Antony of recent times may have been Michael Redgrave, acting under Glen Byam Shaw's direction, with Peggy Ashcroft as Cleopatra, in London and Stratford-upon-Avon in 1953. Together these accomplished theater artists conveyed the fascination of Cleopatra as well as her petty malice and cattiness, her teasing humor, her languidness, her susceptibility to flattery, her despotic fury; Antony was the victim of her wiles but also very masculine, charismatic, generous, and delighted with Cleopatra, both ashamed of his enervating passion and drawn to love as a source of vitality and renewal. The paradoxes of this extraordinary play, and its evocation of the myth of a great love affair amid the ruins of the protagonists' lives, have never been better served in the theater.

Though continuing the practice of simplified staging, recent productions have somewhat shifted the play's traditional romantic focus. Michael Langham's *Antony and Cleopatra* in 1967 at Stratford, Ontario, centered on the play's political dimension. Christopher Plummer and Zoe Caldwell were not so much lovers as skillful game-players, interested more in power than passion. Trevor Nunn directed the play at Stratford-upon-Avon in 1972, similarly moving away from the play's emphasis upon the love story. Antony, played by Richard Johnson, was appealingly honest and generous, aware that his defeat stemmed from his rejection of the political world. Janet Suzman's Cleopatra was sensual and witty, but above all calculating, trying to save herself and her Egypt from Corin Redgrave's puritanical Caesar. At London's Bankside Globe Theatre in 1973, Tony Richardson directed a controversial modern-dress *Antony and Cleopatra*, starring Vanessa Redgrave and Julian Glover. Redgrave's Cleopatra was arrogant and bad-tempered, throwing cola bottles at servants; Glover's Antony was a shallow narcissist. Love, in Richardson's version of the play, was disturbingly irrelevant to a political world destined to fall under Caesar's domination. Peter Brook, in his 1978 production at Stratford-upon-Avon, shared Richardson's estimate of the play's concerns. Brook's *Antony and Cleopatra* was, in his words, a "small, intimate, personal play," starring Glenda Jackson and Alan Howard as lovers whose self-indulgence prevented them from discovering an alternative to the intruding and vicious political world. The single set—a semicircular pavilion formed by six translucent plastic panels—became the center of the lovers' universe. Through the panels the audience was permitted occasional glimpses of the historical world as soldiers, messengers, and servants crossed the rear stage. During one battle scene, soldiers splashed the panels with blood—"the action painting of slaughter and carnage," as the *Newsweek* critic described it.

Peter Hall, in his valedictory production on the Olivier stage at the National Theatre in London in 1987, gave particular emphasis to the interplay of Antony's and Cleopatra's private and public worlds. As portrayed by Anthony Hopkins and Judi Dench—neither of them physically imposing in their parts—Antony and Cleopatra were self-mocking and witty lovers whose personal struggles and brief triumphs were played against the spectacle of a world at war; the unavoidable doom facing the lovers was part of their larger entanglement in the chaos of history. Tim Piggott-Smith's Caesar and Michael Bryant's Enobarbus added weight to the ironies of the historical confrontation from which the lovers finally emerged as legends capable of transcending human vicissitude. The production achieved a cohesiveness of vision that had been lacking for the most part in Toby Robertson's production at the Haymarket Theatre the previous season in London starring Timothy Dalton and Vanessa Redgrave or that of 1985 at the Chichester Festival Theatre with Denis Quilley and Diana Rigg in the title roles.

No play of Shakespeare's illustrates better the inability of conventional theatrical scenery to depict what Shakespeare's original staging achieved on a bare platform and without curtains. The very location of certain key scenes is indeterminately flexible. The play moves all over the Mediterranean, but at what precise points does it shift location? In Act 3, scenes 7 through 10, for example, we are at Actium, historically located on the northwest Adriatic coast of Greece, near modern-day Albania. A battle takes place there in which scene markings are essentially meaningless: Caesar and his army appear, followed swiftly by Antony and his followers, while the battle is suggested in part through offstage sound effects of a sea fight. As Act 3, scene 11, begins we might suppose we are still in the vicinity of Actium, for Antony, having fled by sea, seems to be responding immediately to the crushing news of defeat and shame. Yet by the scene's end, and then in the ensuing action, we realize that we are in Egypt. The logistics of travel or of scenic consistency do not hamper Shakespeare; in an important sense the location is the theater, and the action is wherever Antony is. With a bare stage and uninterrupted movement from scene to scene, the dramatist and his actors can generate the impression they want of headlong haste and continuity. Again, in scenes 12 through 14 of Act 4, the theater provides a fluid and flexible location for the battlefield near Alexandria. Scene 12 begins with Antony clearly in the field, beholding the disastrous surrender of his galleys; then, with Cleopatra's entrance moments later, he speaks as though he is now at the palace in Alexandria. The following scenes move uninterruptedly toward Cleopatra's taking refuge in her monument.

Shakespeare seems positively to exult in the freedom and simplicity of his stage. When the dying Antony is hoisted aloft to Cleopatra in her monument, probably nothing more is needed than the gallery backstage in the Elizabethan playhouse and some attendants to lift Antony up while Cleopatra and her women assist. The opening stage direction in Act 4, scene 15, is explicit about her being *"aloft."* Here and everywhere, *Antony and Cleopatra* is fully conscious of its own theatrical artifice. Cleopatra wryly jests about some "squeaking" actor who will "boy" her greatness in "the posture of a whore" (5.2.220–221)—that is to say, not only a Roman actor in Caesar's triumph but a boy actor in an Elizabethan acting company. This theatrical self-awareness is appropriate to a play so deeply concerned with the complex interplay of history and artistic vision.

The Playhouse

This early copy of a drawing by Johannes de Witt of the Swan Theatre in London (c. 1596), made by his friend Arend van Buchell, is the only surviving contemporary sketch of the interior of a public theater in the 1590s.

From other contemporary evidence, including the stage directions and dialogue of Elizabethan plays, we can surmise that the various public theaters where Shakespeare's plays were produced (the Theatre, the Curtain, the Globe) resembled the Swan in many important particulars, though there must have been some variations as well. The public playhouses were essentially round, or polygonal, and open to the sky, forming an acting arena approximately 70 feet in diameter; they did not have a large curtain with which to open and close a scene, such as we see today in opera and some traditional theater. A platform measuring approximately 43 feet across and 27 feet deep, referred to in the de Witt drawing as the *proscaenium*, projected into the yard, *planities sive arena*. The roof, *tectum*, above the stage and supported by two pillars, could contain machinery for ascents and descents, as were required in several of Shakespeare's late plays. Above this roof was a hut, shown in the drawing with a flag flying atop it and a trumpeter at its door announcing the performance of a play. The underside of the stage roof, called the heavens, was usually richly decorated with symbolic figures of the sun, the moon, and the constellations. The platform stage stood at a height of $5\frac{1}{2}$ feet or so above the yard, providing room under the stage for underworldly effects. A trapdoor, which is not visible in this drawing, gave access to the space below.

The structure at the back of the platform (labeled *mimorum aedes*), known as the tiring-house because it was the actors' attiring (dressing) space, featured at least two doors, as shown here. Some theaters seem to have also had a discovery space, or curtained recessed alcove, perhaps between the two doors—in which Falstaff could have hidden from the sheriff (*1 Henry IV*, 2.4) or Polonius could have eavesdropped on Hamlet and his mother (*Hamlet*, 3.4). This discovery space probably gave the actors a means of access to and from the tiring-house. Curtains may also have been hung in front of the stage doors on occasion. The de Witt drawing shows a gallery above the doors that extends across the back and evidently contains spectators. On occasions when action "above" demanded the use of this space, as when Juliet appears at her "window" (*Romeo and Juliet*, 2.2 and 3.5), the gallery seems to have been used by the actors, but large scenes there were impractical.

The three-tiered auditorium is perhaps best described by Thomas Platter, a visitor to London in 1599 who saw on that occasion Shakespeare's *Julius Caesar* performed at the Globe:

> The playhouses are so constructed that they play on a raised platform, so that everyone has a good view. There are different galleries and places [*orchestra, sedilia, porticus*], however, where the seating is better and more comfortable and therefore more expensive. For whoever cares to stand below only pays one English penny, but if he wishes to sit, he enters by another door [*ingressus*] and pays another penny, while if he desires to sit in the most comfortable seats, which are cushioned, where he not only sees everything well but can also be seen, then he pays yet another English penny at another door. And during the performance food and drink are carried round the audience, so that for what one cares to pay one may also have refreshment.

Scenery was not used, though the theater building itself was handsome enough to invoke a feeling of order and hierarchy that lent itself to the splendor and pageantry onstage. Portable properties, such as thrones, stools, tables, and beds, could be carried or thrust on as needed. In the scene pictured here by de Witt, a lady on a bench, attended perhaps by her waiting-gentlewoman, receives the address of a male figure. If Shakespeare had written *Twelfth Night* by 1596 for performance at the Swan, we could imagine Malvolio appearing like this as he bows before the Countess Olivia and her gentlewoman, Maria.

ANTONY AND CLEOPATRA

MARK ANTONY,
OCTAVIUS CAESAR, } *triumvirs*
LEPIDUS,

CLEOPATRA,
CHARMIAN,
IRAS,
ALEXAS,
MARDIAN, *a eunuch*,
DIOMEDES,
SELEUCUS, *Cleopatra's treasurer*, } *Cleopatra's attendants*

OCTAVIA, *sister of Octavius Caesar and wife of Antony*

DEMETRIUS,
PHILO,
DOMITIUS ENOBARBUS,
VENTIDIUS,
SILIUS,
EROS,
CANIDIUS,
SCARUS,
DERCETUS, } *Antony's friends and followers*

A SCHOOLMASTER, *Antony's* AMBASSADOR *to Caesar*

MAECENAS,
AGRIPPA,
TAURUS,
THIDIAS,
DOLABELLA,
GALLUS,
PROCULEIUS, } *Octavius Caesar's friends and followers*

SEXTUS POMPEIUS *or* POMPEY
MENAS,
MENECRATES, } *Pompey's friends*
VARRIUS,

MESSENGERS *to Antony, Octavius Caesar, and Cleopatra*
A SOOTHSAYER
Two SERVANTS *of Pompey*
SERVANTS *of Antony and Cleopatra*
A BOY
SOLDIERS, SENTRIES, GUARDSMEN *of Antony and Octavius Caesar*
A CAPTAIN *in Antony's army*
An EGYPTIAN
A CLOWN *with figs*

Ladies attending Cleopatra, Eunuchs, Servants, Soldiers,
  Captains, Officers, silent named characters (Rannius,
  Lucillius, Lamprius)

SCENE: *In several parts of the Roman Empire*]

1.1 *Enter Demetrius and Philo.*

PHILO

Nay, but this dotage of our general's   1
O'erflows the measure. Those his goodly eyes,   2
That o'er the files and musters of the war   3
Have glowed like plated Mars, now bend, now turn   4
The office and devotion of their view   5
Upon a tawny front. His captain's heart,   6
Which in the scuffles of great fights hath burst
The buckles on his breast, reneges all temper   8
And is become the bellows and the fan
To cool a gypsy's lust.

> *Flourish. Enter Antony, Cleopatra, her ladies, the*
> *train, with eunuchs fanning her.*

                              Look where they come.   10
Take but good note, and you shall see in him
The triple pillar of the world transformed   12
Into a strumpet's fool. Behold and see.

CLEOPATRA

If it be love indeed, tell me how much.

ANTONY

There's beggary in the love that can be reckoned.   15

CLEOPATRA

I'll set a bourn how far to be beloved.   16

ANTONY

Then must thou needs find out new heaven, new earth.   17

> *Enter a Messenger.*

1.1 Location: Alexandria. Cleopatra's palace.
1 dotage foolish affection, sometimes associated with old age
2 O'erflows the measure exceeds any appropriate limit   **3 files and
musters** orderly formations   **4 plated** clothed in armor   **5 office** function   **6 tawny front** dark face. (Literally, forehead.)   **8 reneges** re-
nounces.   **temper** moderation   **10 gypsy's** (Gypsies were widely
believed to have come from Egypt, and to be lustful and cunning.)
s.d. Flourish trumpet fanfare announcing the arrival or departure of
an important person.   **train** retinue   **12 triple** one of three. (Alludes to
the triumvirate of Antony, Lepidus, and Octavius Caesar; also to tripar-
tite division of the world into Asia, Africa, and Europe.)   **15 There's . . .
reckoned** i.e., love that can be quantified is paltry; ours is infinite
16 bourn boundary, limit   **17 Then . . . earth** i.e., only in some new
universe could you find a limit to my love

MESSENGER   News, my good lord, from Rome.
ANTONY   Grates me! The sum.   19
CLEOPATRA   Nay, hear them, Antony.   20
  Fulvia perchance is angry, or who knows   21
  If the scarce-bearded Caesar have not sent   22
  His powerful mandate to you, "Do this, or this;
  Take in that kingdom, and enfranchise that;   24
  Perform 't, or else we damn thee."   25
ANTONY   How, my love?   26
CLEOPATRA   Perchance? Nay, and most like.   27
  You must not stay here longer; your dismission   28
  Is come from Caesar. Therefore hear it, Antony.
  Where's Fulvia's process? Caesar's, I would say. Both?   30
  Call in the messengers. As I am Egypt's queen,
  Thou blushest, Antony, and that blood of thine
  Is Caesar's homager; else so thy cheek pays shame   33
  When shrill-tongued Fulvia scolds. The messengers!
ANTONY
  Let Rome in Tiber melt and the wide arch
  Of the ranged empire fall! Here is my space.   36
  Kingdoms are clay; our dungy earth alike   37
  Feeds beast as man. The nobleness of life
  Is to do thus; when such a mutual pair   39
  And such a twain can do 't, in which I bind,   40
  On pain of punishment, the world to weet   41
  We stand up peerless.
CLEOPATRA   Excellent falsehood!
  Why did he marry Fulvia, and not love her?   43
  I'll seem the fool I am not. Antony   44

---

19 Grates me it annoys me.   **The sum** i.e., be brief   **20 them** i.e., the
news   **21 Fulvia** Antony's wife   **22 scarce-bearded Caesar** (Octavius
Caesar was twenty-three in 40 B.C., at the time of the play's opening.
Antony was forty-three.)   **24 Take in** conquer.   **enfranchise** set free
25 damn condemn to death   **26 How** i.e., what's that you say?
27 Perchance (Cleopatra reconsiders what she has said in l. 21.)   **like**
likely   **28 dismission** order to depart   **30 process** writ to appear in
court   **33 homager** vassal, one who does homage.   **else so** or else.   **thy
cheek pays shame** i.e., you blush guiltily   **36 ranged** ordered, or possibly, extended   **37 dungy** composed of dung   **39 thus** (May indicate an
embrace; or Antony may refer more generally to their way of life.)
40 bind obligate   **41 pain** penalty.   **weet** know, acknowledge   **43 and
not** if he did not   **44 I'll . . . not** i.e., I'll pretend to be gullible and
believe him, though I know better

  Will be himself.

ANTONY   But stirred by Cleopatra.   45
  Now, for the love of Love and her soft hours,
  Let's not confound the time with conference harsh.   47
  There's not a minute of our lives should stretch   48
  Without some pleasure now. What sport tonight?

CLEOPATRA
  Hear the ambassadors.

ANTONY   Fie, wrangling queen!
  Whom everything becomes—to chide, to laugh,
  To weep; whose every passion fully strives
  To make itself, in thee, fair and admired!
  No messenger but thine; and all alone
  Tonight we'll wander through the streets and note
  The qualities of people. Come, my queen,
  Last night you did desire it.—Speak not to us.
      Exeunt [Antony and Cleopatra] with the train.

DEMETRIUS
  Is Caesar with Antonius prized so slight?   58

PHILO
  Sir, sometimes when he is not Antony
  He comes too short of that great property   60
  Which still should go with Antony.

DEMETRIUS   I am full sorry   61
  That he approves the common liar, who   62
  Thus speaks of him at Rome; but I will hope
  Of better deeds tomorrow. Rest you happy!   *Exeunt.* 64

❖

1.2   *Enter Enobarbus, Lamprius, a Soothsayer,*
        Rannius, Lucillius, Charmian, Iras, Mardian
        the eunuch, and Alexas.

45 be himself i.e., (1) be the Roman Antony (2) be the fool he is (3) be the
deceiver he always is.   **stirred** (1) prompted to noble deeds (2) moved to
folly   **47 confound** ruin, waste.   **conference** conversation   **48 should**
that should.   **stretch** (Suggests that time can be stretched or extended.)   **58 prized** valued   **60 property** quality, distinction   **61 still**
always   **62 approves** corroborates   **64 Of** for

1.2. Location: Alexandria. Cleopatra's palace.
s.d. Lamprius etc. (Lamprius may possibly be the soothsayer, but Rannius and Lucillius have no speaking parts here and do not appear again
in the play. Mardian is mute here but does speak in later scenes.)

CHARMIAN Lord Alexas, sweet Alexas, most anything
Alexas, almost most absolute Alexas, where's the 2
soothsayer that you praised so to the Queen? O, that I
knew this husband, which, you say, must charge his 4
horns with garlands!   5

ALEXAS Soothsayer!

SOOTHSAYER Your will?

CHARMIAN
Is this the man?—Is 't you, sir, that know things?

SOOTHSAYER
In nature's infinite book of secrecy
A little I can read.

ALEXAS [*To Charmian*] Show him your hand.

ENOBARBUS [*To servants within*]
Bring in the banquet quickly; wine enough   12
Cleopatra's health to drink.

CHARMIAN [*Giving hand to Soothsayer*] Good sir, give
me good fortune.

SOOTHSAYER I make not, but foresee.

CHARMIAN Pray, then, foresee me one.

SOOTHSAYER
You shall be yet far fairer than you are.

CHARMIAN He means in flesh.   19

IRAS No, you shall paint when you are old.   20

CHARMIAN Wrinkles forbid!

ALEXAS Vex not his prescience. Be attentive.

CHARMIAN Hush!

SOOTHSAYER
You shall be more beloving than beloved.

CHARMIAN I had rather heat my liver with drinking. 25

ALEXAS Nay, hear him.

CHARMIAN Good now, some excellent fortune! Let me 27
be married to three kings in a forenoon and widow

---

2 absolute perfect   **4–5 must . . . garlands** i.e., must decorate his cuckold's horns with a garland of flowers, like a sacrificial beast. (Cuck-
olded men were derisively thought of as growing horns, as a badge of
their infamy.)   **12 banquet** light repast, dessert   **19 in flesh** i.e., by
putting on weight   **20 paint** i.e., use makeup   **25 heat . . . drinking**
i.e., heat my liver with wine rather than with unrequited love. (The
liver was believed to be the seat of sexual desire.)   **27 Good now** come
on, now

them all. Let me have a child at fifty, to whom Herod 29
of Jewry may do homage. Find me to marry me with 30
Octavius Caesar, and companion me with my mis- 31
tress.

SOOTHSAYER
You shall outlive the lady whom you serve.

CHARMIAN   O, excellent! I love long life better than figs. 34

SOOTHSAYER
You have seen and proved a fairer former fortune   35
Than that which is to approach.

CHARMIAN   Then belike my children shall have no 37
names. Prithee, how many boys and wenches must I 38
have?

SOOTHSAYER
If every of your wishes had a womb,
And fertile every wish, a million.

CHARMIAN   Out, fool! I forgive thee for a witch.   42

ALEXAS   You think none but your sheets are privy to 43
your wishes.

CHARMIAN   Nay, come, tell Iras hers.

ALEXAS   We'll know all our fortunes.

ENOBARBUS   Mine, and most of our fortunes tonight,
shall be—drunk to bed.

IRAS [*Giving her hand to the Soothsayer*] There's a
palm presages chastity, if nothing else.

CHARMIAN   E'en as the o'erflowing Nilus presageth 51
famine.   52

IRAS   Go, you wild bedfellow, you cannot soothsay.   53

CHARMIAN   Nay, if an oily palm be not a fruitful prog- 54
nostication, I cannot scratch mine ear. Prithee, tell her 55
but a workaday fortune.   56

29–30 Herod of Jewry i.e., even the blustering tyrant who massacred the
children of Judea   **31 companion me with** provide as my attendant; or,
give me equal fortune with   **34 better than figs** (Probably a proverbial
expression; with genital suggestion.)   **35 proved** experienced   **37 belike**
probably   **37–38 have no names** be illegitimate   **38 wenches** girls
42 Out . . . witch (Charmian jokingly says that since soothsayers, like
fools, are allowed to speak freely without penalty, she will not charge him
with the crime of wizardry.)   **43 privy to** in on the secret of   **51–52 E'en
. . . famine** (Charmian speaks ironically; the overflowing Nile presaged
abundance. See 2.7.18–24.)   **53 wild** wanton   **54 oily palm** sweaty or
moist palm (indication of a sensual disposition)   **54–55 fruitful prognosti-
cation** omen of fertility   **56 workaday** ordinary

SOOTHSAYER   Your fortunes are alike.

IRAS   But how, but how? Give me particulars.

SOOTHSAYER   I have said.   59

IRAS   Am I not an inch of fortune better than she?

CHARMIAN   Well, if you were but an inch of fortune bet-   61
ter than I, where would you choose it?

IRAS   Not in my husband's nose.   63

CHARMIAN   Our worser thoughts heavens mend! Alexas   64
—come, his fortune, his fortune! O, let him marry
a woman that cannot go, sweet Isis, I beseech thee,   66
and let her die too, and give him a worse, and let
worse follow worse till the worst of all follow him
laughing to his grave, fiftyfold a cuckold! Good Isis,
hear me this prayer, though thou deny me a matter of   70
more weight; good Isis, I beseech thee!

IRAS   Amen, dear goddess, hear that prayer of the people! For, as it is a heart-breaking to see a handsome
man loose-wived, so it is a deadly sorrow to behold a   74
foul knave uncuckolded. Therefore, dear Isis, keep de-   75
corum, and fortune him accordingly!   76

CHARMIAN   Amen.

ALEXAS   Lo now, if it lay in their hands to make me a
cuckold, they would make themselves whores but   79
they'd do 't.   80

    Enter Cleopatra.

ENOBARBUS   Hush! Here comes Antony.

CHARMIAN   Not he. The Queen.

CLEOPATRA   Saw you my lord?

ENOBARBUS   No, lady.

CLEOPATRA   Was he not here?

CHARMIAN   No, madam.

---

59 I have said I have no more to say   **61, 63 inch, nose** (with suggestion
that Iras would prefer her husband to be sexually well-endowed)
64 Our . . . mend (Charmian pretends to be shocked: may heaven im-
prove our dirty minds!)   **66 cannot go** (1) is lame (2) cannot make love
satisfactorily, or cannot bear children.   **Isis** Egyptian goddess usually
identified with fertility and the moon   **70 hear me** hear (on my behalf)   **74 loose-wived** with an unfaithful wife   **75 foul** ugly   **75–76 keep
decorum** deal suitably with the case   **76 fortune him** grant him fortune   **79–80 they . . . do 't** i.e., they would stop at nothing, even becoming whores, to cuckold me

CLEOPATRA
He was disposed to mirth, but on the sudden   87
A Roman thought hath struck him. Enobarbus!
ENOBARBUS   Madam?
CLEOPATRA
Seek him and bring him hither. Where's Alexas?
ALEXAS
Here at your service.—My lord approaches.

    Enter Antony with a Messenger.

CLEOPATRA
We will not look upon him. Go with us.
       Exeunt [all but Antony and the Messenger.]
FIRST MESSENGER
Fulvia thy wife first came into the field.   93
ANTONY   Against my brother Lucius?
FIRST MESSENGER   Ay.
But soon that war had end, and the time's state   96
Made friends of them, jointing their force 'gainst
    Caesar,   97
Whose better issue in the war from Italy   98
Upon the first encounter drave them.   99
ANTONY   Well, what worst?
FIRST MESSENGER
The nature of bad news infects the teller.   101
ANTONY
When it concerns the fool or coward. On.
Things that are past are done with me. 'Tis thus:
Who tells me true, though in his tale lie death,
I hear him as he flattered.
FIRST MESSENGER   Labienus—   105
This is stiff news—hath with his Parthian force
Extended Asia; from Euphrates   107
His conquering banner shook, from Syria

---

87 on the sudden suddenly   **93 field** battlefield   **96 time's state** circumstances prevailing at the moment   **97 jointing** uniting   **98 better issue** success   **98–99 from . . . them** drove them from Italy upon the very first encounter   **101 infects the teller** i.e., makes the teller seem bad   **105 as** as if.   **Labienus** (Brutus and Cassius [see *Julius Caesar*] had sent Quintus Labienus to Orodes, King of Parthia, to seek aid against Antony and Octavius Caesar; with a force thus obtained, he is now overrunning the Roman provinces in the Middle East.)   **107 Extended** seized upon. (A legal phrase.)

To Lydia and to Ionia,
Whilst—

ANTONY   Antony, thou wouldst say.

FIRST MESSENGER   O, my lord!

ANTONY
Speak to me home; mince not the general tongue.   111
Name Cleopatra as she is called in Rome;
Rail thou in Fulvia's phrase, and taunt my faults   113
With such full license as both truth and malice
Have power to utter. O, then we bring forth weeds
When our quick minds lie still, and our ills told us   116
Is as our earing. Fare thee well awhile.   117

FIRST MESSENGER   At your noble pleasure.

                              Exit [First] Messenger.

     Enter another Messenger.

ANTONY
From Sicyon, ho, the news? Speak there.

SECOND MESSENGER
The man from Sicyon—is there such an one?   120

THIRD MESSENGER [*At the door*]
He stays upon your will.

ANTONY   Let him appear.—   121
          [*Exeunt Second and Third Messengers.*]
These strong Egyptian fetters I must break,
Or lose myself in dotage.

     Enter another Messenger, with a letter.

                    What are you?

FOURTH MESSENGER   Fulvia thy wife is dead.

ANTONY   Where died she?

---

111 Speak . . . tongue speak bluntly; don't minimize the common
report   **113 phrase** manner of speech   **116 quick** alive, inventive
116–117 our ills . . . earing hearing our faults told to us improves us, as
plowing (*earing*) improves land by rooting out the weeds   **120 The man
from Sicyon** (The messenger who has just entered, not being from
Sicyon, realizes in some confusion that Antony wants to hear the news
from Sicyon. This second messenger therefore calls out to ask if the
messenger from Sicyon is to be found. Another messenger at the door
replies that such a man is indeed waiting, and in a moment that messenger from Sicyon enters with his report. Some editors change the
second and third messengers into attendants.) *Sicyon* an ancient city in
Greece, where Antony left Fulvia   **121 stays upon** awaits

FOURTH MESSENGER   In Sicyon.
  Her length of sickness, with what else more serious
  Importeth thee to know, this bears. [*He gives a letter.*]
ANTONY   Forbear me.   128
                            [*Exit Fourth Messenger.*]
  There's a great spirit gone! Thus did I desire it.
  What our contempts doth often hurl from us
  We wish it ours again. The present pleasure,
  By revolution lowering, does become   132
  The opposite of itself. She's good, being gone;
  The hand could pluck her back that shoved her on.   134
  I must from this enchanting queen break off.   135
  Ten thousand harms more than the ills I know
  My idleness doth hatch.—How now, Enobarbus!

    Enter Enobarbus.

ENOBARBUS   What's your pleasure, sir?
ANTONY   I must with haste from hence.
ENOBARBUS   Why, then, we kill all our women. We see
  how mortal an unkindness is to them; if they suffer
  our departure, death's the word.
ANTONY   I must be gone.
ENOBARBUS   Under a compelling occasion, let women
  die. It were pity to cast them away for nothing, though
  between them and a great cause they should be es-
  teemed nothing. Cleopatra, catching but the least noise 147
  of this, dies instantly; I have seen her die twenty times 148
  upon far poorer moment. I do think there is mettle in 149
  death, which commits some loving act upon her, she
  hath such a celerity in dying.
ANTONY   She is cunning past man's thought.
ENOBARBUS   Alack, sir, no, her passions are made of
  nothing but the finest part of pure love. We cannot call
  her winds and waters sighs and tears; they are greater 155
  storms and tempests than almanacs can report. This

---

128 Importeth concerns.   **Forbear** leave   **132 By revolution lowering**
losing value by the revolution of Fortune's wheel and the changing of
our opinions   **134 could** would be willing to   **135 enchanting** having
the power of a witch   **147 noise** hint, rumor   **148 dies** (with sexual
suggestion of achieving climax)   **149 poorer moment** lesser cause.
mettle i.e., sexual vigor   **155 sighs** i.e., mere sighs

cannot be cunning in her; if it be, she makes a shower
of rain as well as Jove.

ANTONY   Would I had never seen her!

ENOBARBUS   O, sir, you had then left unseen a wonderful piece of work, which not to have been blessed withal
would have discredited your travel.

ANTONY   Fulvia is dead.

ENOBARBUS   Sir?

ANTONY   Fulvia is dead.

ENOBARBUS   Fulvia?

ANTONY   Dead.

ENOBARBUS   Why, sir, give the gods a thankful sacrifice.
When it pleaseth their deities to take the wife of a man
from him, it shows to man the tailors of the earth;   170
comforting therein, that when old robes are worn out,
there are members to make new. If there were no more   172
women but Fulvia, then had you indeed a cut, and the
case to be lamented. This grief is crowned with con-
solation; your old smock brings forth a new petticoat,
and indeed the tears live in an onion that should water   176
this sorrow.   177

ANTONY
The business she hath broachèd in the state   178
Cannot endure my absence.

ENOBARBUS   And the business you have broached here
cannot be without you, especially that of Cleopatra's,
which wholly depends on your abode.   182

ANTONY
No more light answers. Let our officers   183
Have notice what we purpose. I shall break   184
The cause of our expedience to the Queen   185
And get her leave to part. For not alone   186
The death of Fulvia, with more urgent touches,   187

170 the tailors (The gods are tailors in Enobarbus' figure because they
fashion a new wife to replace a worn-out one just as tailors fashion a new
garment.)   172 members (The word has a bawdy suggestion, pursued in
ll. 173–174 and 178 in *cut, case, business,* and *broachèd; cut* and *case*
suggest the female sexual organs; *broachèd* suggests something that is
stabbed, pricked, opened.)   176–177 the tears . . . sorrow i.e., only an
onion could produce tears on this occasion of Fulvia's death
178 broachèd opened up. (But see note 172.)   182 abode staying   183 light
frivolous, indelicate   184 break i.e., break the news of   185 expedience
haste   186 leave consent   187 urgent touches pressing matters

Do strongly speak to us, but the letters too
Of many our contriving friends in Rome   189
Petition us at home. Sextus Pompeius   190
Hath given the dare to Caesar and commands
The empire of the sea. Our slippery people,   192
Whose love is never linked to the deserver
Till his deserts are past, begin to throw   194
Pompey the Great and all his dignities   195
Upon his son, who—high in name and power,
Higher than both in blood and life—stands up   197
For the main soldier; whose quality, going on,   198
The sides o' the world may danger. Much is breeding   199
Which, like the courser's hair, hath yet but life,   200
And not a serpent's poison. Say our pleasure   201
To such whose places under us require: 202
Our quick remove from hence.   203

ENOBARBUS   I shall do 't.   [*Exeunt.*]

❋

1.3   *Enter Cleopatra, Charmian, Alexas, and Iras.*

CLEOPATRA
Where is he?
CHARMIAN   I did not see him since.   1
CLEOPATRA [*To Alexas*]
See where he is, who's with him, what he does.
I did not send you. If you find him sad,   3

189 Of ... friends from many friends working in our interest   **190 at home**
i.e., to come home.   **Sextus Pompeius** son of Pompey the Great, who,
though outlawed, had been able to exploit the division between Antony and
Octavius and thereby gain command of Sicily and the sea; he appears in
Act 2   **192 slippery** fickle   **194 throw** bestow   **195 Pompey the Great** i.e.,
the title of "Pompey the Great"   **197 blood and life** mettle and vitality
197–198 stands ... soldier is achieving position as, or claims to be, the
leading military leader   **198 quality** character and position.   **going on** i.e.,
if this keeps on   **199 The sides ... danger** may endanger the frame of the
world   **200 like ... hair** (Allusion to the popular belief that a horsehair put
into water would turn to a snake.)   **201–203 Say ... hence** tell my wishes to
those whose place of service under me requires them to know; namely, that
we depart quickly

1.3. Location: Alexandria. Cleopatra's palace.
1 since lately   **3 I did ... you** i.e., do not let him know I sent you.   **sad**
serious

Say I am dancing; if in mirth, report
That I am sudden sick. Quick, and return.   5

                                 [*Exit Alexas.*]

CHARMIAN

Madam, methinks, if you did love him dearly,
You do not hold the method to enforce   7
The like from him.

CLEOPATRA   What should I do I do not?   8

CHARMIAN

In each thing give him way. Cross him in nothing.

CLEOPATRA

Thou teachest like a fool: the way to lose him.

CHARMIAN

Tempt him not so too far. I wish, forbear;   11
In time we hate that which we often fear.

    Enter Antony.

But here comes Antony.

CLEOPATRA   I am sick and sullen.   13

ANTONY

I am sorry to give breathing to my purpose—   14

CLEOPATRA

Help me away, dear Charmian! I shall fall.
It cannot be thus long; the sides of nature   16
Will not sustain it.

ANTONY   Now, my dearest queen—

CLEOPATRA

Pray you, stand farther from me.

ANTONY   What's the matter?   18

CLEOPATRA

I know by that same eye there's some good news.
What, says the married woman you may go?   20
Would she had never given you leave to come!
Let her not say 'tis I that keep you here.
I have no power upon you; hers you are.

---

5 sudden suddenly taken   **7 hold the method** follow the right course
8 I do not that I am not doing   **11 Tempt** try.   **I wish** I wish you
would   **13 sullen** depressed, melancholy   **14 breathing** utterance   **16 It
. . . long** i.e., I can't last long at this rate.   **sides of nature** i.e., human
body, frame   **18 stand farther from me** i.e., give me air   **20 the married
woman** i.e., Fulvia

ANTONY
  The gods best know—
CLEOPATRA   O, never was there queen
  So mightily betrayed! Yet at the first
  I saw the treasons planted.
ANTONY   Cleopatra—
CLEOPATRA
  Why should I think you can be mine, and true—
  Though you in swearing shake the thronèd gods—
  Who have been false to Fulvia? Riotous madness,   29
  To be entangled with those mouth-made vows,
  Which break themselves in swearing!
ANTONY   Most sweet queen— 31
CLEOPATRA
  Nay, pray you, seek no color for your going,   32
  But bid farewell and go. When you sued staying,   33
  Then was the time for words. No going then!
  Eternity was in our lips and eyes,   35
  Bliss in our brows' bent; none our parts so poor   36
  But was a race of heaven. They are so still,   37
  Or thou, the greatest soldier of the world,
  Art turned the greatest liar.
ANTONY   How now, lady?
CLEOPATRA
  I would I had thy inches. Thou shouldst know   40
  There were a heart in Egypt.
ANTONY   Hear me, Queen: 41
  The strong necessity of time commands
  Our services awhile, but my full heart
  Remains in use with you. Our Italy   44
  Shines o'er with civil swords; Sextus Pompeius   45
  Makes his approaches to the port of Rome;
  Equality of two domestic powers   47

29 Who you who **31 in swearing** even while they are being sworn
32 color pretext **33 sued staying** begged to stay **35 our** i.e., my. (The
royal plural.) **36 bent** arch, curve. **none . . . poor** none of my features,
however poor **37 race of heaven** of heavenly origin; or possibly, of the
flavor of heaven **40 inches** (1) height (2) manly strength (with perhaps a
bawdy suggestion) **41 a heart in Egypt** i.e., a mighty courage in the
Queen of Egypt **44 in use with you** for your use **45 Shines o'er**
glitters everywhere. **civil swords** i.e., weapons of civil war
47 Equality . . . powers i.e., the equal splitting of domestic power between two, Caesar and Antony

Breed scrupulous faction; the hated, grown to strength, 48
Are newly grown to love; the condemned Pompey, 49
Rich in his father's honor, creeps apace 50
Into the hearts of such as have not thrived
Upon the present state, whose numbers threaten; 52
And quietness, grown sick of rest, would purge 53
By any desperate change. My more particular, 54
And that which most with you should safe my going, 55
Is Fulvia's death.

CLEOPATRA
Though age from folly could not give me freedom,
It does from childishness. Can Fulvia die?

ANTONY   She's dead, my queen.   [*He offers letters.*]
Look here, and at thy sovereign leisure read
The garboils she awaked; at the last, best, 61
See when and where she died.

CLEOPATRA   O most false love!
Where be the sacred vials thou shouldst fill 63
With sorrowful water? Now I see, I see,
In Fulvia's death how mine received shall be.

ANTONY
Quarrel no more, but be prepared to know
The purposes I bear, which are or cease 67
As you shall give th' advice. By the fire 68
That quickens Nilus' slime, I go from hence 69
Thy soldier, servant, making peace or war
As thou affects.

CLEOPATRA   Cut my lace, Charmian, come! 71
But let it be; I am quickly ill, and well,

---

48 scrupulous carping, concerned with trifles   **49 Are . . . love** have
recently come into favor   **49–50 Pompey . . . honor** i.e., Sextus Pompeius, richly inheriting the honor once accorded Pompey the Great
50 creeps apace quickly insinuates himself   **52 state** government (i.e., of
the triumvirate).   **whose** i.e., those supporting Pompey   **53 purge**
cleanse or purify itself to be rid of sickness. (Peace, long continued,
seems diseased and requires the purging effect of war.)   **54 particular**
personal concern   **55 safe** make safe   **61 garboils** disturbances, commotions.   **best** i.e., best of all   **63 sacred vials** (Alludes to the supposed
Roman custom of putting bottles filled with tears in the tombs of the
departed.)   **67 which are** which will proceed   **68 fire** i.e., sun
69 quickens brings to life.   **Nilus' slime** the mud left by the overflow of
the Nile   **71 thou affects** you desire.   **lace** cord or laces fastening the
bodice. (Cleopatra pretends she is fainting.)

So Antony loves.

ANTONY   My precious queen, forbear,   73
And give true evidence to his love which stands   74
An honorable trial.

CLEOPATRA   So Fulvia told me.   75
I prithee, turn aside and weep for her;
Then bid adieu to me, and say the tears
Belong to Egypt. Good now, play one scene   78
Of excellent dissembling, and let it look
Like perfect honor.

ANTONY   You'll heat my blood. No more.   80

CLEOPATRA
You can do better yet; but this is meetly.   81

ANTONY
Now, by my sword—

CLEOPATRA   And target. Still he mends.   82
But this is not the best. Look, prithee, Charmian,
How this Herculean Roman does become   84
The carriage of his chafe.   85

ANTONY   I'll leave you, lady.

CLEOPATRA   Courteous lord, one word.
Sir, you and I must part, but that's not it;
Sir, you and I have loved, but there's not it;
That you know well. Something it is I would—   90
O, my oblivion is a very Antony,   91
And I am all forgotten.

ANTONY   But that your royalty   92
Holds idleness your subject, I should take you   93
For idleness itself.

---

73 So provided that; or, possibly, "in the same way, with changes as sudden as my own"   **74 evidence** witness (?)   **stands** will sustain **75 told** has taught (by her example of being quickly forgotten by Antony)   **78 Belong to Egypt** are shed for the Queen of Egypt.   **Good now** (An expression of entreaty.)   **80 heat my blood** i.e., anger me   **81 meetly** i.e., fairly well acted   **82 target** shield.   **mends** improves (in his "scene Of excellent dissembling")   **84–85 How . . . chafe** i.e., how Antony, who claims descent from Hercules, plays the role of his enraged ancestor well. (Hercules had become a stock figure of the enraged hero or tyrant.)   **chafe** rage   **90 would** wished to say   **91 my . . . Antony** my forgetful memory is like Antony (who is now leaving and thus forgetting me)   **92 I . . . forgotten** (1) I have forgotten what I was going to say (2) I am entirely forgotten (by Antony)   **92–93 But . . . subject** if your trifling banter were not subject to your control, used by you to serve your royal purposes

CLEOPATRA   'Tis sweating labor
  To bear such idleness so near the heart   95
  As Cleopatra this. But sir, forgive me,
  Since my becomings kill me when they do not   97
  Eye well to you. Your honor calls you hence;   98
  Therefore be deaf to my unpitied folly,
  And all the gods go with you! Upon your sword
  Sit laurel victory, and smooth success   101
  Be strewed before your feet!
ANTONY   Let us go. Come;
  Our separation so abides and flies   103
  That thou, residing here, goes yet with me,
  And I, hence fleeting, here remain with thee.
  Away!   *Exeunt.*

❖

1.4   *Enter Octavius [Caesar], reading a letter,*
          Lepidus, and their train.

CAESAR
  You may see, Lepidus, and henceforth know,
  It is not Caesar's natural vice to hate
  Our great competitor. From Alexandria   3
  This is the news: he fishes, drinks, and wastes
  The lamps of night in revel; is not more manlike
  Than Cleopatra, nor the queen of Ptolemy   6
  More womanly than he; hardly gave audience, or   7
  Vouchsafed to think he had partners. You shall find
    there
  A man who is the abstract of all faults   9
  That all men follow.
LEPIDUS   I must not think there are
  Evils enough to darken all his goodness.

95 such idleness such apparently trifling banter   **97 my becomings** those
qualities that become me (i.e., are attractive in me or are suitable to my
present position); perhaps also, the various roles that I become   **98 Eye**
appear   **101 laurel** wreathed with laurel   **103 so abides and flies** mingles
remaining and going in such a paradoxical fashion

1.4. Location: Rome.
3 competitor partner (with a suggestion also of "rival")   **6 Ptolemy**
(Cleopatra's royal brother, to whom she had been married according to
Egyptian custom.)   **7 gave audience** i.e., received messengers
9 abstract epitome

His faults in him seem as the spots of heaven,   12
More fiery by night's blackness, hereditary
Rather than purchased, what he cannot change   14
Than what he chooses.

CAESAR
You are too indulgent. Let's grant it is not   16
Amiss to tumble on the bed of Ptolemy,
To give a kingdom for a mirth, to sit   18
And keep the turn of tippling with a slave,   19
To reel the streets at noon, and stand the buffet   20
With knaves that smell of sweat. Say this becomes him—
As his composure must be rare indeed   22
Whom these things cannot blemish—yet must Antony
No way excuse his foils when we do bear   24
So great weight in his lightness. If he filled   25
His vacancy with his voluptuousness,   26
Full surfeits and the dryness of his bones   27
Call on him for 't. But to confound such time   28
That drums him from his sport and speaks as loud   29
As his own state and ours, 'tis to be chid   30
As we rate boys who, being mature in knowledge,   31
Pawn their experience to their present pleasure   32
And so rebel to judgment.

    Enter a Messenger.

LEPIDUS   Here's more news.   33
FIRST MESSENGER
Thy biddings have been done, and every hour,
Most noble Caesar, shalt thou have report

---

12 seem as are made conspicuous like. **spots** i.e., stars **14 purchased** acquired **16 Let's grant** even if we were to grant **18 mirth** jest, diversion **19 keep . . . of** take turns **20 stand the buffet** exchange blows **22 As his composure** considering that a man's composition or temperament **24 foils** blemishes **24–25 when . . . lightness** when we have to carry the heavy burden imposed by his levity **26 His vacancy** his leisure time **27–28 Full . . . for 't** i.e., the physical disabilities resulting from such voluptuousness (such as venereal disease) will call him to account. **28 confound** ruin, waste **29 drums** summons (as by a military drum). **sport** amorous pastime **29–30 speaks . . . ours** i.e., summons him urgently in view of his political position and ours as well **30 chid** chided, reprimanded **31 rate** berate. **mature in knowledge** old enough to know what their duty is **32 Pawn . . . pleasure** risk for the sake of immediate gratification what experience tells them will be ultimately painful **33 to judgment** against better judgment

How 'tis abroad. Pompey is strong at sea,
And it appears he is beloved of those   37
That only have feared Caesar. To the ports   38
The discontents repair, and men's reports   39
Give him much wronged.   [*Exit.*]

CAESAR   I should have known no less.   40
It hath been taught us from the primal state   41
That he which is was wished until he were;   42
And the ebbed man, ne'er loved till ne'er worth love,   43
Comes deared by being lacked. This common body,   44
Like to a vagabond flag upon the stream,   45
Goes to and back, lackeying the varying tide   46
To rot itself with motion.

[*Enter a Second Messenger.*]

SECOND MESSENGER   Caesar, I bring thee word
Menecrates and Menas, famous pirates,   49
Makes the sea serve them, which they ear and wound 50
With keels of every kind. Many hot inroads
They make in Italy. The borders maritime   52
Lack blood to think on 't, and flush youth revolt.   53
No vessel can peep forth but 'tis as soon
Taken as seen; for Pompey's name strikes more   55
Than could his war resisted.   [*Exit.*]

CAESAR   Antony,   56
Leave thy lascivious wassails. When thou once   57
Was beaten from Modena, where thou slew'st
Hirtius and Pansa, consuls, at thy heel

---

37 of by   **38 That . . . Caesar** i.e., that have obeyed Caesar only through
fear   **39 discontents** discontented. (See 1.3.48–52.)   **40 Give him** represent him as   **41 from . . . state** since the first government; or possibly,
since the earliest state of being   **42 That . . . were** that the man in
power was desired (by the populace) until he obtained power   **43 ebbed**
decayed in fortune.   **ne'er loved . . . . love** not loved until he was unworthy of love, i.e., until he lost power   **44 Comes deared** becomes loved,
gains value in people's eyes.   **common body** populace   **45 vagabond**
(1) drifting (2) rascally.   **flag** iris   **46 lackeying** following in servile
fashion like a lackey   **49 famous** notorious   **50 ear** plow   **52 borders
maritime** coastal territories   **53 Lack blood** turn pale.   **flush** vigorous;
flushed, ruddy (contrasted with those who *Lack blood*)   **55–56 strikes . . .
resisted** inflicts more damage than his forces could against our resis-
tance   **57 wassails** carousals

Did famine follow, whom thou fought'st against,   60
Though daintily brought up, with patience more
Than savages could suffer. Thou didst drink   62
The stale of horses and the gilded puddle   63
Which beasts would cough at. Thy palate then did deign 64
The roughest berry on the rudest hedge.
Yea, like the stag, when snow the pasture sheets,   66
The barks of trees thou browsèd. On the Alps   67
It is reported thou didst eat strange flesh,
Which some did die to look on. And all this—
It wounds thine honor that I speak it now—
Was borne so like a soldier that thy cheek
So much as lanked not.   72
LEPIDUS 'Tis pity of him.   73
CAESAR   Let his shames quickly
Drive him to Rome. 'Tis time we twain
Did show ourselves i' the field, and to that end
Assemble we immediate council. Pompey
Thrives in our idleness.
LEPIDUS   Tomorrow, Caesar,
I shall be furnished to inform you rightly
Both what by sea and land I can be able   80
To front this present time.
CAESAR   Till which encounter   81
It is my business too. Farewell.
LEPIDUS
Farewell, my lord. What you shall know meantime
Of stirs abroad, I shall beseech you, sir,   84
To let me be partaker.
CAESAR
Doubt not, sir, I knew it for my bond.   86
                            Exeunt [separately].

❖

60 **whom** i.e., famine   62 **suffer** display in suffering   63 **stale** urine.
gilded covered with iridescent slime   64 **deign** not disdain   66 **sheets**
covers   67 **browsèd** fed upon   72 **lanked** became thin   73 **of** about
80 **be able** be capable of mustering   81 **front** confront, deal with
84 **stirs** events   86 **knew** already knew.   **bound** duty, obligation

1.5   *Enter Cleopatra, Charmian, Iras, and Mardian.*

CLEOPATRA   Charmian!

CHARMIAN   Madam?

CLEOPATRA
Ha, ha! Give me to drink mandragora.   3

CHARMIAN   Why, madam?

CLEOPATRA
That I might sleep out this great gap of time
My Antony is away.

CHARMIAN   You think of him too much.

CLEOPATRA
O, 'tis treason!

CHARMIAN   Madam, I trust not so.

CLEOPATRA
Thou, eunuch Mardian!

MARDIAN   What's Your Highness' pleasure?

CLEOPATRA
Not now to hear thee sing. I take no pleasure
In aught an eunuch has. 'Tis well for thee   11
That, being unseminared, thy freer thoughts   12
May not fly forth of Egypt. Hast thou affections?   13

MARDIAN   Yes, gracious madam.

CLEOPATRA   Indeed?   15

MARDIAN
Not in deed, madam, for I can do nothing   16
But what indeed is honest to be done.   17
Yet have I fierce affections, and think
What Venus did with Mars.

CLEOPATRA   O Charmian,
Where think'st thou he is now? Stands he or sits he?
Or does he walk? Or is he on his horse?
O happy horse, to bear the weight of Antony!
Do bravely, horse, for wott'st thou whom thou mov'st?   23

1.5. Location: Egypt. Cleopatra's palace.

3 mandragora juice of the mandrake (a narcotic)   **11 aught** (with bawdy
suggestion)   **12 unseminared** castrated   **13 fly forth of Egypt** i.e., try to
leave as Antony has done.   **affections** passions   **15–16 Indeed? / Not in
deed** i.e., Really? No, not in the physical, sexual sense   **17 honest**
chaste   **23 Do** (with sexual suggestion).   **wott'st thou** do you know

The demi-Atlas of this earth, the arm   24
And burgonet of men. He's speaking now,   25
Or murmuring, "Where's my serpent of old Nile?"
For so he calls me. Now I feed myself
With most delicious poison. Think on me,   28
That am with Phoebus' amorous pinches black   29
And wrinkled deep in time. Broad-fronted Caesar,   30
When thou wast here above the ground, I was
A morsel for a monarch. And great Pompey   32
Would stand and make his eyes grow in my brow;   33
There would he anchor his aspect, and die   34
With looking on his life.   35

    Enter Alexas.

ALEXAS   Sovereign of Egypt, hail!
CLEOPATRA
How much unlike art thou Mark Antony!
Yet, coming from him, that great medicine hath   38
With his tinct gilded thee.   39
How goes it with my brave Mark Antony?   40
ALEXAS   Last thing he did, dear Queen,
He kissed—the last of many doubled kisses—
This orient pearl. [*He gives a pearl.*] His speech sticks in
    my heart.   43
CLEOPATRA
Mine ear must pluck it thence.
ALEXAS   "Good friend," quoth he,
"Say the firm Roman to great Egypt sends   45

---

24 demi-Atlas one who (together with Caesar) supports the weight of the whole world, as Atlas did. (Cleopatra disregards Lepidus as a triumvir.)   **25 burgonet** light helmet or steel cap; i.e., a protector of men **28–30 Think . . . time** (Cleopatra reflects on her ability to attract Antony, given the fact that she is dark-skinned [as from the amorous pinches of her lover, the sun] and increasingly wrinkled with age.)   **Phoebus'** the sun's   **30 Broad-fronted** with broad forehead.   **Caesar** i.e., Julius Caesar   **32 great Pompey** Gnaeus Pompey, oldest son of Pompey the Great. (Shakespeare may conflate the two.)   **33 make . . . brow** i.e., rivet his eyes on my face   **34 aspect** look, gaze.   **die** i.e., suffer the extremity of love   **35 his life** that which he lived for   **38 great medicine** supposed substance by which alchemists hoped to turn all baser metals into gold   **39 his tinct** its alchemical potency; also, its color   **40 brave** splendid   **43 orient** shining, bright. (The best pearls were from the East or Orient.)   **45 firm** constant, true

This treasure of an oyster; at whose foot,
To mend the petty present, I will piece   47
Her opulent throne with kingdoms. All the East,
Say thou, shall call her mistress." So he nodded,
And soberly did mount an arm-gaunt steed,   50
Who neighed so high that what I would have spoke
Was beastly dumbed by him.   52

CLEOPATRA   What was he, sad or merry?

ALEXAS
Like to the time o' the year between the extremes
Of hot and cold, he was nor sad nor merry.   55

CLEOPATRA
O well-divided disposition! Note him,   56
Note him, good Charmian, 'tis the man; but note him. 57
He was not sad, for he would shine on those   58
That make their looks by his; he was not merry,   59
Which seemed to tell them his remembrance lay
In Egypt with his joy; but between both.
O heavenly mingle! Be'st thou sad or merry,
The violence of either thee becomes,   63
So does it no man else.—Mett'st thou my posts?   64

ALEXAS
Ay, madam, twenty several messengers.   65
Why do you send so thick?

CLEOPATRA   Who's born that day   66
When I forget to send to Antony
Shall die a beggar. Ink and paper, Charmian.
Welcome, my good Alexas. Did I, Charmian,
Ever love Caesar so?

CHARMIAN   O that brave Caesar!

CLEOPATRA
Be choked with such another emphasis!   71
Say, "the brave Antony."

47 piece augment   **50 arm-gaunt** made trim and hard by warlike service; or possibly, gaunt of limb, or hungry for battle   **52 dumbed** drowned out, made inaudible   **55 nor sad** neither sad   **56 well-divided disposition** well-balanced temperament   **57 the man** i.e., perfectly characteristic of him.   **but** only   **58 would** wished to   **59 make ... his** model their appearance on his look, or, are dependent on his appearance for their moods   **63 thee becomes** is becoming to you   **64 posts** messengers   **65 several** separate, distinct (also in l. 80)   **66 Who's** anyone who is   **71 emphasis** emphatic expression

CHARMIAN   The valiant Caesar!
CLEOPATRA
  By Isis, I will give thee bloody teeth
  If thou with Caesar paragon again   74
  My man of men.
CHARMIAN   By your most gracious pardon,
  I sing but after you.
CLEOPATRA   My salad days,
  When I was green in judgment, cold in blood,   77
  To say as I said then. But, come, away,
  Get me ink and paper.
  He shall have every day a several greeting,
  Or I'll unpeople Egypt.   *Exeunt.* 81

❖

---

74 paragon match or compare   **77 green** immature   **81 Or . . . Egypt**
i.e., or if not, it will be because I have used up all my subjects as
messengers

2.1   *Enter Pompey, Menecrates, and Menas, in
warlike manner.*

POMPEY
  If the great gods be just, they shall assist
  The deeds of justest men.
MENAS   Know, worthy Pompey,   2
  That what they do delay they not deny.   3
POMPEY
  Whiles we are suitors to their throne, decays   4
  The thing we sue for.
MENAS   We, ignorant of ourselves,   5
  Beg often our own harms, which the wise powers
  Deny us for our good; so find we profit
  By losing of our prayers.
POMPEY   I shall do well.
  The people love me, and the sea is mine;
  My powers are crescent, and my auguring hope   10
  Says it will come to th' full. Mark Antony   11
  In Egypt sits at dinner, and will make
  No wars without doors. Caesar gets money where   13
  He loses hearts. Lepidus flatters both,
  Of both is flattered; but he neither loves,   15
  Nor either cares for him.
MENAS   Caesar and Lepidus
  Are in the field. A mighty strength they carry.   17
POMPEY
  Where have you this? 'Tis false.
MENAS   From Silvius, sir.
POMPEY
  He dreams. I know they are in Rome together
  Looking for Antony. But all the charms of love,   20

2.1. Location: Pompey's camp, probably at Messina, Sicily.
2 Menas (The Folio assigns the speeches in this scene to "Mene.''; some
could be for Menecrates, but Pompey ignores him entirely at ll. 43–52
and Menecrates never reappears in the play.)   **3 not deny** i.e., do not
necessarily deny   **4–5 Whiles . . . for** while we are praying, that for
which we pray is being destroyed   **10 powers** armed forces.   **crescent**
on the increase.   **auguring** prophesying   **11 it** i.e., my, Pompey's,
powers or fortune (seen as a crescent moon, becoming full)   **13 without
doors** outdoors, i.e., in the battlefield, rather than in the bedroom
15 Of by.   **neither loves** loves neither   **17 A . . . carry** they command a
mighty army   **20 Looking for** awaiting.   **charms** spells

Salt Cleopatra, soften thy waned lip!   21
Let witchcraft joined with beauty, lust with both,
Tie up the libertine in a field of feasts,   23
Keep his brain fuming. Epicurean cooks,   24
Sharpen with cloyless sauce his appetite,   25
That sleep and feeding may prorogue his honor   26
Even till a Lethe'd dullness—

    Enter Varrius.

                    How now, Varrius?   27

VARRIUS
This is most certain that I shall deliver: 28
Mark Antony is every hour in Rome
Expected. Since he went from Egypt 'tis
A space for further travel.   31

POMPEY   I could have given less matter   32
A better ear. Menas, I did not think
This amorous surfeiter would have donned his helm   34
For such a petty war. His soldiership
Is twice the other twain. But let us rear   36
The higher our opinion, that our stirring   37
Can from the lap of Egypt's widow pluck   38
The ne'er-lust-wearied Antony.

MENAS   I cannot hope   39
Caesar and Antony shall well greet together.   40
His wife that's dead did trespasses to Caesar;   41
His brother warred upon him, although, I think,   42
Not moved by Antony.

POMPEY   I know not, Menas,   43
How lesser enmities may give way to greater.
Were 't not that we stand up against them all,

---

21 Salt lustful. **waned** faded, withered   **23 Tie . . . feasts** i.e., tether
him like an animal in a rich pasture   **24 Epicurean** i.e., let epicurean
25 cloyless which will not satiate   **26 prorogue** defer the operation of
27 Lethe'd oblivious. (From the river of the underworld whose waters
cause forgetfulness in those who drink.)   **28 deliver** report   **31 space
. . . travel** time enough for an even longer journey   **32 less** less important   **34 helm** helmet   **36 rear** raise   **37 opinion** i.e., of ourselves
38 Egypt's widow i.e., Cleopatra, widow of the young King Ptolemy
39 hope expect   **40 well greet** greet one another kindly   **41 did trespasses to** wronged   **42 brother** i.e., Lucius Antonius. (See 1.2.94 ff.)
43 moved provoked, incited

'Twere pregnant they should square between
   themselves,   46
For they have entertainèd cause enough   47
To draw their swords. But how the fear of us
May cement their divisions and bind up
The petty difference, we yet not know.
Be 't as our gods will have 't! It only stands   51
Our lives upon to use our strongest hands.   52
Come, Menas.   *Exeunt.*

❧

2.2 *Enter Enobarbus and Lepidus.*

LEPIDUS
Good Enobarbus, 'tis a worthy deed,
And shall become you well, to entreat your captain
To soft and gentle speech.
ENOBARBUS   I shall entreat him
To answer like himself. If Caesar move him,   4
Let Antony look over Caesar's head   5
And speak as loud as Mars. By Jupiter,
Were I the wearer of Antonio's beard,
I would not shave 't today.   8
LEPIDUS
'Tis not a time for private stomaching.
ENOBARBUS   Every time   9
Serves for the matter that is then born in 't.
LEPIDUS
But small to greater matters must give way.
ENOBARBUS
Not if the small come first.
LEPIDUS   Your speech is passion;

---

46 pregnant likely. **square** quarrel **47 entertainèd** maintained **51–52 It**
. . . hands our very lives depend upon our using our greatest strength

2.2. Location: Rome. Furniture is put out on which Antony and Caesar
are to sit.
4 like himself i.e., in a way befitting his greatness. **move him** i.e., to
anger **5 look . . . head** i.e., condescend to Caesar as a smaller man
8 I . . . shave 't i.e., I would continue to wear it and thereby dare Caesar
to pluck it (in a symbolic gesture for starting a fight) **9 private stomaching** personal resentment

But pray you stir no embers up. Here comes   13
The noble Antony.

Enter Antony and Ventidius [in conversation].

ENOBARBUS   And yonder, Caesar.

*Enter Caesar, Maecenas, and Agrippa, [also in
conversation, by another door].*

ANTONY
If we compose well here, to Parthia.   15
Hark, Ventidius.
CAESAR
I do not know, Maecenas. Ask Agrippa.
LEPIDUS   Noble friends,
That which combined us was most great, and let not
A leaner action rend us. What's amiss,   20
May it be gently heard. When we debate
Our trivial difference loud, we do commit
Murder in healing wounds. Then, noble partners,   23
The rather for I earnestly beseech,   24
Touch you the sourest points with sweetest terms,
Nor curstness grow to th' matter.
ANTONY   'Tis spoken well.   26
Were we before our armies, and to fight,   27
I should do thus.   *Flourish.*
CAESAR   Welcome to Rome.
ANTONY   Thank you.
CAESAR   Sit.
ANTONY   Sit, sir.
CAESAR   Nay, then.   [*They sit.*]
ANTONY
I learn you take things ill which are not so,
Or being, concern you not.
CAESAR   I must be laughed at   35
If, or for nothing or a little, I   36
Should say myself offended, and with you

---

13 embers i.e., old quarrels **15 compose** come to an agreement
20 leaner lesser, more trivial. **rend** divide. **What's** whatever is
23 healing i.e., attempting to heal **24 The rather for** all the more
because **26 Nor . . . grow** nor let ill humor be added **27 to** about to
35 being being so, i.e., even if they are amiss **36 or . . . or** either . . . or

Chiefly i' the world; more laughed at that I should   38
Once name you derogately, when to sound your name   39
It not concerned me.   40

ANTONY
My being in Egypt, Caesar, what was 't to you?

CAESAR
No more than my residing here at Rome
Might be to you in Egypt. Yet if you there
Did practice on my state, your being in Egypt   44
Might be my question.

ANTONY   How intend you "practiced"?   45

CAESAR
You may be pleased to catch at mine intent   46
By what did here befall me. Your wife and brother
Made wars upon me, and their contestation
Was theme for you. You were the word of war.   49

ANTONY
You do mistake your business. My brother never
Did urge me in his act. I did inquire it,   51
And have my learning from some true reports   52
That drew their swords with you. Did he not rather   53
Discredit my authority with yours,   54
And make the wars alike against my stomach,   55
Having alike your cause? Of this my letters   56
Before did satisfy you. If you'll patch a quarrel,   57
As matter whole you have to make it with,   58
It must not be with this.

CAESAR   You praise yourself   59
By laying defects of judgment to me, but
You patched up your excuses.

38 i' the world of all people   **39 Once** under any circumstances.   **derogately** disparagingly   **39–40 when . . . concerned me** i.e., if, as you say, it were none of my business   **44 practice on my state** plot against my position   **45 question** business.   **How intend you** what do you mean   **46 catch at** infer   **49 Was . . . war** provided you with a theme, had you for its theme (or perhaps, operated on your behalf); your name was the watchword, i.e., the central cause, of that conflict   **51 urge . . . act** claim that he was fighting in my behalf.   **inquire** inquire into   **52 reports** reporters   **53 drew . . . you** i.e., fought in your army   **54 Discredit** injure. **with** along with   **55 stomach** desire   **56 Having . . . cause** i.e., I having just as much reason as you to deplore Lucius' action   **57–59 If . . . this** if you insist on manufacturing a quarrel out of shreds and patches, even though you have substantial material to make it with, you've chosen a weak matter to use

ANTONY   Not so, not so.

I know you could not lack, I am certain on 't,   62
Very necessity of this thought, that I,   63
Your partner in the cause 'gainst which he fought,   64
Could not with graceful eyes attend those wars   65
Which fronted mine own peace. As for my wife,   66
I would you had her spirit in such another.   67
The third o' the world is yours, which with a snaffle   68
You may pace easy, but not such a wife.   69

ENOBARBUS   Would we had all such wives, that the men
might go to wars with the women!

ANTONY

So much uncurbable, her garboils, Caesar,   72
Made out of her impatience—which not wanted   73
Shrewdness of policy too—I grieving grant   74
Did you too much disquiet. For that you must   75
But say I could not help it.

CAESAR   I wrote to you   76
When rioting in Alexandria; you   77
Did pocket up my letters and with taunts
Did gibe my missive out of audience.

ANTONY   Sir,   79
He fell upon me ere admitted, then.   80
Three kings I had newly feasted, and did want   81
Of what I was i' the morning. But next day   82
I told him of myself, which was as much   83
As to have asked him pardon. Let this fellow
Be nothing of our strife; if we contend,   85
Out of our question wipe him.

CAESAR   You have broken   86

62–63 I know . . . thought I'm certain you must have known   **64 he** i.e.,
Lucius   **65 with . . . attend** regard favorably   **66 fronted** confronted,
opposed   **67 her . . . another** i.e., a wife such as she was   **68 snaffle**
bridle bit   **69 pace** put through its paces, manage   **72–75 So . . . disquiet** I unhappily concede that her unmanageable commotions, caused
by her impatience but not lacking in keenness of stratagem, did too
much to disquiet you, Caesar   **76 But** only   **77 When** while you were
79 gibe taunt.   **missive** messenger.   **out of audience** out of your presence   **80 fell** burst in   **81–82 did want . . . morning** was not at my best
as I had been earlier in the day   **83 of myself** i.e., of my having had a
lot to drink   **85 Be nothing of** have nothing to do with   **86 question**
contention

The article of your oath, which you shall never   87
Have tongue to charge me with.

LEPIDUS   Soft, Caesar!   89

ANTONY   No, Lepidus, let him speak.
The honor is sacred which he talks on now,
Supposing that I lacked it. But, on, Caesar: 92
The article of my oath—

CAESAR
To lend me arms and aid when I required them,   94
The which you both denied.

ANTONY   Neglected, rather;
And then when poisoned hours had bound me up
From mine own knowledge. As nearly as I may   97
I'll play the penitent to you, but mine honesty   98
Shall not make poor my greatness nor my power   99
Work without it. Truth is that Fulvia,   100
To have me out of Egypt, made wars here,
For which myself, the ignorant motive, do   102
So far ask pardon as befits mine honor
To stoop in such a case.

LEPIDUS   'Tis noble spoken.   104

MAECENAS
If it might please you to enforce no further
The griefs between ye; to forget them quite   106
Were to remember that the present need
Speaks to atone you.

LEPIDUS   Worthily spoken, Maecenas.   108

ENOBARBUS   Or, if you borrow one another's love for the
instant, you may, when you hear no more words of
Pompey, return it again. You shall have time to wran-
gle in when you have nothing else to do.

ANTONY
Thou art a soldier only. Speak no more.

---

87 article terms   **89 Soft** gently, go easy   **92 Supposing . . . it** i.e., which
Caesar implies that I lacked   **94 required** requested   **97 From . . .
knowledge** from knowing myself   **98–100 mine . . . it** my honesty (in
admitting my overindulgence) will not go so far as to dishonor my
greatness, nor, conversely, will my great power function without honesty   **102 motive** moving or inciting cause   **104 noble** nobly   **106 griefs**
grievances   **108 atone** reconcile

ENOBARBUS   That truth should be silent I had almost
  forgot.

ANTONY
  You wrong this presence. Therefore speak no more.   116

ENOBARBUS   Go to, then; your considerate stone.   117

CAESAR
  I do not much dislike the matter, but
  The manner of his speech; for 't cannot be
  We shall remain in friendship, our conditions   120
  So differing in their acts. Yet, if I knew
  What hoop should hold us staunch, from edge to edge   122
  O' the world I would pursue it.

AGRIPPA   Give me leave, Caesar.

CAESAR   Speak, Agrippa.

AGRIPPA
  Thou hast a sister by the mother's side,
  Admired Octavia. Great Mark Antony
  Is now a widower.

CAESAR   Say not so, Agrippa.
  If Cleopatra heard you, your reproof
  Were well deserved of rashness.   130

ANTONY
  I am not married, Caesar. Let me hear
  Agrippa further speak.

AGRIPPA
  To hold you in perpetual amity,
  To make you brothers, and to knit your hearts
  With an unslipping knot, take Antony
  Octavia to his wife, whose beauty claims
  No worse a husband than the best of men,
  Whose virtue and whose general graces speak   138
  That which none else can utter. By this marriage   139
  All little jealousies, which now seem great,   140

---

116 presence company   **117 Go to, then** i.e., all right, all right.   **your
considerate stone** i.e., I shall continue to think (consider), but be as
silent as a stone   **120 conditions** temperaments, dispositions   **122 hoop**
barrel hoop.   **staunch** firm, watertight   **130 of rashness** because of
your rashness (in overlooking Cleopatra's claim to Antony)   **138–139 graces
. . . utter** i.e., virtues speak for themselves in a way that no one else can
do justice to   **140 jealousies** misunderstandings, suspicions

And all great fears, which now import their dangers,   141
Would then be nothing. Truths would be tales,   142
Where now half tales be truths. Her love to both   143
Would each to other and all loves to both
Draw after her. Pardon what I have spoke,
For 'tis a studied, not a present thought,
By duty ruminated.

ANTONY   Will Caesar speak?
CAESAR
Not till he hears how Antony is touched   148
With what is spoke already.   149
ANTONY   What power is in Agrippa
If I would say, "Agrippa, be it so,"
To make this good?
CAESAR   The power of Caesar and
His power unto Octavia.
ANTONY   May I never   153
To this good purpose, that so fairly shows,   154
Dream of impediment! Let me have thy hand
Further this act of grace, and from this hour   156
The heart of brothers govern in our loves
And sway our great designs!
CAESAR   There's my hand.
                              [They clasp hands.]
A sister I bequeath you whom no brother
Did ever love so dearly. Let her live
To join our kingdoms and our hearts; and never   161
Fly off our loves again!
LEPIDUS   Happily, amen!   162
ANTONY
I did not think to draw my sword 'gainst Pompey,
For he hath laid strange courtesies and great   164
Of late upon me. I must thank him only,   165

141 **import** carry with them   142–143 **Truths . . . truths** true reports (no matter how distressing) would then be discounted as mere rumors, whereas at present half-true reports are taken for the whole truth   148–149 **touched With** affected by   153 **unto** over   154 **fairly shows** looks so promising   156 **Further** i.e., in furtherance of   161–162 **never . . . again** may our amity never desert us again   164 **strange** remarkable   165 **only** at least

Lest my remembrance suffer ill report;   166
At heel of that, defy him.

LEPIDUS   Time calls upon 's.   167
Of us must Pompey presently be sought,   168
Or else he seeks out us.

ANTONY   Where lies he?

CAESAR
About the mount Misena.

ANTONY   What is his strength   171
By land?

CAESAR   Great and increasing; but by sea
He is an absolute master.

ANTONY   So is the fame.   173
Would we had spoke together! Haste we for it.   174
Yet, ere we put ourselves in arms, dispatch we
The business we have talked of.

CAESAR   With most gladness,   176
And do invite you to my sister's view,   177
Whither straight I'll lead you.   178

ANTONY
Let us, Lepidus, not lack your company.

LEPIDUS
Noble Antony, not sickness should detain me.   180

> *Flourish. Exeunt. Manent Enobarbus, Agrippa,*
> *Maecenas.*

MAECENAS   Welcome from Egypt, sir.

ENOBARBUS   Half the heart of Caesar, worthy Maecenas!   182
My honorable friend, Agrippa!

AGRIPPA   Good Enobarbus!

MAECENAS   We have cause to be glad that matters are so
well digested. You stayed well by 't in Egypt.   186

---

166 remembrance readiness to remember or acknowledge favors done
167 At heel of immediately after   **168 Of** by.   **presently** at once
171 Misena i.e., Misenum, in southern Italy (not in Sicily, where 2.1
perhaps takes place)   **173 So is the fame** so it is reported   **174 Would
. . . together** i.e., would the negotiations with Pompey were already over
(?)   **176 most** the greatest   **177 to my sister's view** to see my sister
178 straight straightway   **180 s.d. Manent** they remain onstage
182 Half the heart i.e., one of Caesar's two closest advisers, along with
Agrippa; or, simply, a very close friend of Caesar's   **186 digested** disposed.   **stayed well by 't** kept at it

ENOBARBUS Ay, sir, we did sleep day out of counte- 187
nance and made the night light with drinking. 188

MAECENAS Eight wild boars roasted whole at a break-
fast, and but twelve persons there; is this true?

ENOBARBUS This was but as a fly by an eagle. We had 191
much more monstrous matter of feast, which worthily
deserved noting.

MAECENAS She's a most triumphant lady, if report be 194
square to her. 195

ENOBARBUS When she first met Mark Antony, she
pursed up his heart upon the river of Cydnus. 197

AGRIPPA There she appeared indeed, or my reporter de- 198
vised well for her. 199

ENOBARBUS I will tell you.
The barge she sat in, like a burnished throne, 201
Burnt on the water. The poop was beaten gold; 202
Purple the sails, and so perfumèd that
The winds were lovesick with them. The oars were silver,
Which to the tune of flutes kept stroke, and made
The water which they beat to follow faster,
As amorous of their strokes. For her own person, 207
It beggared all description: she did lie
In her pavilion—cloth-of-gold of tissue— 209
O'erpicturing that Venus where we see
The fancy outwork nature. On each side her 211
Stood pretty dimpled boys, like smiling Cupids,
With divers-colored fans, whose wind did seem 213
To glow the delicate cheeks which they did cool, 214
And what they undid did.

AGRIPPA   O, rare for Antony!

ENOBARBUS
Her gentlewomen, like the Nereides, 216

187–188 we . . . countenance we insulted day by sleeping right through
it   188 light giddy and debauched (with play on the commoner meaning
of "bright")   191 by beside, compared with   194 triumphant magnificent   195 square just   197 pursed up pocketed up, put in her purse
198–199 devised invented   201 burnished lustrous, shiny   202 poop a
short deck built over the main deck at the stern of the vessel   207 As as
if.   For as for   209 cloth-of-gold of tissue cloth made of gold thread
and silk woven together   211 fancy imagination   213 divers-colored
multicolored   214 glow cause to glow   216 Nereides sea nymphs

So many mermaids, tended her i' th' eyes,   217
And made their bends adornings. At the helm   218
A seeming mermaid steers. The silken tackle
Swell with the touches of those flower-soft hands,
That yarely frame the office. From the barge   221
A strange invisible perfume hits the sense
Of the adjacent wharfs. The city cast   223
Her people out upon her; and Antony,
Enthroned i' the marketplace, did sit alone,
Whistling to th' air, which, but for vacancy,   226
Had gone to gaze on Cleopatra too
And made a gap in nature.

AGRIPPA   Rare Egyptian!

ENOBARBUS
Upon her landing, Antony sent to her,
Invited her to supper. She replied
It should be better he became her guest,
Which she entreated. Our courteous Antony,
Whom ne'er the word of "No" woman heard speak,
Being barbered ten times o'er, goes to the feast,
And for his ordinary pays his heart   235
For what his eyes eat only.

AGRIPPA   Royal wench!   236
She made great Caesar lay his sword to bed;   237
He plowed her, and she cropped.

ENOBARBUS   I saw her once   238
Hop forty paces through the public street,
And having lost her breath, she spoke and panted,
That she did make defect perfection,   241
And, breathless, power breathe forth.

MAECENAS
Now Antony must leave her utterly.

ENOBARBUS Never. He will not.

---

217 So many i.e., as if they were so many. **i' th' eyes** in her sight, watching and obeying her every look (?) **218 made ... adornings** made their graceful bowings beautiful, as in a work of art **221 yarely frame** nimbly perform. **office** task **223 wharfs** banks **226 but for vacancy** except that it would have created a vacuum **235 ordinary** meal, supper (such as one might obtain at a public table in a tavern) **236 eat** ate. (Pronounced *et*.) **237 Caesar** i.e., Julius Caesar, by whom Cleopatra had a son named Caesarion **238 cropped** bore fruit (a son) **241 That** so that

Age cannot wither her, nor custom stale   245
Her infinite variety. Other women cloy
The appetites they feed, but she makes hungry
Where most she satisfies; for vilest things
Become themselves in her, that the holy priests   249
Bless her when she is riggish.   250

MAECENAS
If beauty, wisdom, modesty can settle
The heart of Antony, Octavia is
A blessèd lottery to him.

AGRIPPA   Let us go.   253
Good Enobarbus, make yourself my guest
Whilst you abide here.

ENOBARBUS   Humbly, sir, I thank you.
                                        Exeunt.

                            ❖

2.3   *Enter Antony, Caesar, Octavia between them.*

ANTONY
The world and my great office will sometimes
Divide me from your bosom.

OCTAVIA   All which time
Before the gods my knee shall bow my prayers
To them for you.

ANTONY   Good night, sir. My Octavia,
Read not my blemishes in the world's report.   5
I have not kept my square, but that to come   6
Shall all be done by th' rule. Good night, dear lady.
Good night, sir.

CAESAR   Good night.   *Exit [with Octavia].*

        Enter Soothsayer.

---

245 custom repeated experience.   **stale** make stale   **249 Become themselves** are becoming, attractive.   **that** so that   **250 riggish** lustful
253 lottery prize, gift of fortune

2.3. Location: Rome.
5 Read interpret.   **in** according to   **6 kept my square** kept to a straight
course (as guided by a carpenter's square; with pun on *rule*, "ruler" in
next line).   **that** that which is

ANTONY
  Now, sirrah: you do wish yourself in Egypt?   10
SOOTHSAYER   Would I had never come from thence, nor
  you thither!   12
ANTONY   If you can, your reason?
SOOTHSAYER   I see it in my motion, have it not in my   14
  tongue; but yet hie you to Egypt again.   15
ANTONY
  Say to me, whose fortunes shall rise higher,
  Caesar's or mine?
SOOTHSAYER   Caesar's.
  Therefore, O Antony, stay not by his side.
  Thy daemon—that thy spirit which keeps thee—is   20
  Noble, courageous, high unmatchable,   21
  Where Caesar's is not; but near him thy angel   22
  Becomes afeard, as being o'erpowered. Therefore
  Make space enough between you.
ANTONY   Speak this no more.
SOOTHSAYER
  To none but thee; no more but when to thee.   25
  If thou dost play with him at any game,
  Thou art sure to lose; and of that natural luck   27
  He beats thee 'gainst the odds. Thy luster thickens   28
  When he shines by. I say again, thy spirit   29
  Is all afraid to govern thee near him;
  But, he away, 'tis noble.
ANTONY   Get thee gone.
  Say to Ventidius I would speak with him.
                          Exit [Soothsayer].
  He shall to Parthia.—Be it art or hap,   33
  He hath spoken true. The very dice obey him,
  And in our sports my better cunning faints   35
  Under his chance. If we draw lots, he speeds.   36
  His cocks do win the battle still of mine   37

---

10 sirrah (A form of address to a social inferior.)   **12 thither** to that
place   **14 in my motion** intuitively, by inward prompting   **15 hie** hasten
20 daemon guardian spirit.   **that thy spirit** that spirit of yours.   **keeps**
protects   **21 high unmatchable** unmatchable in the extreme   **22 Where**
whereas   **25 no more but when** only when   **27 of** by   **28 thickens** grows
dim   **29 by** nearby   **33 art or hap** skill or luck   **35 cunning** skill
36 chance luck.   **speeds** wins   **37 still** always.   **of** from

When it is all to naught, and his quails ever   38
Beat mine, inhooped, at odds. I will to Egypt;   39
And though I make this marriage for my peace,
I' th' East my pleasure lies.

    Enter Ventidius.

                       O, come, Ventidius.
You must to Parthia. Your commission's ready;
Follow me and receive 't.   *Exeunt.*

❖

2.4   *Enter Lepidus, Maecenas, and Agrippa.*

LEPIDUS
  Trouble yourselves no further. Pray you, hasten
  Your generals after.
AGRIPPA   Sir, Mark Antony   2
  Will e'en but kiss Octavia, and we'll follow.   3
LEPIDUS
  Till I shall see you in your soldier's dress,   4
  Which will become you both, farewell.
MAECENAS   We shall,   5
  As I conceive the journey, be at the Mount   6
  Before you, Lepidus.
LEPIDUS   Your way is shorter;
  My purposes do draw me much about.   8
  You'll win two days upon me.
MAECENAS, AGRIPPA   Sir, good success!
LEPIDUS Farewell.   *Exeunt.*

❖

2.5   *Enter Cleopatra, Charmian, Iras, and Alexas.*

38 When . . . naught when the odds are everything to nothing (in my favor) **39 inhooped** (The birds were enclosed in hoops to make them fight.) **at odds** i.e., the odds being in my favor

2.4. Location: Rome.
2 Your generals after after your generals **3 e'en but** only, just **4 dress** garb, apparel **5 become** suit **6 conceive** understand. **the Mount** i.e., Mount Misenum **8 about** roundabout

2.5. Location: Alexandria. Cleopatra's palace.

CLEOPATRA

Give me some music; music, moody food   1
Of us that trade in love.

ALL   The music, ho!

Enter Mardian the eunuch.

CLEOPATRA

Let it alone. Let's to billiards. Come, Charmian.

CHARMIAN

My arm is sore. Best play with Mardian.

CLEOPATRA

As well a woman with an eunuch played
As with a woman. Come, you'll play with me, sir?

MARDIAN   As well as I can, madam.

CLEOPATRA

And when good will is showed, though 't come too short,   8
The actor may plead pardon. I'll none now.   9
Give me mine angle; we'll to the river. There,   10
My music playing far off, I will betray
Tawny-finned fishes. My bended hook shall pierce
Their slimy jaws, and as I draw them up
I'll think them every one an Antony
And say, "Aha! You're caught."

CHARMIAN   'Twas merry when
You wagered on your angling, when your diver
Did hang a salt fish on his hook, which he   17
With fervency drew up.

CLEOPATRA   That time—O times!—   18
I laughed him out of patience; and that night
I laughed him into patience. And next morn,
Ere the ninth hour, I drunk him to his bed,   21
Then put my tires and mantles on him, whilst   22
I wore his sword Philippan.

Enter a Messenger.

O, from Italy!   23

1 **moody** melancholy   8 **too short** (A bawdy joke on Mardian's being
castrated; *will* suggests "sexual desire," *come* suggests "reach orgasm.")   9 **I'll none now** i.e., I won't play billiards after all   10 **angle**
rod and line   17 **salt** dried, preserved in salt   18 **With fervency** excit-
edly   21 **ninth hour** i.e., 9 A.M.   **drunk** drank   22 **tires** headdresses, or
perhaps attire   23 **Philippan** (Named for Antony's victory over Brutus
and Cassius at Philippi.)

Ram thou thy fruitful tidings in mine ears,
That long time have been barren.
MESSENGER   Madam, madam—
CLEOPATRA
Antonio's dead! If thou say so, villain,
Thou kill'st thy mistress; but well and free,
If thou so yield him, there is gold, and here   28
My bluest veins to kiss—a hand that kings
Have lipped, and trembled kissing.
               [*She offers him gold, and her hand to kiss.*]
MESSENGER   First, madam, he is well.
CLEOPATRA
Why, there's more gold. But, sirrah, mark, we use
To say the dead are well. Bring it to that,   33
The gold I give thee will I melt and pour
Down thy ill-uttering throat.
MESSENGER   Good madam, hear me.
CLEOPATRA   Well, go to, I will.   37
But there's no goodness in thy face, if Antony
Be free and healthful—so tart a favor   39
To trumpet such good tidings! If not well,
Thou shouldst come like a Fury crowned with snakes,   41
Not like a formal man.
MESSENGER   Will 't please you hear me?   42
CLEOPATRA
I have a mind to strike thee ere thou speak'st.
Yet, if thou say Antony lives, is well,
Or friends with Caesar, or not captive to him,
I'll set thee in a shower of gold and hail
Rich pearls upon thee.
MESSENGER   Madam, he's well.
CLEOPATRA   Well said.
MESSENGER
And friends with Caesar.
CLEOPATRA   Thou'rt an honest man.   48
MESSENGER
Caesar and he are greater friends than ever.

---

28 yield grant   **33 well** i.e., well out of it, in heaven.   **Bring it to that** if
that is your meaning   **37 go to** i.e., all right, then. (Said remonstrat-
ingly.)   **39 tart a favor** sour a face   **41 Fury** avenging goddess of classical
mythology   **42 like . . . man** in ordinary human form   **48 honest** worthy

CLEOPATRA
Make thee a fortune from me.

MESSENGER   But yet, madam—

CLEOPATRA
I do not like "But yet"; it does allay   51
The good precedence. Fie upon "But yet"!   52
"But yet" is as a jailer to bring forth
Some monstrous malefactor. Prithee, friend,
Pour out the pack of matter to mine ear,   55
The good and bad together. He's friends with Caesar,
In state of health, thou sayst, and, thou sayst, free.

MESSENGER
Free, madam? No, I made no such report.
He's bound unto Octavia.

CLEOPATRA   For what good turn?   59

MESSENGER
For the best turn i' the bed.

CLEOPATRA   I am pale, Charmian.

MESSENGER
Madam, he's married to Octavia.

CLEOPATRA
The most infectious pestilence upon thee!
                        Strikes him down.

MESSENGER
Good madam, patience.

CLEOPATRA   What say you?   *Strikes him.*
                         Hence,
Horrible villain, or I'll spurn thine eyes   64
Like balls before me! I'll unhair thy head!   65
              She hales him up and down.
Thou shalt be whipped with wire and stewed in brine,
Smarting in lingering pickle!

MESSENGER   Gracious madam,   67
I that do bring the news made not the match.

CLEOPATRA
Say 'tis not so, a province I will give thee
And make thy fortunes proud. The blow thou hadst

51–52 allay . . . precedence annul the good news that preceded it
55 pack of matter entire contents (as of a peddler's pack)   **59 turn**
favor, purpose. (But the Messenger replies in the sense of "feat, bout,"
with sexual suggestion.)   **64 spurn** kick   **65 s.d. hales** drags   **67 pickle**
pickling solution

Shall make thy peace for moving me to rage,   71
And I will boot thee with what gift besides   72
Thy modesty can beg.
MESSENGER   He's married, madam.
CLEOPATRA
Rogue, thou hast lived too long!   *Draw[s] a knife.*
MESSENGER   Nay then, I'll run.
What mean you, madam? I have made no fault.   *Exit.*
CHARMIAN
Good madam, keep yourself within yourself.   76
The man is innocent.
CLEOPATRA
Some innocents scape not the thunderbolt.
Melt Egypt into Nile, and kindly creatures   79
Turn all to serpents! Call the slave again.
Though I am mad, I will not bite him. Call!   81
CHARMIAN
He is afeard to come.
CLEOPATRA   I will not hurt him.
                    [*The Messenger is sent for.*]
These hands do lack nobility, that they strike
A meaner than myself, since I myself   84
Have given myself the cause.

                Enter the Messenger again.

                                Come hither, sir.   85
Though it be honest, it is never good
To bring bad news. Give to a gracious message
An host of tongues, but let ill tidings tell   88
Themselves when they be felt.   89
MESSENGER   I have done my duty.
CLEOPATRA   Is he married?
I cannot hate thee worser than I do
If thou again say "Yes."

71 make thy peace compensate, mollify me   **72 boot thee with** give you
into the bargain, or make amends with.   **what** whatever   **76 keep . . .
yourself** i.e., control yourself   **79 kindly** endowed with innately good
qualities   **81 mad** (1) angry (2) insane, and so apt to bite   **84 A meaner**
one of lower social station   **84–85 since . . . cause** since I am the one I
ought to blame   **85 the cause** i.e., by loving Antony   **88 host** multitude   **89 when . . . felt** i.e., when they occur, making themselves known
by the occurrence

MESSENGER   He's married, madam.

CLEOPATRA
The gods confound thee! Dost thou hold there still?   94

MESSENGER
Should I lie, madam?

CLEOPATRA   O, I would thou didst,
So half my Egypt were submerged and made   96
A cistern for scaled snakes! Go, get thee hence.   97
Hadst thou Narcissus in thy face, to me   98
Thou wouldst appear most ugly. He is married?

MESSENGER
I crave Your Highness' pardon.

CLEOPATRA   He is married?

MESSENGER
Take no offense that I would not offend you.   101
To punish me for what you make me do
Seems much unequal. He's married to Octavia.   103

CLEOPATRA
O, that his fault should make a knave of thee,   104
That art not what thou'rt sure of! Get thee hence.   105
The merchandise which thou hast brought from Rome
Are all too dear for me. Lie they upon thy hand,   107
And be undone by 'em!   [Exit Messenger.]

CHARMIAN   Good Your Highness, patience.   108

CLEOPATRA
In praising Antony, I have dispraised Caesar.

CHARMIAN   Many times, madam.

CLEOPATRA
I am paid for 't now. Lead me from hence;
I faint. O Iras, Charmian! 'Tis no matter.
Go to the fellow, good Alexas. Bid him
Report the feature of Octavia: her years,

---

94 confound destroy.   **hold there still** stick to your story   **96 So** even
if   **97 cistern** tank.   **scaled** scaly   **98 Narcissus** beautiful youth of
Greek mythology who fell in love with his own reflected image
101 Take . . . offend you don't be offended that I hesitate to offend you
(by telling bad news); or, don't interpret as offense what is not meant to
offend   **103 much unequal** most unjust   **104–105 O, that . . . sure of**
i.e., it's too bad that Antony's fault puts you in the wrong, you who
shouldn't be equated with the bad news you report as true   **107 dear**
(1) expensive (2) emotionally precious   **107–108 Lie . . . undone** may
they remain in your possession unsold, and may you be bankrupt,
financially ruined (i.e., may you never profit from your bad tidings)

Her inclination. Let him not leave out   115
The color of her hair. Bring me word quickly.
                              [*Exit Alexas.*]
Let him forever go!—Let him not, Charmian.   117
Though he be painted one way like a Gorgon,   118
The other way's a Mars. [*To Mardian.*] Bid you Alexas   119
Bring me word how tall she is.—Pity me, Charmian,
But do not speak to me. Lead me to my chamber.
                              Exeunt.

❖

2.6   *Flourish. Enter Pompey [and Menas] at one
        door, with drum and trumpet; at another,
        Caesar, Lepidus, Antony, Enobarbus, Maecenas,
        Agrippa, with soldiers marching.*

POMPEY
  Your hostages I have, so have you mine,
  And we shall talk before we fight.
CAESAR   Most meet   2
  That first we come to words; and therefore have we
  Our written purposes before us sent,
  Which, if thou hast considered, let us know
  If 'twill tie up thy discontented sword   6
  And carry back to Sicily much tall youth   7
  That else must perish here.
POMPEY   To you all three,
  The senators alone of this great world,   9

115 **inclination** disposition   117 **him** i.e., Antony   118–119 **Though . . .
Mars** (Alludes to a type of picture known as a perspective, which shows
different objects when looked at from different angles of vision.)
a Gorgon a female monster with serpents in her hair; her head was
capable of turning to stone anything that met her gaze

2.6. **Location: Near Misenum, in southern Italy near modern Naples.
(But 2.1 perhaps took place in Messina, Sicily.)**
2 **meet** fitting   6 **tie . . . sword** i.e., satisfy your concerns and allow you
to forgo a fight   7 **tall** brave   9 **senators alone** i.e., sole rulers of the
empire (and those who have thus supplanted the Senate)

Chief factors for the gods: I do not know   10
Wherefore my father should revengers want,   11
Having a son and friends, since Julius Caesar,   12
Who at Philippi the good Brutus ghosted,   13
There saw you laboring for him. What was 't   14
That moved pale Cassius to conspire? And what
Made all-honored, honest Roman Brutus,   16
With the armed rest, courtiers of beauteous freedom,   17
To drench the Capitol, but that they would   18
Have one man but a man? And that is it   19
Hath made me rig my navy, at whose burden
The angered ocean foams, with which I meant
To scourge th' ingratitude that despiteful Rome   22
Cast on my noble father.
CAESAR   Take your time.
ANTONY
Thou canst not fear us, Pompey, with thy sails;   24
We'll speak with thee at sea. At land thou know'st   25
How much we do o'ercount thee.
POMPEY   At land indeed   26
Thou dost o'ercount me of my father's house;
But since the cuckoo builds not for himself,   28
Remain in 't as thou mayst.
LEPIDUS   Be pleased to tell us—   29

10 factors agents 10–14 I do . . . for him (Julius Caesar defeated
Pompey's father, Pompey the Great, and was subsequently assassinated
by Brutus and Cassius among others. Caesar's ghost appeared to Brutus at Philippi, where the combined forces of Antony, Octavius, and
Lepidus defeated Brutus and Cassius. [See *Julius Caesar*.] Since Antony,
Octavius, and Lepidus thus defeated the avengers of Pompey the Great's
death, Pompey the Great's sons and friends should become his avengers
by continuing to war on Antony, Octavius, and Lepidus.) 11 want
lack 13 ghosted haunted 16 honest honorable 17 the armed rest i.e.,
the rest of those who were armed. courtiers wooers, those who serve
freedom only 18 drench bathe in blood 19 Have . . . a man (The
republican conspirators acted to keep Julius Caesar from accepting the
crown.) 22 despiteful cruel, malicious 24 fear frighten 25 speak
with confront 26 o'ercount outnumber. (But Pompey's use of the word
in the next line implies that Antony has cheated him. Plutarch informs
us that Antony bought the elder Pompey's house at auction and later
refused to pay for it.) 28 cuckoo a bird that builds no nest for itself
but lays its eggs in other birds' nests. (Perhaps suggests also that Antony is a cuckold maker.) 29 as thou mayst as long as you can, or since
you can

For this is from the present—how you take   30
The offers we have sent you.

CAESAR   There's the point.

ANTONY
Which do not be entreated to, but weigh   32
What it is worth embraced.

CAESAR   And what may follow,   33
To try a larger fortune.

POMPEY   You have made me offer   34
Of Sicily, Sardinia; and I must
Rid all the sea of pirates; then, to send   36
Measures of wheat to Rome. This 'greed upon,
To part with unhacked edges and bear back   38
Our targes undinted.

CAESAR, ANTONY, LEPIDUS   That's our offer.

POMPEY   Know then   39
I came before you here a man prepared
To take this offer, but Mark Antony
Put me to some impatience. Though I lose
The praise of it by telling, you must know,   43
When Caesar and your brother were at blows,
Your mother came to Sicily and did find
Her welcome friendly.

ANTONY   I have heard it, Pompey,
And am well studied for a liberal thanks   47
Which I do owe you.

POMPEY   Let me have your hand.
                          [*They shake hands.*]
I did not think, sir, to have met you here.

ANTONY
The beds i' th' East are soft; and thanks to you,
That called me timelier than my purpose hither,   51
For I have gained by 't.

CAESAR   Since I saw you last
There's a change upon you.

---

30 from the present digressing from the business at hand.   **take** i.e.,
respond to   **32 do . . . to** i.e., do not accept merely because we ask
33 embraced if accepted by you   **34 To . . . fortune** i.e., if you decide to
risk war with the triumvirs; or, if you join with us to share a greater
fortune   **36 to send** I am to send   **38 To part** we are to part company.
edges swords   **39 targes** shields   **43 praise of** credit for   **47 well
studied for** well prepared to deliver   **51 timelier** earlier

POMPEY   Well, I know not
What counts harsh Fortune casts upon my face,   54
But in my bosom shall she never come
To make my heart her vassal.
LEPIDUS   Well met here.
POMPEY
I hope so, Lepidus. Thus we are agreed.
I crave our composition may be written   58
And sealed between us.
CAESAR   That's the next to do.   59
POMPEY
We'll feast each other ere we part, and let's
Draw lots who shall begin.
ANTONY   That will I, Pompey.   61
POMPEY
No, Antony, take the lot. But, first or last,   62
Your fine Egyptian cookery shall have
The fame. I have heard that Julius Caesar
Grew fat with feasting there.
ANTONY   You have heard much.
POMPEY   I have fair meanings, sir.   67
ANTONY   And fair words to them.   68
POMPEY   Then so much have I heard.   69
And I have heard Apollodorus carried—   70
ENOBARBUS
No more of that. He did so.
POMPEY   What, I pray you?   71
ENOBARBUS
A certain queen to Caesar in a mattress.   72
POMPEY
I know thee now. How far'st thou, soldier?
ENOBARBUS   Well,

54 counts tally marks. (From the practice of casting accounts or reckon-
ings by means of marks or notches on tallies.)   **casts** calculates
58 composition agreement   **59 sealed between us** stamped with the
official seal of each cosigner   **61 That will I** i.e., I will begin   **62 take
the lot** draw lots with the rest of us, accept the results of the lottery.
first or last whether you win the lottery to go first or last   **67 fair** i.e.,
friendly   **68 fair** i.e., well-chosen   **69 Then . . . heard** i.e., I am not
implying more about Antony in Egypt than my words honestly mean
70–72 Apollodorus . . . mattress (Alludes to a tale told by Plutarch
according to which Cleopatra had herself rolled up in a mattress and
carried secretly by Apollodorus to meet Julius Caesar.)

And well am like to do, for I perceive
Four feasts are toward.

POMPEY   Let me shake thy hand.   75
                         [*They shake hands.*]
I never hated thee. I have seen thee fight
When I have envied thy behavior.

ENOBARBUS   Sir,
I never loved you much, but I ha' praised ye
When you have well deserved ten times as much
As I have said you did.

POMPEY   Enjoy thy plainness;   80
It nothing ill becomes thee.   81
Aboard my galley I invite you all.
Will you lead, lords?

CAESAR, ANTONY, LEPIDUS   Show 's the way, sir.

POMPEY   Come.   83
          Exeunt. Manent Enobarbus and Menas.

MENAS [*Aside*] Thy father, Pompey, would ne'er have
made this treaty.—You and I have known, sir.   85

ENOBARBUS   At sea, I think.

MENAS   We have, sir.

ENOBARBUS   You have done well by water.

MENAS   And you by land.

ENOBARBUS   I will praise any man that will praise me,
though it cannot be denied what I have done by land.

MENAS   Nor what I have done by water.

ENOBARBUS   Yes, something you can deny for your own
safety: you have been a great thief by sea.

MENAS   And you by land.

ENOBARBUS   There I deny my land service. But give me 96
your hand, Menas. [*They shake hands.*] If our eyes had
authority, here they might take two thieves kissing.   98

MENAS   All men's faces are true, whatsoe'er their
hands are.

ENOBARBUS   But there is never a fair woman has a true 101
face.

---

75 toward coming up   **80 plainness** bluntness   **81 nothing . . . thee**
suits you not at all badly   **83 s.d. Manent** they remain onstage
85 known known each other   **96 There** in respect to that   **98 authority**
i.e., to make arrests, like a constable.   **take** arrest.   **two thieves kissing**
(1) our two thieving hands shaking (2) two thieves greeting each other
101 true honest (because women use cosmetic art to conceal defects)

MENAS   No slander; they steal hearts.   103

ENOBARBUS   We came hither to fight with you.

MENAS   For my part, I am sorry it is turned to a drinking.   105
Pompey doth this day laugh away his fortune.

ENOBARBUS   If he do, sure he cannot weep 't back
again.

MENAS   You've said, sir. We looked not for Mark An-   109
tony here. Pray you, is he married to Cleopatra?

ENOBARBUS   Caesar's sister is called Octavia.

MENAS   True, sir. She was the wife of Caius Marcellus.

ENOBARBUS   But she is now the wife of Marcus
Antonius.

MENAS   Pray ye, sir?   115

ENOBARBUS   'Tis true.

MENAS   Then is Caesar and he forever knit together.

ENOBARBUS   If I were bound to divine of this unity, I   118
would not prophesy so.

MENAS   I think the policy of that purpose made more in   120
the marriage than the love of the parties.

ENOBARBUS   I think so too. But you shall find the band
that seems to tie their friendship together will be the
very strangler of their amity. Octavia is of a holy, cold,
and still conversation.   125

MENAS   Who would not have his wife so?

ENOBARBUS   Not he that himself is not so, which is
Mark Antony. He will to his Egyptian dish again.
Then shall the sighs of Octavia blow the fire up in
Caesar, and, as I said before, that which is the strength
of their amity shall prove the immediate author of   131
their variance. Antony will use his affection where it   132
is; he married but his occasion here.   133

MENAS   And thus it may be. Come, sir, will you
aboard? I have a health for you.   135

ENOBARBUS   I shall take it, sir. We have used our throats
in Egypt.

---

103 No slander i.e., you speak true (since women in their own way are
thieves also)   **105 a drinking** an occasion for drinking   **109 You've said**
i.e., you've spoken truly   **115 Pray ye** are you in earnest   **118 divine of**
prophesy about   **120 made more** played more of a role   **125 conversation** demeanor   **131–132 author ... variance** cause of their falling
out   **132–133 use ... it is** i.e., satisfy his passion in Egypt   **133 his
occasion** what his interests demanded   **135 health** toast

MENAS   Come, let's away.   *Exeunt.*

❖

2.7   *Music plays. Enter two or three Servants with
          a banquet.*

FIRST SERVANT   Here they'll be, man. Some o' their
plants are ill-rooted already; the least wind i' the world 2
will blow them down.
SECOND SERVANT   Lepidus is high-colored.   4
FIRST SERVANT   They have made him drink alms drink.   5
SECOND SERVANT   As they pinch one another by the dis-   6
position, he cries out, "No more," reconciles them to   7
his entreaty, and himself to the drink.   8
FIRST SERVANT   But it raises the greater war between
him and his discretion.
SECOND SERVANT   Why, this it is to have a name in great   11
men's fellowship. I had as lief have a reed that will do   12
me no service as a partisan I could not heave.   13
FIRST SERVANT   To be called into a huge sphere and not   14
to be seen to move in 't, are the holes where eyes   15
should be, which pitifully disaster the cheeks.   16

   *A sennet sounded. Enter Caesar, Antony, Pompey,
   Lepidus, Agrippa, Maecenas, Enobarbus, Menas,
   with other captains [and a Boy].*

**2.7. Location: On board Pompey's galley, off Misenum in southern Italy.
A table and stools are brought on.**
s.d. banquet a course of the feast, probably dessert   **2 plants** soles of
the feet (with pun on usual sense)   **4 high-colored** flushed   **5 alms
drink** drink given or taken in charity (?), i.e., to further the business of
reconciliation (as indicated in the following speech)   **6–7 pinch . . .
disposition** chafe one another, fall to bickering as prompted by their
contrasting temperaments. (Lepidus stops them but has to join them in
fresh rounds of drink.)   **8 his entreaty** i.e., that they stop quarreling
11 a name a name only   **12 had as lief** would just as soon   **13 partisan**
long-bladed spear. (Here, metaphorically, too large a weapon for Lepidus to wield.)   **14–16 To . . . cheeks** to be summoned by fortune to
greatness and yet not be able to fulfill the role greatly is like having eye
sockets with no eyes in them, a defect that will disfigure (*disaster*) the
cheeks. (The underlying image is of a heavenly body that cannot move
properly in its sphere, causing *disaster*, meaning both disfigurement and
the evil effects of unfavorable aspect of a planet.)   **16 s.d. sennet** trumpet call signaling the approach of a procession

ANTONY [*To Caesar*]
Thus do they, sir: they take the flow o' the Nile   17
By certain scales i' the pyramid. They know   18
By the height, the lowness, or the mean if dearth   19
Or foison follow. The higher Nilus swells   20
The more it promises; as it ebbs, the seedsman
Upon the slime and ooze scatters his grain,
And shortly comes to harvest.

LEPIDUS   You've strange serpents there.

ANTONY   Ay, Lepidus.

LEPIDUS   Your serpent of Egypt is bred now of your   26
mud by the operation of your sun; so is your crocodile.

ANTONY   They are so.

POMPEY   Sit—and some wine. A health to Lepidus!   29
                                    [*They sit and drink.*]

LEPIDUS   I am not so well as I should be, but I'll   30
ne'er out.   31

ENOBARBUS   Not till you have slept; I fear me you'll be
in till then.   33

LEPIDUS   Nay, certainly, I have heard the Ptolemies'
pyramises are very goodly things; without contradic-   35
tion I have heard that.

MENAS [*Aside to Pompey*]   Pompey, a word.

POMPEY [*To Menas*]   Say in mine ear. What is 't?

MENAS (*Whispers in 's ear*)
Forsake thy seat, I do beseech thee, captain,
And hear me speak a word.

POMPEY [*To Menas*]
Forbear me till anon.—This wine for Lepidus!   41

LEPIDUS   What manner o' thing is your crocodile?

ANTONY   It is shaped, sir, like itself, and it is as broad as
it hath breadth. It is just so high as it is, and moves
with its own organs. It lives by that which nourisheth
it, and, the elements once out of it, it transmigrates.   46

---

17 take measure   **18 scales** graduated markings   **19 mean** middle
20 foison plenty   **26 Your serpent** i.e., this serpent that people talk
about. (The colloquial indefinite *your*.)   **29 health** toast. (Lepidus is
obliged to drink up every time a toast is proposed to him.)   **30–31 I'll
ne'er out** i.e., I'll never refuse a toast, never quit   **33 in** (1) in drink, in
your cups (2) indoors. (Enobarbus quibbles on *in* as the antithesis of *out*
in l. 33.)   **35 pyramises** (Lepidus' drunken error for *pyramides*, plural of
pyramis or pyramid.)   **41 Forbear** leave.   **till anon** for a moment
46 elements vital elements

LEPIDUS   What color is it of?

ANTONY   Of its own color too.

LEPIDUS   'Tis a strange serpent.

ANTONY   'Tis so. And the tears of it are wet.   50

CAESAR   Will this description satisfy him?

ANTONY   With the health that Pompey gives him, else
he is a very epicure.   [*Menas whispers again.*]   53

POMPEY [*Aside to Menas*]
Go hang, sir, hang! Tell me of that? Away!
Do as I bid you.—Where's this cup I called for?

MENAS [*Aside to Pompey*]
If for the sake of merit thou wilt hear me,   56
Rise from thy stool.

POMPEY [*To Menas*]   I think thou'rt mad. [*He rises, and
they walk aside.*] The matter?

MENAS
I have ever held my cap off to thy fortunes.   58

POMPEY
Thou hast served me with much faith. What's else to
say?—   59
Be jolly, lords.

ANTONY   These quicksands, Lepidus,
Keep off them, for you sink.

MENAS
Wilt thou be lord of all the world?

POMPEY   What sayst thou?

MENAS
Wilt thou be lord of the whole world? That's twice.

POMPEY
How should that be?

MENAS   But entertain it,   64
And, though thou think me poor, I am the man
Will give thee all the world.

POMPEY   Hast thou drunk well?

---

50 tears (Alludes to the ancient belief that the crocodile wept insincere
"crocodile tears" over its victim before devouring it.)   **53 epicure** i.e.,
atheist. (The Epicureans did not believe in an afterlife.)   **56 merit** i.e.,
my merits as a loyal follower, or the merit of my ideas   **58 held . . . off**
i.e., been a respectful and faithful servant   **59 faith** faithfulness
64 But entertain it only accept the possibility

MENAS
No, Pompey, I have kept me from the cup.
Thou art, if thou dar'st be, the earthly Jove.
Whate'er the ocean pales or sky inclips   69
Is thine, if thou wilt ha 't.

POMPEY   Show me which way.

MENAS
These three world-sharers, these competitors,   71
Are in thy vessel. Let me cut the cable,
And, when we are put off, fall to their throats.   73
All there is thine.

POMPEY   Ah, this thou shouldst have done
And not have spoke on 't! In me 'tis villainy,   75
In thee 't had been good service. Thou must know,
'Tis not my profit that does lead mine honor;
Mine honor, it. Repent that e'er thy tongue   78
Hath so betrayed thine act. Being done unknown,   79
I should have found it afterwards well done,
But must condemn it now. Desist, and drink.

                          [He returns to the feast.]

MENAS [Aside]   For this,
I'll never follow thy palled fortunes more.   83
Who seeks and will not take when once 'tis offered   84
Shall never find it more.

POMPEY   This health to Lepidus!

ANTONY
Bear him ashore. I'll pledge it for him, Pompey.   86

ENOBARBUS
Here's to thee, Menas!   [They drink.]

MENAS   Enobarbus, welcome!

POMPEY   Fill till the cup be hid.

ENOBARBUS   There's a strong fellow, Menas.

                [Pointing to one who carries off Lepidus.]

MENAS   Why?

---

69 pales impales, fences in.   inclips embraces   71 competitors partners
(with secondary sense of "rivals")   73 are put off have put to sea
75 on 't of it   78 Mine honor, it i.e., my honor comes before my personal profit.   Repent regret   79 unknown i.e., without my knowledge
83 palled decayed, darkened   84 Who he who   86 pledge it i.e., drink
the toast (since Lepidus is too far gone to drink)

ENOBARBUS   'A bears the third part of the world, man;   91
  seest not?

MENAS
  The third part, then, is drunk. Would it were all,
  That it might go on wheels!   94

ENOBARBUS   Drink thou; increase the reels.   95

MENAS   Come.

POMPEY
  This is not yet an Alexandrian feast.

ANTONY
  It ripens towards it. Strike the vessels, ho!   98
  Here's to Caesar!

CAESAR   I could well forbear 't.
  It's monstrous labor when I wash my brain
  And it grows fouler.

ANTONY   Be a child o' the time.

CAESAR   Possess it, I'll make answer.   102
  But I had rather fast from all four days   103
  Than drink so much in one.

ENOBARBUS [To Antony]   Ha, my brave emperor!   104
  Shall we dance now the Egyptian Bacchanals   105
  And celebrate our drink?   106

POMPEY   Let's ha 't, good soldier.

ANTONY   Come, let's all take hands
  Till that the conquering wine hath steeped our sense   109
  In soft and delicate Lethe.

ENOBARBUS   All take hands.   110
  Make battery to our ears with the loud music,   111
  The while I'll place you; then the boy shall sing.
  The holding every man shall bear as loud   113
  As his strong sides can volley.
      Music plays. Enobarbus places them hand in hand.

                The Song.

91 'A he   94 go on wheels go fast or easily. (Proverbial.)   95 reels
(1) revels (2) reeling and whirling of drunkenness   98 Strike the vessels
broach or tap the casks   102 Possess it drink it off.   make answer
drink in return (? Or Caesar may be saying, "My answer is, 'Be master
of the time.'")   103 all all nourishment   104 brave splendid
105 Bacchanals drunken dance to Bacchus, god of wine   106 celebrate
consecrate with observances   109 Till that until   110 Lethe i.e., forgetfulness. (Literally, the river of oblivion in Hades.)   111 Make battery to
assault   113 holding refrain.   bear carry, sing

BOY [*Sings*]
    Come, thou monarch of the vine,
    Plumpy Bacchus with pink eyne!   116
    In thy fats our cares be drowned,   117
    With thy grapes our hairs be crowned.
ALL Cup us till the world go round,   119
    Cup us till the world go round!

CAESAR
  What would you more? Pompey, good night.—Good
    brother,
  Let me request you off. Our graver business   122
  Frowns at this levity. Gentle lords, let's part;
  You see we have burnt our cheeks. Strong Enobarb 124
  Is weaker than the wine, and mine own tongue
  Splits what it speaks. The wild disguise hath almost 126
  Anticked us all. What needs more words? Good night. 127
  Good Antony, your hand.

POMPEY   I'll try you on the shore. 128

ANTONY
  And shall, sir. Give 's your hand.

POMPEY   O Antony,
  You have my father's house. But what? We are friends.
  Come down into the boat.

ENOBARBUS   Take heed you fall not.
      [*Exeunt all but Enobarbus and Menas.*]
  Menas, I'll not on shore.

MENAS   No, to my cabin.
  These drums, these trumpets, flutes! What!
  Let Neptune hear we bid a loud farewell
  To these great fellows. Sound and be hanged, sound
    out!   *Sound a flourish, with drums.*

ENOBARBUS Hoo! says 'a. There's my cap.
              [*He flings it in the air.*]

MENAS Hoo! Noble captain, come.   *Exeunt.*

❖

116 **pink eyne** (i.e., eyes half shut, from drinking)   117 **fats** vats, vessels
119 **Cup** intoxicate   122 **off** to come away   124 **we . . . cheeks** our com-
plexions are flushed with drinking   126 **disguise** (1) masque (2) drunkenness as a disguise   127 **Anticked us** (1) made dancers of us in a
masque (2) made buffoons or fools of us   128 **try you** i.e., take you on
in a drinking contest

3.1   *Enter Ventidius as it were in triumph [with*
Silius, and other Romans, officers, and
soldiers], the dead body of Pacorus borne
before him.

VENTIDIUS
Now, darting Parthia, art thou struck, and now   1
Pleased fortune does of Marcus Crassus' death   2
Make me revenger. Bear the King's son's body
Before our army. Thy Pacorus, Orodes,   4
Pays this for Marcus Crassus.
SILIUS   Noble Ventidius,
Whilst yet with Parthian blood thy sword is warm,
The fugitive Parthians follow. Spur through Media,   7
Mesopotamia, and the shelters whither
The routed fly. So thy grand captain, Antony,
Shall set thee on triumphant chariots and   10
Put garlands on thy head.
VENTIDIUS   O Silius, Silius,
I have done enough. A lower place, note well,   12
May make too great an act. For learn this, Silius:
Better to leave undone than by our deed
Acquire too high a fame when him we serve's away.
Caesar and Antony have ever won
More in their officer than person. Sossius,   17
One of my place in Syria, his lieutenant,   18
For quick accumulation of renown,
Which he achieved by the minute, lost his favor.   20
Who does i' the wars more than his captain can   21
Becomes his captain's captain; and ambition,
The soldier's virtue, rather makes choice of loss   23

3.1. Location: The Middle East.
1 darting (The Parthians were famous for archery and for the Parthian
dart which they discharged as they fled.)   **Parthia** i.e., Orodes, King of
Parthia   **2 Crassus' death** (Crassus, member of the first triumvirate with
Pompey the Great and Julius Caesar, was overthrown and treacherously
murdered by Orodes in 53 B.C.)   **4 Pacorus, Orodes** (Pacorus was
the son of Orodes.)   **7 The . . . follow** follow the fleeing Parthians
10 triumphant triumphal   **12 A lower place** i.e., one of lower rank
17 More . . . person more through the actions of their lieutenants than by
their own efforts   **18 of my place** of the same rank as I.   **his lieutenant**
i.e., the commanding officer acting for Antony   **20 by the minute** minute
by minute, continually   **21 Who** he who   **23 makes choice of** chooses

Than gain which darkens him.　　　　24
I could do more to do Antonius good,
But 'twould offend him, and in his offense　　　　26
Should my performance perish.
SILIUS　Thou hast, Ventidius, that　　　　28
Without the which a soldier and his sword　　　　29
Grants scarce distinction. Thou wilt write to Antony?　　　30
VENTIDIUS
I'll humbly signify what in his name,
That magical word of war, we have effected:　　　　32
How with his banners and his well-paid ranks
The ne'er-yet-beaten horse of Parthia　　　　34
We have jaded out o' the field.
SILIUS　　　　　　　　　　　Where is he now?　　　　35
VENTIDIUS
He purposeth to Athens, whither, with what haste
The weight we must convey with 's will permit,　　　　37
We shall appear before him.—On, there. Pass along!
　　　　　　　　　　　　　　　　　　　Exeunt.

❖

3.2　*Enter Agrippa at one door, Enobarbus at
another.*

AGRIPPA　What, are the brothers parted?　　　　1
ENOBARBUS
They have dispatched with Pompey; he is gone.　　　　2
The other three are sealing. Octavia weeps　　　　3
To part from Rome; Caesar is sad; and Lepidus,　　　　4
Since Pompey's feast, as Menas says, is troubled

---

24 which darkens him achieved at the expense of darkening his reputation　**26 offense** taking offense　**28–30 that . . . distinction** i.e., discretion, without the which a soldier can scarcely be distinguished from the
sword he uses.　**Grants scarce** scarcely admits of　**32 word of war**
watchword.　**effected** achieved　**34 horse** cavalry　**35 jaded** driven
exhausted like jades, inferior horses　**37 with 's** with us

3.2. Location: Rome.
1 brothers brothers-in-law.　**parted** departed　**2 dispatched** concluded
the business　**3 sealing** affixing seals to their agreements, settling
matters　**4 sad** sober

With the greensickness.

AGRIPPA   'Tis a noble Lepidus.   6

ENOBARBUS
A very fine one. O, how he loves Caesar!   7

AGRIPPA
Nay, but how dearly he adores Mark Antony!

ENOBARBUS
Caesar? Why, he's the Jupiter of men.

AGRIPPA
What's Antony? The god of Jupiter.

ENOBARBUS
Spake you of Caesar? How, the nonpareil!

AGRIPPA
O Antony, O thou Arabian bird!   12

ENOBARBUS
Would you praise Caesar, say "Caesar"; go no further.

AGRIPPA
Indeed, he plied them both with excellent praises.

ENOBARBUS
But he loves Caesar best; yet he loves Antony.
Hoo! Hearts, tongues, figures, scribes, bards, poets,
    cannot   16
Think, speak, cast, write, sing, number, hoo!   17
His love to Antony. But as for Caesar,
Kneel down, kneel down, and wonder.

AGRIPPA   Both he loves.

ENOBARBUS
They are his shards, and he their beetle. [*Trumpets
    within.*] So;   20
This is to horse. Adieu, noble Agrippa.   21

AGRIPPA
Good fortune, worthy soldier, and farewell.

---

6 greensickness a kind of anemia supposed to affect young women,
especially those afflicted with love-longing. (Used ironically here to refer
to Lepidus' hangover and to his love for Antony and Caesar.)   **7 fine**
Lepidus in Latin means "fine," "elegant"   **12 Arabian bird** i.e., the
fabled phoenix. (Only one existed at a time; it recreated itself by arising
from its ashes.)   **16 figures** figures of speech   **17 cast** calculate.
number write verses   **20 shards** patches of dung, or perhaps wings or
wing-cases, i.e., protectors, patrons   **21 This is to horse** i.e., the trumpet
call gives the signal to depart

Enter Caesar, Antony, Lepidus, and Octavia.

ANTONY   No further, sir.   23

CAESAR
You take from me a great part of myself;
Use me well in 't.—Sister, prove such a wife
As my thoughts make thee, and as my farthest bond   26
Shall pass on thy approof.—Most noble Antony,   27
Let not the piece of virtue, which is set   28
Betwixt us as the cement of our love
To keep it builded, be the ram to batter
The fortress of it; for better might we
Have loved without this mean, if on both parts   32
This be not cherished.

ANTONY   Make me not offended
In your distrust.

CAESAR   I have said.

ANTONY   You shall not find,   34
Though you be therein curious, the least cause   35
For what you seem to fear. So the gods keep you,
And make the hearts of Romans serve your ends!
We will here part.

CAESAR
Farewell, my dearest sister, fare thee well.
The elements be kind to thee, and make
Thy spirits all of comfort! Fare thee well.

OCTAVIA [*Weeping*]   My noble brother!

ANTONY
The April's in her eyes; it is love's spring,
And these the showers to bring it on.—Be cheerful.

OCTAVIA [*To Caesar*]
Sir, look well to my husband's house; and—

CAESAR   What,   45
Octavia?

OCTAVIA   I'll tell you in your ear.

---

23 No further i.e., you need not go on urging your point; or, you need
accompany me no further   **26–27 as . . . approof** such that my utmost
bond shall be justified in certifying what you will prove to be   **28 piece**
masterpiece   **32 mean** intermediary, or means   **34 In** by.   **I have said**
i.e., I stand by what I've said   **35 curious** overly inquisitive or touchy
45 husband's house i.e., Antony's house, as at 2.7.130, though Octavia is
also a widow; see 3.3.29

[She whispers to Caesar.]

ANTONY

Her tongue will not obey her heart, nor can   47
Her heart inform her tongue—the swan's down feather,   48
That stands upon the swell at full of tide,   49
And neither way inclines.   50

ENOBARBUS [*Aside to Agrippa*]   Will Caesar weep?

AGRIPPA [*Aside to Enobarbus*]   He has a cloud in 's face.

ENOBARBUS [*Aside to Agrippa*]

He were the worse for that, were he a horse;   53
So is he, being a man.

AGRIPPA [*Aside to Enobarbus*]   Why, Enobarbus,
When Antony found Julius Caesar dead,
He cried almost to roaring; and he wept
When at Philippi he found Brutus slain.

ENOBARBUS [*Aside to Agrippa*]

That year indeed he was troubled with a rheum.   58
What willingly he did confound he wailed,   59
Believe 't, till I wept too.

CAESAR   No, sweet Octavia,
You shall hear from me still. The time shall not   61
Outgo my thinking on you.

ANTONY   Come, sir, come,   62
I'll wrestle with you in my strength of love.
Look, here I have you [*Embracing him*]; thus I let you go,
And give you to the gods.

CAESAR   Adieu. Be happy!

LEPIDUS

Let all the number of the stars give light
To thy fair way!

CAESAR   Farewell, farewell!   *Kisses Octavia.*

ANTONY   Farewell!

Trumpets sound. Exeunt [in separate groups].

❖

47–50 Her . . . inclines i.e., her conflicting emotions make her unable to
speak aloud, like a swan's down feather floating at full tide, moving
neither up nor down stream   **53 He . . . horse** (Alludes to the belief that
a horse without any light coloring on its face was apt to be bad-
tempered.)   **58 rheum** i.e., running at the eyes. (Said of any discharge
of secretion from the head.)   **59 confound** destroy.   **wailed** bewailed
61 still regularly   **61–62 The time . . . you** time itself will not outlast my
thinking of you

3.3   *Enter Cleopatra, Charmian, Iras, and Alexas.*

CLEOPATRA
Where is the fellow?
ALEXAS   Half afeard to come.
CLEOPATRA
Go to, go to.

Enter the Messenger as before.

                    Come hither, sir.
ALEXAS   Good Majesty,   2
Herod of Jewry dare not look upon you   3
But when you are well pleased.
CLEOPATRA   That Herod's head
I'll have; but how, when Antony is gone,
Through whom I might command it?—Come thou near.
MESSENGER   Most gracious Majesty!
CLEOPATRA   Didst thou behold Octavia?
MESSENGER
Ay, dread Queen.
CLEOPATRA   Where?
MESSENGER   Madam, in Rome.
I looked her in the face, and saw her led
Between her brother and Mark Antony.
CLEOPATRA
Is she as tall as me?
MESSENGER   She is not, madam.
CLEOPATRA
Didst hear her speak? Is she shrill-tongued or low?
MESSENGER
Madam, I heard her speak. She is low-voiced.
CLEOPATRA
That's not so good. He cannot like her long.   15
CHARMIAN
Like her! O Isis, 'tis impossible.
CLEOPATRA
I think so, Charmian. Dull of tongue, and dwarfish.—

3.3. Location: Alexandria. Cleopatra's palace.
2 Go to (An expression of impatience.)   **3 Herod of Jewry** i.e., even the
famous tyrant who slaughtered the children. (See 1.2.29–30.)   **15 not so
good** i.e., not so good for her

What majesty is in her gait? Remember,
If e'er thou lookedst on majesty.
MESSENGER   She creeps:
  Her motion and her station are as one.   20
  She shows a body rather than a life,   21
  A statue than a breather.
CLEOPATRA   Is this certain?   22
MESSENGER
  Or I have no observance.
CHARMIAN   Three in Egypt   23
  Cannot make better note.
CLEOPATRA   He's very knowing,   24
  I do perceive 't. There's nothing in her yet.
  The fellow has good judgment.
CHARMIAN   Excellent.
CLEOPATRA   Guess at her years, I prithee.
MESSENGER   Madam,
  She was a widow—
CLEOPATRA   Widow? Charmian, hark.
MESSENGER   And I do think she's thirty.
CLEOPATRA
  Bear'st thou her face in mind? Is 't long or round?
MESSENGER   Round, even to faultiness.
CLEOPATRA
  For the most part, too, they are foolish that are so.
  Her hair, what color?
MESSENGER   Brown, madam, and her forehead
  As low as she would wish it.   36
CLEOPATRA [Giving money]   There's gold for thee.
  Thou must not take my former sharpness ill.
  I will employ thee back again; I find thee   39
  Most fit for business. Go make thee ready;
  Our letters are prepared.   [Exit Messenger.]
CHARMIAN   A proper man.   41
CLEOPATRA
  Indeed, he is so. I repent me much

20 motion moving.   **station** manner of standing   **21 shows** appears as
22 breather living being   **23–24 Three . . . note** there are not three
people in Egypt who are better observers   **36 As . . . it** i.e., as low as
could be. (A colloquial way of suggesting she is ugly; high foreheads
were thought more beautiful.)   **39 employ . . . again** send you back with
a message   **41 proper** good

That so I harried him. Why, methinks, by him,   43
This creature's no such thing.

CHARMIAN   Nothing, madam.   44

CLEOPATRA
The man hath seen some majesty, and should know.

CHARMIAN
Hath he seen majesty? Isis else defend,   46
And serving you so long!   47

CLEOPATRA
I have one thing more to ask him yet, good Charmian—
But 'tis no matter; thou shalt bring him to me
Where I will write. All may be well enough.

CHARMIAN   I warrant you, madam.   *Exeunt.* 51

❖

3.4   *Enter Antony and Octavia.*

ANTONY
Nay, nay, Octavia, not only that—
That were excusable, that and thousands more
Of semblable import—but he hath waged   3
New wars 'gainst Pompey; made his will, and read it   4
To public ear;
Spoke scantly of me; when perforce he could not   6
But pay me terms of honor, cold and sickly
He vented them, most narrow measure lent me;   8
When the best hint was given him, he not took 't, 9
Or did it from his teeth.

OCTAVIA   O my good lord,   10
Believe not all, or, if you must believe,
Stomach not all. A more unhappy lady,   12
If this division chance, ne'er stood between,   13

---

43 harried maltreated. **by** according to   **44 no such thing** nothing
much   **46 else defend** forbid that it be otherwise. (An interjection.)
47 serving i.e., he having served   **51 warrant** assure

3.4. Location: Athens.
3 semblable similar   **4 read it** (to win the populace by showing them what
benefits they might expect from him)   **6 scantly** slightingly   **8 vented** gave
vent to, expressed.   **narrow measure lent me** gave me small credit   **9 hint**
occasion (to praise Antony)   **10 from his teeth** i.e., between clenched
teeth, not from the heart   **12 Stomach** resent   **13 chance** occur

Praying for both parts.
The good gods will mock me presently   15
When I shall pray "O, bless my lord and husband!"
Undo that prayer by crying out as loud   17
"O, bless my brother!" Husband win, win brother
Prays and destroys the prayer; no midway
Twixt these extremes at all.

ANTONY   Gentle Octavia,
Let your best love draw to that point which seeks   21
Best to preserve it. If I lose mine honor,   22
I lose myself; better I were not yours
Than yours so branchless. But, as you requested,   24
Yourself shall go between 's. The meantime, lady,   25
I'll raise the preparation of a war   26
Shall stain your brother. Make your soonest haste;   27
So your desires are yours.

OCTAVIA   Thanks to my lord.   28
The Jove of power make me, most weak, most weak,
Your reconciler! Wars twixt you twain would be
As if the world should cleave, and that slain men   31
Should solder up the rift.   32

ANTONY
When it appears to you where this begins,   33
Turn your displeasure that way, for our faults   34
Can never be so equal that your love   35
Can equally move with them. Provide your going;   36
Choose your own company and command what cost
Your heart has mind to.   *Exeunt.*

✤

15 **presently** immediately   17 **Undo** i.e., and then undo; or, I shall
undo   21–22 **Let . . . it** let your warmest love be given to that one of us
who seeks to preserve it (your love) best   24 **branchless** pruned (of
honor)   25 **The meantime** in the meantime   26–27 **I'll . . . brother** I'll
raise an army that will deprive your brother of his luster   28 **So . . .
yours** i.e., thus you have obtained your desire (to go). (Or, *so* may mean
"as long as.")   31 **cleave** split   32 **Should** would be needed to
33 **where this begins** who started this quarrel   34 **our** i.e., Caesar's and
mine   34–36 **our faults . . . them** i.e., you will have to judge between
our faults and choose   36 **Provide** make arrangements for

3.5   *Enter Enobarbus and Eros, [meeting].*

ENOBARBUS   How now, friend Eros?

EROS   There's strange news come, sir.

ENOBARBUS   What, man?

EROS   Caesar and Lepidus have made wars upon Pompey.

ENOBARBUS   This is old. What is the success?   6

EROS   Caesar, having made use of him in the wars   7
'gainst Pompey, presently denied him rivality, would   8
not let him partake in the glory of the action; and, not
resting here, accuses him of letters he had formerly   10
wrote to Pompey; upon his own appeal seizes him.   11
So the poor third is up, till death enlarge his confine.   12

ENOBARBUS
Then, world, thou hast a pair of chops, no more;   13
And throw between them all the food thou hast,
They'll grind the one the other. Where's Antony?   15

EROS
He's walking in the garden—thus, and spurns   16
The rush that lies before him; cries, "Fool Lepidus!"   17
And threats the throat of that his officer   18
That murdered Pompey.

ENOBARBUS   Our great navy's rigged.   19

EROS
For Italy and Caesar. More, Domitius: 20
My lord desires you presently. My news   21

3.5. Location: Athens.

6 success outcome, result   **7 him** i.e., Lepidus   **8 presently** immediately.   **rivality** rights of a partner. (Caesar and Lepidus have newly gone to war against Pompey and have defeated him.)   **10 resting here** i.e., stopping with this insult   **11 his own appeal** Caesar's own accusation   **12 up** shut up (in prison).   **enlarge his confine** set him free   **13 pair of chops** two jaws.   **no more** i.e., no more than one pair, no third partner   **15 They'll . . . other** i.e., the jaws will still grind against each other, grind each other down   **16 thus** (Eros imitates Antony's angry walk.)   **spurns** kicks   **17 rush** strewn rushes   **18 threats the throat** i.e., threatens the life.   **that his officer** that officer of his (Antony's)   **19 Pompey** (After his defeat by Caesar and Lepidus, Pompey was murdered—perhaps, according to history, on Antony's orders; but here Antony blames his officer for killing Pompey because he might have been a useful ally against Caesar.)   **20 More** I have more to say   **21 presently** immediately

I might have told hereafter.

ENOBARBUS   'Twill be naught,
But let it be. Bring me to Antony.

EROS   Come, sir.

Exeunt.

❖

3.6   *Enter Agrippa, Maecenas, and Caesar.*

CAESAR
Contemning Rome, he has done all this and more   1
In Alexandria. Here's the manner of 't:
I' the marketplace, on a tribunal silvered,   3
Cleopatra and himself in chairs of gold
Were publicly enthroned. At the feet sat
Caesarion, whom they call my father's son,   6
And all the unlawful issue that their lust
Since then hath made between them. Unto her
He gave the stablishment of Egypt, made her   9
Of lower Syria, Cyprus, Lydia,
Absolute queen.

MAECENAS   This in the public eye?

CAESAR
I' the common showplace, where they exercise.   12
His sons he there proclaimed the kings of kings:
Great Media, Parthia, and Armenia
He gave to Alexander; to Ptolemy he assigned
Syria, Cilicia, and Phoenicia. She
In th' habiliments of the goddess Isis   17
That day appeared, and oft before gave audience,
As 'tis reported, so.   19

MAECENAS   Let Rome be thus informed.

AGRIPPA
Who, queasy with his insolence already,   21
Will their good thoughts call from him.

3.6. Location: Rome.
1 Contemning disdaining   **3 tribunal** seat of state, dais   **6 my father's**
i.e., Julius Caesar's. (Julius Caesar had adopted his grandnephew Octavius as his son.)   **9 stablishment** settled possession   **12 exercise** perform ceremonial functions   **17 habiliments** attire   **19 so** i.e., dressed as
Isis   **21 queasy** disgusted. (Refers to the Roman people.)

CAESAR
  The people knows it, and have now received
  His accusations.
AGRIPPA   Who does he accuse?
CAESAR
  Caesar, and that, having in Sicily
  Sextus Pompeius spoiled, we had not rated him   26
  His part o' th' isle. Then does he say he lent me   27
  Some shipping, unrestored. Lastly, he frets   28
  That Lepidus of the triumvirate   29
  Should be deposed, and, being, that we detain   30
  All his revenue.
AGRIPPA   Sir, this should be answered.
CAESAR
  'Tis done already, and the messenger gone.
  I have told him Lepidus was grown too cruel,
  That he his high authority abused
  And did deserve his change. For what I have conquered, 35
  I grant him part; but then in his Armenia,
  And other of his conquered kingdoms, I
  Demand the like.
MAECENAS   He'll never yield to that.
CAESAR
  Nor must not then be yielded to in this.

    Enter Octavia with her train.

OCTAVIA
  Hail, Caesar, and my lord! Hail, most dear Caesar!
CAESAR
  That ever I should call thee castaway!
OCTAVIA
  You have not called me so, nor have you cause.
CAESAR
  Why have you stol'n upon us thus? You come not
  Like Caesar's sister. The wife of Antony
  Should have an army for an usher and
  The neighs of horse to tell of her approach   46

---

26 spoiled despoiled, plundered.　**rated him** allotted to Antony　**27 th'
isle** i.e., Sicily　**28 unrestored** i.e., that I did not return to him　**29 of**
from　**30 being** i.e., having been deposed　**35 For** as for　**46 horse**
horses

Long ere she did appear. The trees by the way   47
Should have borne men, and expectation fainted,
Longing for what it had not. Nay, the dust
Should have ascended to the roof of heaven,
Raised by your populous troops. But you are come
A market maid to Rome, and have prevented   52
The ostentation of our love, which, left unshown,   53
Is often left unloved. We should have met you   54
By sea and land, supplying every stage   55
With an augmented greeting.

OCTAVIA   Good my lord,
To come thus was I not constrained, but did it
On my free will. My lord, Mark Antony,
Hearing that you prepared for war, acquainted
My grievèd ear withal, whereon I begged
His pardon for return.

CAESAR   Which soon he granted,   61
Being an obstruct 'tween his lust and him.   62

OCTAVIA
Do not say so, my lord.

CAESAR   I have eyes upon him,
And his affairs come to me on the wind.
Where is he now?

OCTAVIA   My lord, in Athens.

CAESAR
No, my most wrongèd sister. Cleopatra
Hath nodded him to her. He hath given his empire
Up to a whore; who now are levying   69
The kings o' th' earth for war. He hath assembled
Bocchus, the King of Libya; Archelaus,
Of Cappadocia; Philadelphos, King
Of Paphlagonia; the Thracian king, Adallas;
King Manchus of Arabia; King of Pont;
Herod of Jewry; Mithridates, King
Of Comagene; Polemon and Amyntas,

---

47 by along   **52 prevented** forestalled (by your too-early arrival)
53 ostentation ceremonial display   **53-54 which . . . unloved** i.e., a love
that is not given proper outward display often remains unexercised and
dwindles into neglect. (Also, Caesar wants the display of love to be seen
publicly.)   **55 stage** stage of your journey   **61 pardon** permission
62 Being . . . him i.e., since your return to Rome removed the obstacle
between him and the gratification of his desires   **69 who** i.e., and they

The Kings of Mede and Lycaonia,
With a more larger list of scepters.   78

OCTAVIA Ay me, most wretched,
That have my heart parted betwixt two friends
That does afflict each other!

CAESAR   Welcome hither.
Your letters did withhold our breaking forth   82
Till we perceived both how you were wrong led
And we in negligent danger. Cheer your heart.   84
Be you not troubled with the time, which drives   85
O'er your content these strong necessities,   86
But let determined things to destiny   87
Hold unbewailed their way. Welcome to Rome,   88
Nothing more dear to me. You are abused   89
Beyond the mark of thought, and the high gods,   90
To do you justice, makes his ministers   91
Of us and those that love you. Best of comfort,   92
And ever welcome to us.

AGRIPPA Welcome, lady.

MAECENAS Welcome, dear madam.
Each heart in Rome does love and pity you.
Only th' adulterous Antony, most large   97
In his abominations, turns you off   98
And gives his potent regiment to a trull   99
That noises it against us.

OCTAVIA   Is it so, sir?   100

CAESAR
Most certain. Sister, welcome. Pray you
Be ever known to patience. My dear'st sister! *Exeunt.* 102

❖

78 **a more larger** an even longer   82 **withhold** restrain.   **breaking forth**
attacking   84 **negligent danger** danger through negligence   85 **the time**
the present state of affairs   85–86 **drives . . . necessities** drives these
strong necessities over your happiness as a team of animals might drive
a chariot, trampling your happiness underfoot   87–88 **let . . . way** allow
inevitable events to go unbewailed to their destined conclusion   89 **No-**
thing . . . me i.e., you who are more dear to me than anything   90 **mark**
reach   90–92 **the high . . . you** i.e., the high gods (here a single concept)
make us and those that love you their ministers of justice in your
cause   97 **large** unrestrained   98 **turns you off** rejects you
99 **regiment** government, rule.   **trull** prostitute   100 **noises it** is clamor-
ous   102 **known to patience** i.e., patient

3.7   *Enter Cleopatra and Enobarbus.*

CLEOPATRA
  I will be even with thee, doubt it not.
ENOBARBUS   But why, why, why?
CLEOPATRA
  Thou hast forspoke my being in these wars,   3
  And sayst it is not fit.
ENOBARBUS   Well, is it, is it?   4
CLEOPATRA
  If not denounced against us, why should not we   5
  Be there in person?
ENOBARBUS [*Aside*]   Well, I could reply.
  If we should serve with horse and mares together,   7
  The horse were merely lost; the mares would bear   8
  A soldier and his horse.
CLEOPATRA   What is 't you say?
ENOBARBUS
  Your presence needs must puzzle Antony,   10
  Take from his heart, take from his brain, from 's time
  What should not then be spared. He is already
  Traduced for levity, and 'tis said in Rome   13
  That Photinus, an eunuch, and your maids   14
  Manage this war.
CLEOPATRA   Sink Rome, and their tongues rot
  That speak against us! A charge we bear i' the war,   16
  And as the president of my kingdom will
  Appear there for a man. Speak not against it.   18
  I will not stay behind.

      Enter Antony and Canidius.

ENOBARBUS   Nay, I have done.
  Here comes the Emperor.

3.7. Location: Near Actium, on the northwestern coast of Greece. Antony's camp.
3 forspoke spoken against   **4 fit** appropriate   **5 If . . . us** i.e., even if the war were not declared against me (which it is)   **7 horse** horses
8 merely utterly   **10 puzzle** bewilder   **13 Traduced** criticized, censured   **14 an eunuch** (Probably Mardian. In North's Plutarch, Caesar complains that "Mardian the eunuch, Photinus, and Iras . . . and Charmian . . . ruled the affairs of Antonius' empire." But Photinus [or Pothinus] was a eunuch too.)   **16 charge** responsibility, cost   **18 for** in the capacity of

ANTONY   Is it not strange, Canidius,
  That from Tarentum and Brundusium
  He could so quickly cut the Ionian sea   22
  And take in Toryne?—You have heard on 't, sweet?   23
CLEOPATRA
  Celerity is never more admired   24
  Than by the negligent.
ANTONY   A good rebuke,
  Which might have well becomed the best of men,   26
  To taunt at slackness. Canidius, we
  Will fight with him by sea.
CLEOPATRA   By sea, what else?
CANIDIUS   Why will my lord do so?
ANTONY   For that he dares us to 't.   30
ENOBARBUS
  So hath my lord dared him to single fight.
CANIDIUS
  Ay, and to wage this battle at Pharsalia,
  Where Caesar fought with Pompey. But these offers,
  Which serve not for his vantage, he shakes off,
  And so should you.
ENOBARBUS   Your ships are not well manned;
  Your mariners are muleteers, reapers, people   36
  Engrossed by swift impress. In Caesar's fleet   37
  Are those that often have 'gainst Pompey fought;
  Their ships are yare, yours heavy. No disgrace   39
  Shall fall you for refusing him at sea,   40
  Being prepared for land.
ANTONY   By sea, by sea.
ENOBARBUS
  Most worthy sir, you therein throw away
  The absolute soldiership you have by land,
  Distract your army, which doth most consist   44
  Of war-marked footmen, leave unexecuted   45

22 Ionian (Often applied to the Aegean, but here the Adriatic. Tarentum
and Brundusium or Brundisium are in the "heel" of Italy, across the
Adriatic from Actium and Toryne.)   **23 take in** conquer   **24 Celerity**
swiftness.   **admired** wondered at   **26 becomed** become, suited   **30 For
that** because   **36 muleteers** mule-drivers, peasants   **37 Engrossed**
collected wholesale.   **impress** impressment, conscription   **39 yare**
quick, maneuverable   **40 fall** befall   **44 Distract** divide, divert, confuse
the purpose of.   **most** for the most part   **45 footmen** foot soldiers.
unexecuted unused

Your own renownèd knowledge, quite forgo
The way which promises assurance, and
Give up yourself merely to chance and hazard   48
From firm security.

ANTONY   I'll fight at sea.

CLEOPATRA
I have sixty sails, Caesar none better.

ANTONY
Our overplus of shipping will we burn,
And with the rest full-manned, from the head of Actium 52
Beat th' approaching Caesar. But if we fail,
We then can do 't at land.

            Enter a Messenger.

                        Thy business?

MESSENGER
The news is true, my lord; he is descried.   55
Caesar has taken Toryne.

ANTONY
Can he be there in person? 'Tis impossible;
Strange that his power should be. Canidius,   58
Our nineteen legions thou shalt hold by land,
And our twelve thousand horse. We'll to our ship.
Away, my Thetis!

            Enter a Soldier.

                    How now, worthy soldier?   61

SOLDIER
O noble Emperor, do not fight by sea;
Trust not to rotten planks. Do you misdoubt   63
This sword and these my wounds? Let th' Egyptians
And the Phoenicians go a-ducking; we   65
Have used to conquer standing on the earth   66
And fighting foot to foot.

ANTONY   Well, well, away!
            Exeunt Antony, Cleopatra, and Enobarbus.

---

48 merely entirely   **52 head** promontory   **55 he is descried** he has been
sighted   **58 his power** i.e., his army, let alone himself   **61 Thetis** sea
goddess, the mother of Achilles   **63 misdoubt** disbelieve   **65 go a-
ducking** (1) get drenched (2) cringe   **66 Have used** are accustomed.
standing on the earth (1) fighting on land (2) standing upright, not
ducking or cringing

SOLDIER
  By Hercules, I think I am i' the right.
CANIDIUS
  Soldier, thou art; but his whole action grows   69
  Not in the power on 't. So our leader's led,   70
  And we are women's men.
SOLDIER   You keep by land   71
  The legions and the horse whole, do you not?   72
CANIDIUS
  Marcus Octavius, Marcus Justeius,
  Publicola, and Caelius are for sea;
  But we keep whole by land. This speed of Caesar's
  Carries beyond belief.   76
SOLDIER   While he was yet in Rome
  His power went out in such distractions as   78
  Beguiled all spies.
CANIDIUS   Who's his lieutenant, hear you?
SOLDIER
  They say, one Taurus.
CANIDIUS   Well I know the man.

        Enter a Messenger.

MESSENGER   The Emperor calls Canidius.
CANIDIUS
  With news the time's with labor, and throws forth   82
  Each minute some.   *Exeunt.* 83

                    ✤

3.8   *Enter Caesar [and Taurus] with his army,*
          marching.

CAESAR   Taurus!
TAURUS   My lord?

69–70 his . . . on 't his whole strategy has been developed without
regard to where his power really lies   71 men servingmen   72 horse
cavalry.   whole undivided, held in reserve   76 Carries surpasses
(like an arrow in archery)   78 distractions detachments, divisions
82–83 With news . . . some more news is born each minute.   throws
forth gives birth

3.8. Location: A field near Actium, as before.

CAESAR
  Strike not by land; keep whole. Provoke not battle
  Till we have done at sea. Do not exceed
  The prescript of this scroll. [*He gives a scroll.*] Our
    fortune lies   5
  Upon this jump.   *Exit* [*with army*]. 6

3.9   *Enter Antony and Enobarbus.*

ANTONY
  Set we our squadrons on yond side o' the hill,
  In eye of Caesar's battle, from which place   2
  We may the number of the ships behold
  And so proceed accordingly.   *Exit* [*with Enobarbus*].

3.10   *Canidius marcheth with his land army one
            way over the stage, and Taurus, the lieutenant
            of Caesar, the other way. After their going in
            is heard the noise of a sea fight.*

        Alarum. Enter Enobarbus.

ENOBARBUS
  Naught, naught, all naught! I can behold no longer.   1
  Th' *Antoniad*, the Egyptian admiral,   2
  With all their sixty, fly and turn the rudder.
  To see 't mine eyes are blasted.

        Enter Scarus.

SCARUS   Gods and goddesses,
  All the whole synod of them!
ENOBARBUS   What's thy passion?   5

5 **prescript** orders 6 **jump** chance, hazard

3.9. Location: A field near Actium, as before.
2 **eye** sight. **battle** battle line

3.10. Location: A field near Actium, as before.
1 **Naught** i.e., all has come to naught 2 **admiral** flagship 5 **synod**
assembly. **What's** what is the cause of

SCARUS

  The greater cantle of the world is lost   6

  With very ignorance; we have kissed away   7

  Kingdoms and provinces.

ENOBARBUS   How appears the fight?

SCARUS

  On our side like the tokened pestilence,   9

  Where death is sure. Yon ribaudred nag of Egypt—   10

  Whom leprosy o'ertake!—i' the midst o' the fight,

  When vantage like a pair of twins appeared   12

  Both as the same, or rather ours the elder,   13

  The breeze upon her, like a cow in June,   14

  Hoists sails and flies.

ENOBARBUS   That I beheld.

  Mine eyes did sicken at the sight, and could not

  Endure a further view.

SCARUS   She once being loofed,   18

  The noble ruin of her magic, Antony,   19

  Claps on his sea wing and, like a doting mallard,   20

  Leaving the fight in height, flies after her.   21

  I never saw an action of such shame.

  Experience, manhood, honor, ne'er before

  Did violate so itself.

ENOBARBUS   Alack, alack!

   Enter Candidus.

CANIDIUS

  Our fortune on the sea is out of breath,

  And sinks most lamentably. Had our general

  Been what he knew himself, it had gone well.

  O, he has given example for our flight

  Most grossly by his own!

---

6 **cantle** corner; hence, piece or part   7 **With very ignorance** through utter stupidity   9 **tokened pestilence** (Certain red spots appeared on the bodies of the plague-smitten, called tokens.)   10 **ribaudred** foul, obscene   12–13 **When . . . same** i.e., when the advantage was equal on either side   13 **elder** i.e., more advanced, more likely to inherit 14 **breeze** (1) gadfly (2) light wind   18 **loofed** luffed, with ship's head brought close to the wind (with a pun on *aloofed*, becoming distant) 19 **ruin** object ruined by   20 **Claps . . . sea wing** i.e., hoists sail, preparing for flight like a water bird.   **mallard** drake   21 **in** at its

ENOBARBUS
  Ay, are you thereabouts? Why then, good night indeed. 30
CANIDIUS
  Toward Peloponnesus are they fled.   31
SCARUS
  'Tis easy to 't, and there I will attend   32
  What further comes.
CANIDIUS   To Caesar will I render   33
  My legions and my horse. Six kings already   34
  Show me the way of yielding.
ENOBARBUS   I'll yet follow
  The wounded chance of Antony, though my reason   36
  Sits in the wind against me.   [*Exeunt separately.*]   37

❖

3.11   *Enter Antony with attendants.*

ANTONY
  Hark! The land bids me tread no more upon 't;
  It is ashamed to bear me. Friends, come hither.
  I am so lated in the world that I   3
  Have lost my way forever. I have a ship
  Laden with gold. Take that, divide it; fly,   5
  And make your peace with Caesar.
ALL   Fly? Not we.
ANTONY
  I have fled myself, and have instructed cowards
  To run and show their shoulders. Friends, begone.   8
  I have myself resolved upon a course
  Which has no need of you. Begone.
  My treasure's in the harbor. Take it. O,

30 **thereabouts** i.e., of that mind, thinking of desertion. **good night
indeed** i.e., it's all over 31 **Peloponnesus** southern Greece (from which
Antony then crosses the Mediterranean to Egypt) 32 **to 't** to get to it.
attend await 33 **render** surrender 34 **horse** cavalry 36 **wounded
chance** broken fortunes 37 **Sits . . . me** i.e., is on my windward side,
tracking me and hunting me down

3.11. **Location: Historically, events such as dispatching the Schoolmaster to Caesar took place in Egypt; however, the dramatic impression of
this scene is that it occurs soon after the battle.**
3 **lated** belated, like a traveler still journeying when night falls 5 **fly**
flee 8 **shoulders** i.e., backs

I followed that I blush to look upon!   12
My very hairs do mutiny, for the white   13
Reprove the brown for rashness, and they them   14
For fear and doting. Friends, begone. You shall
Have letters from me to some friends that will
Sweep your way for you. Pray you, look not sad,   17
Nor make replies of loathness. Take the hint   18
Which my despair proclaims. Let that be left   19
Which leaves itself. To the seaside straightway!   20
I will possess you of that ship and treasure.
Leave me, I pray, a little. Pray you now,   22
Nay, do so, for indeed I have lost command.   23
Therefore I pray you. I'll see you by and by.   24
          [*Exeunt attendants. Antony*] *sits down.*

          Enter Cleopatra led by Charmian, [*Iras,*]
          and Eros.

EROS
  Nay, gentle madam, to him, comfort him.
IRAS   Do, most dear Queen.
CHARMIAN   Do; why, what else?
CLEOPATRA   Let me sit down. O Juno!
ANTONY   No, no, no, no, no.
EROS   See you here, sir?
ANTONY   O fie, fie, fie!
CHARMIAN   Madam!
IRAS   Madam, O good Empress!
EROS   Sir, sir!
ANTONY
  Yes, my lord, yes. He at Philippi kept   35
  His sword e'en like a dancer, while I struck   36
  The lean and wrinkled Cassius, and 'twas I
  That the mad Brutus ended. He alone   38

12 that that which   **13 mutiny** contend among themselves   **14 they
them** i.e., the brown hairs reprove the white   **17 Sweep your way** clear
your way (to Caesar)   **18 loathness** unwillingness.   **hint** opportunity
19 that i.e., Antony and his cause   **20 leaves** is untrue to, deserts   **22 a
little** for a moment   **23 lost command** (1) lost command of myself
(2) lost command of my troops and my right to command   **24 pray** entreat   **35 He** i.e., Octavius.   **kept** kept in its sheath   **36 e'en . . . dancer**
i.e., as though for ornament only, in a dance   **38 ended** i.e., defeated.
(Not *killed*; Brutus and Cassius committed suicide.)

Dealt on lieutenantry, and no practice had   39
In the brave squares of war; yet now—no matter.   40
CLEOPATRA
Ah, stand by.
EROS   The Queen, my lord, the Queen.   41
IRAS
Go to him, madam, speak to him.
He's unqualitied with very shame.   43
CLEOPATRA   Well then, sustain me. O!
EROS
Most noble sir, arise. The Queen approaches.
Her head's declined, and death will seize her but   46
Your comfort makes the rescue.
ANTONY
I have offended reputation,
A most unnoble swerving.
EROS   Sir, the Queen.   49
ANTONY
O, whither hast thou led me, Egypt? See   50
How I convey my shame out of thine eyes   51
By looking back what I have left behind   52
'Stroyed in dishonor.
CLEOPATRA   O my lord, my lord,   53
Forgive my fearful sails! I little thought   54
You would have followed.
ANTONY   ·   Egypt, thou knew'st too well
My heart was to thy rudder tied by the strings,   56
And thou shouldst tow me after. O'er my spirit
Thy full supremacy thou knew'st, and that
Thy beck might from the bidding of the gods
Command me.
CLEOPATRA   O, my pardon!
ANTONY   Now I must

---

39 Dealt on lieutenantry let his subordinates do the fighting   **40 brave
squares** splendid squadrons, bodies of troops drawn up in square forma-
tion   **41 stand by** (Cleopatra indicates she is about to faint and needs
assistance.)   **43 unqualitied** dispossessed of his own nature, i.e., not
himself   **46 but** unless   **49 swerving** lapse, transgression   **50–53 See . . .
dishonor** i.e., see how I avert my eyes in shame from your gaze as though
looking back on the ruin of my fortunes and honor   **54 fearful** fright-
ened   **56 the strings** (1) the heartstrings (2) towing cable

To the young man send humble treaties, dodge   61
And palter in the shifts of lowness, who   62
With half the bulk o' the world played as I pleased,
Making and marring fortunes. You did know
How much you were my conqueror, and that
My sword, made weak by my affection, would   66
Obey it on all cause.
CLEOPATRA   Pardon, pardon!   67
ANTONY
Fall not a tear, I say; one of them rates   68
All that is won and lost. Give me a kiss.   [*They kiss.*]
Even this repays me.—We sent our schoolmaster;   70
Is 'a come back?—Love, I am full of lead.—
Some wine, within there, and our viands! Fortune
    knows   72
We scorn her most when most she offers blows.
                                             Exeunt.

✣

3.12   *Enter Caesar, Agrippa, [Thidias,] and
            Dolabella, with others.*

CAESAR
Let him appear that's come from Antony.
Know you him?
DOLABELLA   Caesar, 'tis his schoolmaster—
An argument that he is plucked, when hither   3
He sends so poor a pinion of his wing,   4
Which had superfluous kings for messengers   5
Not many moons gone by.

    Enter Ambassador from Antony.

---

61 treaties entreaties, propositions for settlement.   **dodge** shuffle,
cringe   **62 palter** use trickery, prevaricate, equivocate.   **shifts of lowness**
pitiful evasions used by those lacking power   **66 affection** passion
67 on all cause whatever the reason   **68 Fall** let fall.   **rates** equals
70 Even this this by itself.   **schoolmaster** (Identified in Plutarch as
Euphronius, tutor to Antony's children by Cleopatra.)   **72 viands** food

3.12. Location: Egypt. Caesar's camp.
3 An argument an indication   **4 pinion** i.e., pinion-feather, outer
feather   **5 Which** who

CAESAR   Approach and speak.
AMBASSADOR
  Such as I am, I come from Antony.
  I was of late as petty to his ends   8
  As is the morn-dew on the myrtle leaf
  To his grand sea.
CAESAR   Be 't so. Declare thine office.   10
AMBASSADOR
  Lord of his fortunes he salutes thee, and
  Requires to live in Egypt; which not granted,   12
  He lessens his requests, and to thee sues   13
  To let him breathe between the heavens and earth   14
  A private man in Athens. This for him.
  Next, Cleopatra does confess thy greatness,
  Submits her to thy might, and of thee craves
  The circle of the Ptolemies for her heirs,   18
  Now hazarded to thy grace.
CAESAR   For Antony,   19
  I have no ears to his request. The Queen
  Of audience nor desire shall fail, so she   21
  From Egypt drive her all-disgracèd friend
  Or take his life there. This if she perform
  She shall not sue unheard. So to them both.   24
AMBASSADOR
  Fortune pursue thee!
CAESAR   Bring him through the bands.   25
                          [Exit Ambassador, attended.]
  [To Thidias] To try thy eloquence now 'tis time. Dispatch.
  From Antony win Cleopatra. Promise,
  And in our name, what she requires; add more,   28
  From thine invention, offers. Women are not   29
  In their best fortunes strong, but want will perjure   30

---

8 petty to insignificant in terms of   **10 To . . . sea** compared to its, the
dewdrop's, great source, the sea.   **thine office** your official business
12 Requires asks.   **which not granted** and if that request is not
granted   **13 sues** petitions   **14 breathe** i.e., live   **18 circle** crown
19 hazarded . . . grace dependent on your favor.   **For** as for   **21 Of
audience** neither of hearing.   **so** provided that   **24 So** with these
terms, go   **25 Bring** escort.   **bands** troops on guard, military lines
28 requires asks   **28–29 add . . . offers** add ideas of your own   **30 In
. . . fortunes** even when at the height of their fortune.   **want** lack,
need.   **perjure** cause to break her vows (of chastity)

The ne'er touched vestal. Try thy cunning, Thidias.   31
Make thine own edict for thy pains, which we   32
Will answer as a law.
THIDIAS   Caesar, I go.   33
CAESAR
Observe how Antony becomes his flaw,   34
And what thou think'st his very action speaks   35
In every power that moves.
THIDIAS   Caesar, I shall. *Exeunt.* 36

✤

3.13   *Enter Cleopatra, Enobarbus, Charmian, and*
           Iras.

CLEOPATRA
What shall we do, Enobarbus?
ENOBARBUS   Think, and die.   1
CLEOPATRA
Is Antony or we in fault for this?   2
ENOBARBUS
Antony only, that would make his will   3
Lord of his reason. What though you fled
From that great face of war, whose several ranges   5
Frighted each other? Why should he follow?
The itch of his affection should not then   7
Have nicked his captainship, at such a point,   8
When half to half the world opposed, he being   9
The merèd question. 'Twas a shame no less   10
Than was his loss, to course your flying flags   11
And leave his navy gazing.

---

31 vestal priestess of Vesta, committed to chastity; or, simply, "vir-
gin." **cunning** skill **32 Make . . . edict** decree your own reward
33 answer as a law confirm as if it were a law **34 becomes his flaw**
bears his misfortune and disgrace **35 speaks** signifies **36 power that
moves** faculty or passion that manifests itself

3.13. Location: Alexandria. Cleopatra's palace.
1 Think i.e., reflect on our grievous situation **2 we** I **3 will** desire
(especially sexual) **5 ranges** ranks, lines (of ships) **7 affection** sexual
passion **8 nicked** cut short or damaged (from being nicked), or (from
gaming) got the better of, since a *nick* was a winning throw in a game of
chance. **point** crisis **9 half to . . . opposed** the two halves of the world
found themselves in conflict **10 merèd question** sole ground of quarrel **11 course** pursue (as in hunting)

CLEOPATRA   Prithee, peace.

Enter the Ambassador with Antony.

ANTONY   Is that his answer?

AMBASSADOR   Ay, my lord.

ANTONY
  The Queen shall then have courtesy, so she   15
  Will yield us up.

AMBASSADOR   He says so.

ANTONY   Let her know 't.—
  To the boy Caesar send this grizzled head,
  And he will fill thy wishes to the brim
  With principalities.

CLEOPATRA   That head, my lord?

ANTONY
  To him again. Tell him he wears the rose
  Of youth upon him, from which the world should note
  Something particular. His coin, ships, legions,   22
  May be a coward's, whose ministers would prevail   23
  Under the service of a child as soon
  As i' the command of Caesar. I dare him therefore
  To lay his gay comparisons apart   26
  And answer me declined, sword against sword,   27
  Ourselves alone. I'll write it. Follow me.
                    [*Exeunt Antony and Ambassador.*]

ENOBARBUS [*Aside*]
  Yes, like enough, high-battled Caesar will   29
  Unstate his happiness and be staged to the show   30
  Against a sworder! I see men's judgments are   31
  A parcel of their fortunes, and things outward   32
  Do draw the inward quality after them   33
  To suffer all alike. That he should dream,   34

---

15 so provided   **22 Something particular** some achievement or exploit
of his own   **23 May be** could as well be.   **ministers** agents, subordinates   **26 gay comparisons** i.e., the wealth and splendor just mentioned
(as compared with Antony's poverty); or, the comparisons between them
that Caesar makes on the basis of his wealth and power   **27 declined**
i.e., lowered in fortune and advanced in years   **29 high-battled** provided
with or raised up by noble armies   **30 Unstate** depose.   **happiness** good
fortune.   **staged** exhibited publicly   **31 sworder** one fighting with a
sword   **32 A parcel of** of a piece with   **33 quality** nature   **34 To . . .
alike** i.e., so that they deteriorate simultaneously

Knowing all measures, the full Caesar will   35
Answer his emptiness! Caesar, thou hast subdued
His judgment too.

    Enter a Servant.

SERVANT   A messenger from Caesar.

CLEOPATRA
What, no more ceremony? See, my women,
Against the blown rose may they stop their nose,   39
That kneeled unto the buds.—Admit him, sir.

                       [Exit Servant.]

ENOBARBUS *[Aside]*
Mine honesty and I begin to square.   41
The loyalty well held to fools does make
Our faith mere folly; yet he that can endure   43
To follow with allegiance a fall'n lord
Does conquer him that did his master conquer   45
And earns a place i' the story.

    Enter Thidias.

CLEOPATRA   Caesar's will?

THIDIAS
Hear it apart.

CLEOPATRA   None but friends. Say boldly.   47

THIDIAS
So haply are they friends to Antony.   48

ENOBARBUS
He needs as many, sir, as Caesar has,   49
Or needs not us. If Caesar please, our master   50
Will leap to be his friend. For us, you know   51
Whose he is we are, and that is Caesar's.

THIDIAS   So.   52
Thus then, thou most renowned: Caesar entreats

---

35 Knowing all measures i.e., having experienced every degree of fortune   **39 blown** overblown, starting to decay   **41 honesty** (with meaning
also of "honor").   **square** quarrel   **43 faith** fidelity   **45 Does . . . conquer** i.e., achieves a moral victory surpassing in honor the military
victory of the winner   **47 apart** in private   **48 haply** perhaps
49–50 He . . . us i.e., Antony would need as many followers as Caesar to
be a threat to him; otherwise, as things stand, we few would be of no
use to him in opposing Caesar and thus are not dangerous   **51 For** as
for   **52 Whose . . . Caesar's** i.e., we are Antony's friends, and he is
Caesar's, so that we too are Caesar's

Not to consider in what case thou stand'st   54
Further than he is Caesar.

CLEOPATRA   Go on: right royal.   55

THIDIAS
He knows that you embrace not Antony
As you did love, but as you feared him.

CLEOPATRA   O!

THIDIAS
The scars upon your honor therefore he
Does pity as constrainèd blemishes,   59
Not as deserved.

CLEOPATRA   He is a god and knows
What is most right. Mine honor was not yielded,   61
But conquered merely.

ENOBARBUS [Aside]   To be sure of that,   62
I will ask Antony. Sir, sir, thou art so leaky
That we must leave thee to thy sinking, for
Thy dearest quit thee.   Exit Enobarbus.

THIDIAS   Shall I say to Caesar
What you require of him? For he partly begs   66
To be desired to give. It much would please him
That of his fortunes you should make a staff
To lean upon; but it would warm his spirits
To hear from me you had left Antony
And put yourself under his shroud,   71
The universal landlord.

CLEOPATRA   What's your name?

THIDIAS
My name is Thidias.

CLEOPATRA   Most kind messenger,
Say to great Caesar this in deputation: 74
I kiss his conquering hand. Tell him I am prompt   75
To lay my crown at 's feet, and there to kneel.
Tell him, from his all-obeying breath I hear   77

54–55 Not . . . Caesar i.e., not to worry about your situation other than
to consider that you are dealing with Caesar, the embodiment of magna-
nimity   **55 right royal** i.e., that is very magnanimous   **59 constrainèd**
forced upon you   **61 right** true   **62 merely** utterly   **66 require** ask.
partly (Caesar's begging can be understood only as it befits his dignity.)   **71 shroud** shelter, protection   **74 in deputation** by you as
deputy   **75 prompt** ready   **77 all-obeying** obeyed by all

The doom of Egypt.

THIDIAS 'Tis your noblest course. 78
Wisdom and fortune combating together, 79
If that the former dare but what it can, 80
No chance may shake it. Give me grace to lay 81
My duty on your hand. [*He kisses her hand.*]

CLEOPATRA Your Caesar's father oft, 83
When he hath mused of taking kingdoms in, 84
Bestowed his lips on that unworthy place,
As it rained kisses.

Enter Antony and Enobarbus.

ANTONY Favors? By Jove that thunders! 86
What art thou, fellow?

THIDIAS One that but performs
The bidding of the fullest man, and worthiest 88
To have command obeyed.

ENOBARBUS [*Aside*] You will be whipped.

ANTONY [*Calling for Servants*]
Approach, there!—Ah, you kite!—Now, gods and devils! 90
Authority melts from me. Of late, when I cried "Ho!"
Like boys unto a muss kings would start forth 92
And cry, "Your will?"—Have you no ears? I am
Antony yet.

Enter a Servant [followed by others].

Take hence this Jack and whip him. 94

ENOBARBUS [*Aside*]
'Tis better playing with a lion's whelp 95
Than with an old one dying.

ANTONY Moon and stars!
Whip him. Were 't twenty of the greatest tributaries 97

78 **The doom of Egypt** i.e., my fate 79 **Wisdom . . . together** i.e., when fortune afflicts the wise 80 **If . . . can** if wise persons will only persist in being strong 81 **No . . . it** i.e., no ill fortune can harm those who are wise enough to accept the inevitable; if you submit to the fortunate Caesar, you will be all right 83 **Your Caesar's father** i.e., Julius Caesar. (See note at 3.6.6.) 84 **mused . . . in** thought about occupying kingdoms 86 **As** as if 88 **fullest** most fortunate, best 90 **kite** a rapacious bird of prey that feeds on ignoble objects, and a slang word for "whore." (Said of Cleopatra.) 92 **muss** game in which small objects are thrown down to be scrambled for 94 **Jack** fellow. (Contemptuous.) 95 **whelp** cub 97 **tributaries** rulers who paid tribute (to Rome)

That do acknowledge Caesar, should I find them
So saucy with the hand of she here—what's her name
Since she was Cleopatra? Whip him, fellows,
Till like a boy you see him cringe his face   101
And whine aloud for mercy. Take him hence.

THIDIAS
Mark Antony—

ANTONY   Tug him away! Being whipped,
Bring him again. This Jack of Caesar's shall
Bear us an errand to him.

          Exeunt [Servants] with Thidias.

[*To Cleopatra.*] You were half blasted ere I knew you. Ha? 106
Have I my pillow left unpressed in Rome,
Forborne the getting of a lawful race,   108
And by a gem of women, to be abused   109
By one that looks on feeders?   110

CLEOPATRA   Good my lord—

ANTONY   You have been a boggler ever.   112
But when we in our viciousness grow hard—
O misery on 't!—the wise gods seel our eyes,   114
In our own filth drop our clear judgments, make us
Adore our errors, laugh at 's while we strut
To our confusion.

CLEOPATRA   O, is 't come to this?   117

ANTONY
I found you as a morsel cold upon
Dead Caesar's trencher; nay, you were a fragment   119
Of Gnaeus Pompey's, besides what hotter hours,   120
Unregistered in vulgar fame, you have   121
Luxuriously picked out. For I am sure,   122
Though you can guess what temperance should be,
You know not what it is.

CLEOPATRA   Wherefore is this?   124

---

101 cringe contract in pain   **106 blasted** withered, blighted   **108 getting**
begetting.   **lawful** legitimate   **109 abused** deceived, betrayed
110 feeders servants   **112 boggler** waverer, shifty person. (Often used of
shying horses.)   **114 seel** blind. (A term in falconry for sewing shut the
eyes of wild hawks in order to tame them.)   **117 confusion** destruction   **119 trencher** wooden plate.   **fragment** leftover   **120 Gnaeus
Pompey's** (See 1.5.32 and note.)   **121 vulgar fame** common gossip
122 Luxuriously lustfully   **124 Wherefore is this** i.e., what brought
this on

ANTONY
   To let a fellow that will take rewards
   And say "God quit you!" be familiar with   126
   My playfellow, your hand, this kingly seal
   And plighter of high hearts! O, that I were   128
   Upon the hill of Basan, to outroar   129
   The hornèd herd! For I have savage cause,   130
   And to proclaim it civilly were like
   A haltered neck which does the hangman thank
   For being yare about him.

       Enter a Servant with Thidias.

                     Is he whipped?   133
SERVANT   Soundly, my lord.
ANTONY   Cried he? And begged 'a pardon?
SERVANT   He did ask favor.
ANTONY [*To Thidias*]
   If that thy father live, let him repent
   Thou wast not made his daughter; and be thou sorry
   To follow Caesar in his triumph, since
   Thou hast been whipped for following him. Henceforth
   The white hand of a lady fever thee;   141
   Shake thou to look on 't. Get thee back to Caesar.
   Tell him thy entertainment. Look thou say   143
   He makes me angry with him; for he seems
   Proud and disdainful, harping on what I am,
   Not what he knew I was. He makes me angry,
   And at this time most easy 'tis to do 't,
   When my good stars, that were my former guides,
   Have empty left their orbs and shot their fires   149
   Into th' abysm of hell. If he mislike   150
   My speech and what is done, tell him he has
   Hipparchus, my enfranchèd bondman, whom   152
   He may at pleasure whip, or hang, or torture,

---

126 quit reward. (*God quit you* is said obsequiously to acknowledge a tip.)   **128 plighter** pledger   **129–130 hill of Basan . . . The hornèd herd** (Allusion to the strong bulls of Bashan, Psalms 22:12 and 68:15. Antony imagines himself as the greatest horned beast, i.e., cuckold, of that herd.)   **133 yare** deft, quick   **141 fever thee** make you shiver **143 entertainment** reception.   **Look** be sure that   **149 orbs** spheres **150 abysm** abyss   **152 Hipparchus** (According to Plutarch, the man was a deserter to Caesar's side.)   **enfranchèd** enfranchised, freed

As he shall like, to quit me. Urge it thou.   154
Hence with thy stripes, begone!   *Exit Thidias.*
CLEOPATRA   Have you done yet?
ANTONY
Alack, our terrene moon is now eclipsed,   156
And it portends alone the fall of Antony.
CLEOPATRA I must stay his time.   158
ANTONY
To flatter Caesar, would you mingle eyes
With one that ties his points?
CLEOPATRA   Not know me yet?   160
ANTONY
Coldhearted toward me?
CLEOPATRA   Ah, dear, if I be so,
From my cold heart let heaven engender hail,
And poison it in the source, and the first stone
Drop in my neck; as it determines, so   164
Dissolve my life! The next Caesarion smite,
Till by degrees the memory of my womb,   166
Together with my brave Egyptians all,   167
By the discandying of this pelleted storm   168
Lie graveless till the flies and gnats of Nile
Have buried them for prey!
ANTONY   I am satisfied.   170
Caesar sits down in Alexandria, where   171
I will oppose his fate. Our force by land   172
Hath nobly held; our severed navy too
Have knit again, and fleet, threat'ning most sealike.   174
Where hast thou been, my heart? Dost thou hear, lady?   175
If from the field I shall return once more
To kiss these lips, I will appear in blood;   177

154 **quit** requite, pay back   156 **terrene** earthly.   **moon** (with an allusion to Cleopatra; she is contrasted with the moon in 5.2.240–241)
158 **stay his time** i.e., be patient until his fury has subsided   160 **his**
Caesar's.   **points** laces by which articles of clothing were secured
164 **neck** throat or head.   **determines** comes to an end, dissolves (see
l. 168)   166 **memory of my womb** i.e., my offspring   167 **brave** splendid
(also at l. 180)   168 **discandying** melting.   **pelleted** falling in pellets
170 **for prey** i.e., by eating them   171 **sits down in** lays siege to
172 **oppose his fate** confront his (seemingly irresistible) fortune
174 **fleet** float   175 **heart** courage   177 **in blood** (1) bloody from battle
(2) full-spirited

I and my sword will earn our chronicle.　　　178
There's hope in 't yet.

CLEOPATRA　That's my brave lord!

ANTONY

I will be treble-sinewed, hearted, breathed,　　　181
And fight maliciously. For when mine hours　　　182
Were nice and lucky, men did ransom lives　　　183
Of me for jests; but now I'll set my teeth　　　184
And send to darkness all that stop me. Come,　　　185
Let's have one other gaudy night. Call to me　　　186
All my sad captains. Fill our bowls once more;
Let's mock the midnight bell.

CLEOPATRA　　　　　　　　　It is my birthday.
I had thought t' have held it poor; but since my lord　　　189
Is Antony again, I will be Cleopatra.

ANTONY　We will yet do well.

CLEOPATRA [To attendants]
Call all his noble captains to my lord.

ANTONY
Do so. We'll speak to them, and tonight I'll force
The wine peep through their scars. Come on, my queen,
There's sap in 't yet. The next time I do fight　　　195
I'll make Death love me, for I will contend　　　196
Even with his pestilent scythe.　　　197

　　　　　　　　　　Exeunt [all but Enobarbus].

ENOBARBUS
Now he'll outstare the lightning. To be furious　　　198
Is to be frighted out of fear, and in that mood
The dove will peck the estridge; and I see still　　　200
A diminution in our captain's brain
Restores his heart. When valor preys on reason,
It eats the sword it fights with. I will seek
Some way to leave him.　　　　　　　Exit.

❖

178 **chronicle** place in history　181 **hearted** treble-hearted.　**breathed**
treble-breathed　182 **maliciously** violently, fiercely　183 **nice** delicate,
fastidious, able to appreciate chivalrous niceties　183–184 **men . . . jests**
i.e., I allowed enemies to be ransomed for trifles or as a magnanimous
gesture　185 **to darkness** i.e., to death, the underworld　186 **gaudy**
festive　189 **held it poor** celebrated it simply　195 **sap in 't** i.e., life in
me　196–197 **I will . . . scythe** i.e., I will outdo even Death himself and
his scythe of *pestilence* or plague　198 **outstare** stare down.　**furious**
frenzied　200 **estridge** kind of hawk.

4.1   *Enter Caesar, Agrippa, and Maecenas, with his army, Caesar reading a letter.*

CAESAR
  He calls me boy, and chides as he had power   1
  To beat me out of Egypt. My messenger
  He hath whipped with rods, dares me to personal
    combat,
  Caesar to Antony. Let the old ruffian know
  I have many other ways to die, meantime
  Laugh at his challenge.   6
MAECENAS Caesar must think,
  When one so great begins to rage, he's hunted   8
  Even to falling. Give him no breath, but now   9
  Make boot of his distraction. Never anger   10
  Made good guard for itself.
CAESAR   Let our best heads   11
  Know that tomorrow the last of many battles
  We mean to fight. Within our files there are,   13
  Of those that served Mark Antony but late,   14
  Enough to fetch him in. See it done,   15
  And feast the army; we have store to do 't,   16
  And they have earned the waste. Poor Antony!   17

                                      Exeunt.

❖

4.2   *Enter Antony, Cleopatra, Enobarbus, Charmian, Iras, Alexas, with others.*

ANTONY
  He will not fight with me, Domitius?
ENOBARBUS No.
ANTONY Why should he not?

4.1. Location: Before Alexandria. Caesar's camp.
1 as as if **6 Laugh** i.e., let him know I laugh **8 rage** rave **9 breath**
breathing space **10 boot** advantage. **distraction** frenzy **11 best heads**
commanding officers **13 files** (as in "rank and file") **14 late** lately
15 fetch him in surround, capture him **16 store** provisions **17 waste**
lavish expenditure

4.2. Location: Alexandria. Cleopatra's palace.

ENOBARBUS
 He thinks, being twenty times of better fortune,
 He is twenty men to one.
ANTONY   Tomorrow, soldier,
 By sea and land I'll fight. Or I will live   6
 Or bathe my dying honor in the blood
 Shall make it live again. Woo't thou fight well?   8
ENOBARBUS
 I'll strike, and cry, "Take all."
ANTONY   Well said. Come on!   9
 Call forth my household servants. Let's tonight
 Be bounteous at our meal.

          Enter three or four servitors.

                         Give me thy hand.   11
 Thou hast been rightly honest—so hast thou—   12
 Thou—and thou—and thou. You have served me well,
 And kings have been your fellows.
CLEOPATRA [*Aside to Enobarbus*]   What means this?   14
ENOBARBUS [*Aside to Cleopatra*]
 'Tis one of those odd tricks which sorrow shoots
 Out of the mind.
ANTONY   And thou art honest too.
 I wish I could be made so many men,   17
 And all of you clapped up together in   18
 An Antony, that I might do you service
 So good as you have done.
ALL   The gods forbid!
ANTONY
 Well, my good fellows, wait on me tonight:
 Scant not my cups, and make as much of me   22
 As when mine empire was your fellow too,   23
 And suffered my command.
CLEOPATRA [*Aside to Enobarbus*]   What does he mean?   24

___

6 Or either   **8 Shall** that shall.   **Woo't** wilt   **9 strike . . . Take all**
(1) fight to the finish, crying, "Winner take all" (2) strike sail and surrender   **11 s.d. servitors** attendants   **12 honest** true, loyal   **14 fellows**
i.e., fellow servants of me   **17 made . . . men** divided into as many men
as you are   **18 clapped up** combined   **22 Scant not my cups** i.e., provide generously   **23 fellow** i.e., fellow servant   **24 suffered** acknowledged, submitted to

ENOBARBUS [*Aside to Cleopatra*]
  To make his followers weep.
ANTONY   Tend me tonight;
  May be it is the period of your duty.   26
  Haply you shall not see me more, or if,   27
  A mangled shadow. Perchance tomorrow   28
  You'll serve another master. I look on you
  As one that takes his leave. Mine honest friends,
  I turn you not away, but, like a master
  Married to your good service, stay till death.
  Tend me tonight two hours, I ask no more,
  And the gods yield you for 't!
ENOBARBUS   What mean you, sir,   34
  To give them this discomfort? Look, they weep,
  And I, an ass, am onion-eyed. For shame,
  Transform us not to women.
ANTONY   Ho, ho, ho!
  Now the witch take me if I meant it thus!   38
  Grace grow where those drops fall! My hearty friends,   39
  You take me in too dolorous a sense,
  For I spake to you for your comfort, did desire you
  To burn this night with torches. Know, my hearts,
  I hope well of tomorrow, and will lead you
  Where rather I'll expect victorious life
  Than death and honor. Let's to supper, come,
  And drown consideration.   *Exeunt.*   46

❖

4.3   *Enter a company of Soldiers.*

FIRST SOLDIER
  Brother, good night. Tomorrow is the day.
SECOND SOLDIER
  It will determine one way. Fare you well.   2
  Heard you of nothing strange about the streets?   3

26 period end   **27 if** i.e., if you do   **28 shadow** ghost   **34 yield** reward
38 the witch take me may I be bewitched   **39 Grace grow** (1) may rue or
herb of grace grow (2) may gracious fortune flourish.   **hearty** loving
46 consideration thinking, brooding

4.3. Location: Alexandria. Before the palace.
2 determine be decided, come to an end   **3 about** in

FIRST SOLDIER   Nothing. What news?
SECOND SOLDIER
  Belike 'tis but a rumor. Good night to you.   5
FIRST SOLDIER   Well, sir, good night.

        They meet other Soldiers.

SECOND SOLDIER   Soldiers, have careful watch.
FIRST SOLDIER   And you. Good night, good night.   8
                    [*Exeunt First and Second Soldiers.*]

        They [*the Soldiers coming on watch*] *place
        themselves in every corner of the stage.*

FOURTH SOLDIER   Here we. An if tomorrow   9
  Our navy thrive, I have an absolute hope
  Our landmen will stand up.
THIRD SOLDIER   'Tis a brave army, and full of purpose.   12
                Music of the hautboys is under the stage.
FOURTH SOLDIER   Peace! What noise?
THIRD SOLDIER   List, list!   14
FOURTH SOLDIER   Hark!
THIRD SOLDIER   Music i' th' air.
FIFTH SOLDIER   Under the earth.
SIXTH SOLDIER   It signs well, does it not?   18
FIFTH SOLDIER   No.
THIRD SOLDIER   Peace, I say! What should this mean?
FOURTH SOLDIER
  'Tis the god Hercules, whom Antony loved,
  Now leaves him.
THIRD SOLDIER   Walk; let's see if other watchmen
  Do hear what we do.
              [*They advance toward their fellow watchmen.*]
FOURTH SOLDIER   How now, masters?
ALL (*Speak together*)   How now? How now? Do you hear
  this?
THIRD SOLDIER   Ay. Is 't not strange?
FIFTH SOLDIER   Do you hear, masters? Do you hear?   28

5 Belike probably   **8 And you** (The First Soldier probably is speaking to
those coming on watch, as the Second Soldier has done.)   **9 Here we**
here's our station.   **An if** if   **12 brave** splendid, gallant   **s.d. hautboys**
oboelike instruments   **14 List** listen   **18 signs well** is a good sign
28 masters i.e., sirs

THIRD SOLDIER
  Follow the noise so far as we have quarter;   29
  Let's see how it will give off.   30
ALL   Content. 'Tis strange.

                                                  Exeunt.

                              ✤

4.4   *Enter Antony and Cleopatra, with [Charmian*
           and] others [attending].

ANTONY
  Eros! Mine armor, Eros!
CLEOPATRA   Sleep a little.
ANTONY
  No, my chuck. Eros, come, mine armor, Eros!   2

       Enter Eros [with armor].

  Come, good fellow, put thine iron on.   3
  If fortune be not ours today, it is
  Because we brave her. Come.
CLEOPATRA   Nay, I'll help too.   5
  What's this for?   [*She helps to arm him.*]
ANTONY   Ah, let be, let be! Thou art
  The armorer of my heart. False, false; this, this.   7
CLEOPATRA
  Sooth, la, I'll help. Thus it must be.
ANTONY   Well, well,   8
  We shall thrive now. Seest thou, my good fellow?
  Go, put on thy defenses.
EROS   Briefly, sir.   10
CLEOPATRA
  Is not this buckled well?
ANTONY   Rarely, rarely.   11

29 as we have quarter as our watch post extends   **30 give off** cease

4.4. Location: Alexandria. The palace.
2 chuck (A term of endearment.)   **3 thine iron** i.e., my armor that you
have there. (Or perhaps he is telling Eros to arm.)   **5 brave** defy
7 False you're putting it on wrong   **8 Sooth** in truth   **10 defenses**
armor.   **Briefly** in a moment   **11 Rarely** excellently

He that unbuckles this, till we do please   12
To doff 't for our repose, shall hear a storm.   13
Thou fumblest, Eros, and my queen's a squire   14
More tight at this than thou. Dispatch. O love,   15
That thou couldst see my wars today, and knew'st
The royal occupation! Thou shouldst see
A workman in 't.

    Enter an armed Soldier.

                Good morrow to thee. Welcome.   18
Thou look'st like him that knows a warlike charge.   19
To business that we love we rise betimes   20
And go to 't with delight.

SOLDIER   A thousand, sir,
Early though 't be, have on their riveted trim   22
And at the port expect you.   *Shout. Trumpets flourish.*   23

    Enter Captains and Soldiers.

CAPTAIN
The morn is fair. Good morrow, General.
ALL
Good morrow, General.
ANTONY   'Tis well blown, lads.   25
This morning, like the spirit of a youth
That means to be of note, begins betimes.
So, so. Come, give me that. This way. Well said.   28
Fare thee well, dame. Whate'er becomes of me,
This is a soldier's kiss. [*He kisses her.*] Rebukable,
And worthy shameful check it were, to stand   31
On more mechanic compliment. I'll leave thee   32

12–13 He . . . storm i.e., anyone who attempts to burst my armor in the
fight, before I choose myself to unarm and rest, will be greeted by a
storm of blows   **13 doff 't** take it off   **14 squire** officer charged with
attendance on a knight or noble   **15 tight** deft, skillful.   **Dispatch** finish
up   **18 workman** craftsman, professional   **19 charge** duty, responsibility   **20 betimes** early   **22 riveted trim** i.e., armor   **23 port** gate   **25 'Tis
well blown** i.e., the morning begins well; or, refers to trumpets in l. 23
28 said done   **31 check** reproof   **31–32 stand On** be particular about,
insist on   **32 mechanic** dwelling on technicalities; vulgar.   **compliment**
exchange of courtesies

Now like a man of steel.—You that will fight,
Follow me close. I'll bring you to 't. Adieu.
          Exeunt [Antony, Eros, Captains, and Soldiers].
CHARMIAN
Please you, retire to your chamber?
CLEOPATRA   Lead me.
He goes forth gallantly. That he and Caesar might
Determine this great war in single fight!
Then Antony—but now—Well, on.   *Exeunt.*

❖

4.5   *Trumpets sound. Enter Antony and Eros;*
           [a Soldier meeting them].

SOLDIER
The gods make this a happy day to Antony!   1
ANTONY
Would thou and those thy scars had once prevailed   2
To make me fight at land!
SOLDIER   Hadst thou done so,
The kings that have revolted, and the soldier   4
That has this morning left thee, would have still
Followed thy heels.
ANTONY   Who's gone this morning?
SOLDIER   Who?
One ever near thee. Call for Enobarbus,
He shall not hear thee, or from Caesar's camp
Say, "I am none of thine."
ANTONY   What sayest thou?
SOLDIER   Sir,
He is with Caesar.
EROS   Sir, his chests and treasure
He has not with him.
ANTONY   Is he gone?
SOLDIER   Most certain.
ANTONY
Go, Eros, send his treasure after. Do it.
Detain no jot, I charge thee. Write to him—

4.5. Location: Before Alexandria. Antony's camp.
1 happy fortunate   **2 once** formerly   **4 revolted** deserted

I will subscribe—gentle adieus and greetings.   14
Say that I wish he never find more cause
To change a master. O, my fortunes have
Corrupted honest men! Dispatch.—Enobarbus!   17
                    Exit [*with Eros and Soldier*].

❖

4.6   *Flourish. Enter Agrippa, Caesar, with
          Enobarbus, and Dolabella.*

CAESAR
  Go forth, Agrippa, and begin the fight.
  Our will is Antony be took alive;
  Make it so known.
AGRIPPA   Caesar, I shall.   [*Exit.*]
CAESAR
  The time of universal peace is near.   5
  Prove this a prosperous day, the three-nooked world 6
  Shall bear the olive freely.

        Enter a Messenger.

MESSENGER   Antony   7
  Is come into the field.
CAESAR   Go charge Agrippa   8
  Plant those that have revolted in the van,   9
  That Antony may seem to spend his fury
  Upon himself.   *Exeunt* [*all but Enobarbus*].
ENOBARBUS
  Alexas did revolt and went to Jewry on   12
  Affairs of Antony, there did dissuade   13
  Great Herod to incline himself to Caesar
  And leave his master Antony. For this pains,

---

14 subscribe sign   **17 Dispatch** make haste, get done with it

4.6. Location: Before Alexandria. Caesar's camp.

5 The . . . near (The Renaissance identified Octavius Caesar, or the
Emperor Augustus as he was subsequently titled, with this *Pax Ro-
mana,* peace under the Roman Empire.)   **6 Prove this** if this prove.
three-nooked three-cornered. (Refers to Asia, Europe, and Africa.)
7 bear (1) bring forth (2) wear as a triumphal garland   **8 charge Agrippa**
order Agrippa to   **9 van** vanguard, front lines   **12 Jewry** Judaea
13 dissuade i.e., from following Antony

Caesar hath hanged him. Canidius and the rest
That fell away have entertainment but   17
No honorable trust. I have done ill,
Of which I do accuse myself so sorely   19
That I will joy no more.

    Enter a Soldier of Caesar's.

SOLDIER   Enobarbus, Antony
Hath after thee sent all thy treasure, with
His bounty overplus. The messenger   22
Came on my guard, and at thy tent is now   23
Unloading of his mules.
ENOBARBUS   I give it you.
SOLDIER   Mock not, Enobarbus,
I tell you true. Best you safed the bringer   27
Out of the host. I must attend mine office,   28
Or would have done 't myself. Your emperor
Continues still a Jove.   *Exit.*

ENOBARBUS
I am alone the villain of the earth,   31
And feel I am so most. O Antony,   32
Thou mine of bounty, how wouldst thou have paid   33
My better service when my turpitude
Thou dost so crown with gold! This blows my heart.   35
If swift thought break it not, a swifter mean   36
Shall outstrike thought; but thought will do 't, I feel.   37
I fight against thee? No, I will go seek
Some ditch wherein to die. The foul'st best fits
My latter part of life.   *Exit.*

               ❖

17 entertainment employment, maintenance   **19 sorely** heavily
22 overplus in addition   **23 on my guard** while I was standing guard
27 Best you safed it would be best for you to provide safe-conduct for
28 host army.   **attend mine office** see to my duties   **31 alone the** the
only, the greatest   **32 And . . . most** and am the one who feels it most
33 mine i.e., abundant store   **35 blows** causes to swell to the bursting
point   **36 mean** i.e., suicide   **37 thought** melancholy.   **do 't** i.e., break
my heart

4.7   *Alarum. Drums and trumpets. Enter Agrippa*
[and others].

AGRIPPA

Retire! We have engaged ourselves too far.   1
Caesar himself has work, and our oppression   2
Exceeds what we expected.   *Exeunt.* 3

    Alarums. Enter Antony, and Scarus wounded.

SCARUS

O my brave Emperor, this is fought indeed!
Had we done so at first, we had droven them home   5
With clouts about their heads.

ANTONY   Thou bleed'st apace.   6

SCARUS

I had a wound here that was like a T,
But now 'tis made an H.   *[Sound retreat] far off.*

ANTONY   They do retire.   8

SCARUS

We'll beat 'em into bench holes. I have yet   9
Room for six scotches more.   10

    Enter Eros.

EROS

They are beaten, sir, and our advantage serves   11
For a fair victory.

SCARUS   Let us score their backs   12
And snatch 'em up, as we take hares, behind!
'Tis sport to maul a runner.

ANTONY   I will reward thee   14
Once for thy spritely comfort and tenfold
For thy good valor. Come thee on.

SCARUS   I'll halt after.   *Exeunt.* 17

4.7. Location: Field of battle between the camps.

1 Retire retreat **2 has work** is hard pressed. **our oppression** the heavy
attacks against us **3 Exeunt** (The cleared stage technically marks a
new scene.) **5 droven** driven **6 clouts** (1) bandages (2) blows and
knocks **8 H** i.e., the bottom of the *T* has been cut across to make an H
lying on its side. (There is a pun on *ache*, pronounced *aitch*.) **9 bench
holes** the holes of privies, i.e., any desperate place to hide **10 scotches**
cuts **11–12 our . . . victory** i.e., we are in such a favorable position that
a complete victory seems in prospect **12 score** mark by cuts from a
whip **14 a runner** i.e., in retreat **17 halt** limp

4.8   *Alarum. Enter Antony again in a march;*
         Scarus, with others.

ANTONY
  We have beat him to his camp. Run one before   1
  And let the Queen know of our gests. [*Exit a Soldier.*]
    Tomorrow,   2
  Before the sun shall see 's, we'll spill the blood
  That has today escaped. I thank you all,
  For doughty-handed are you, and have fought   5
  Not as you served the cause, but as 't had been   6
  Each man's like mine; you have shown all Hectors.   7
  Enter the city, clip your wives, your friends,   8
  Tell them your feats, whilst they with joyful tears
  Wash the congealment from your wounds and kiss
  The honored gashes whole.

         Enter Cleopatra [attended].

                        [*To Scarus.*] Give me thy hand;
  To this great fairy I'll commend thy acts,   12
  Make her thanks bless thee. [*To Cleopatra.*] O thou day o'
    the world,   13
  Chain mine armed neck; leap thou, attire and all,
  Through proof of harness to my heart, and there   15
  Ride on the pants triumphing!   [*They embrace.*]
CLEOPATRA   Lord of lords,   16
  O infinite virtue, com'st thou smiling from   17
  The world's great snare uncaught?
ANTONY   My nightingale,
  We have beat them to their beds. What, girl, though gray
  Do something mingle with our younger brown, yet
    ha' we   20
  A brain that nourishes our nerves and can   21

4.8. Location: Before Alexandria. The action is virtually continuous.
1 beat driven.   **Run one** let someone run   **2 gests** deeds   **5 doughty-
handed** valiant   **6 as . . . as 't** as if . . . as if it.   **the cause** merely the
general cause   **7 shown** shown yourselves   **8 clip** embrace   **12 fairy**
enchantress, dispenser of good fortune   **13 day** i.e., sun; or, span, time
of existence (? i.e., the world exists through her)   **15 proof of harness**
proof-armor, tested armor   **16 pants** heartbeats   **17 virtue** valor
20 something somewhat   **21 nerves** sinews, tendons

Get goal for goal of youth. Behold this man;   22
Commend unto his lips thy favoring hand.—   23
Kiss it, my warrior. [*Scarus kisses Cleopatra's hand.*]
    He hath fought today
As if a god, in hate of mankind, had
Destroyed in such a shape.

CLEOPATRA   I'll give thee, friend,
An armor all of gold; it was a king's.

ANTONY
He has deserved it, were it carbuncled   28
Like holy Phoebus' car. Give me thy hand.   29
Through Alexandria make a jolly march;
Bear our hacked targets like the men that owe them.   31
Had our great palace the capacity
To camp this host, we all would sup together   33
And drink carouses to the next day's fate,   34
Which promises royal peril. Trumpeters,   35
With brazen din blast you the city's ear;
Make mingle with our rattling taborins,   37
That heaven and earth may strike their sounds together,   38
Applauding our approach. [*Trumpets sound.*] *Exeunt.*

❖

4.9   *Enter a Sentry and his company. Enobarbus
follows.*

SENTRY
If we be not relieved within this hour,
We must return to the court of guard. The night   2
Is shiny, and they say we shall embattle   3
By the second hour i' the morn.

FIRST WATCH   This last day was a shrewd one to 's.   5

---

22 Get . . . of i.e., stay competitively equal with.   **this man** i.e., Scarus
23 Commend entrust, commit   **28 carbuncled** set with jewels
29 Phoebus' car the chariot of the sun   **31 targets** shields.   **like** as
becomes.   **owe** own   **33 camp this host** accommodate this army
34 carouses toasts   **35 royal peril** i.e., war, the sport of monarchs
37 taborins drums   **38 That . . . together** i.e., the heavens are to echo
the loud noise of the drums, augmenting the acclaim

4.9. Location: Caesar's camp.
2 court of guard guardroom   **3 shiny** bright, moonlit.   **embattle** fall in
for the combat   **5 shrewd** unlucky

ENOBARBUS   O, bear me witness, night—
SECOND WATCH   What man is this?
FIRST WATCH   Stand close and list him. [*They stand aside.*] 8
ENOBARBUS
  Be witness to me, O thou blessèd moon,
  When men revolted shall upon record   10
  Bear hateful memory: poor Enobarbus did
  Before thy face repent.
SENTRY   Enobarbus?
SECOND WATCH   Peace! Hark further.
ENOBARBUS
  O sovereign mistress of true melancholy,   15
  The poisonous damp of night dispunge upon me, 16
  That life, a very rebel to my will,
  May hang no longer on me. Throw my heart
  Against the flint and hardness of my fault,
  Which, being dried with grief, will break to powder 20
  And finish all foul thoughts. O Antony,
  Nobler than my revolt is infamous,
  Forgive me in thine own particular,   23
  But let the world rank me in register   24
  A master-leaver and a fugitive.   25
  O Antony! O Antony!   [*He dies.*]
FIRST WATCH   Let's speak to him.
SENTRY
  Let's hear him, for the things he speaks
  May concern Caesar.
SECOND WATCH   Let's do so. But he sleeps.
SENTRY
  Swoons rather, for so bad a prayer as his
  Was never yet for sleep.
FIRST WATCH   Go we to him.   31
                [*They approach Enobarbus.*]

---

8 close concealed.   **list** listen to   **10 revolted** who have broken their
allegiance.   **upon record** in the record of history   **15 mistress . . .
melancholy** i.e., the moon, so addressed because of her supposed influence in causing lunacy   **16 dispunge** pour down (as from a squeezed
sponge)   **20 Which** i.e., the heart.   **dried with grief** (Elizabethans
thought that the spirits of a man in Enobarbus' state of mind would
descend into his bowels, leaving his heart dry.)   **23 in . . . particular** in
your own person   **24 rank me in register** put me down in its records
25 fugitive deserter   **31 for** a prelude to

SECOND WATCH   Awake, sir, awake. Speak to us.
FIRST WATCH   Hear you, sir?
SENTRY   The hand of death hath raught him.   34

                              Drums afar off.
Hark, the drums demurely wake the sleepers.   35
Let us bear him to the court of guard;
He is of note. Our hour is fully out.   37
SECOND WATCH
Come on, then. He may recover yet.
                              Exeunt [with the body].

❖

4.10   *Enter Antony and Scarus, with their army.*

ANTONY
Their preparation is today by sea;
We please them not by land.
SCARUS   For both, my lord.
ANTONY
I would they'd fight i' the fire or i' the air;   3
We'd fight there too. But this it is: our foot   4
Upon the hills adjoining to the city
Shall stay with us. Order for sea is given;   6
They have put forth the haven,   7
Where their appointment we may best discover   8
And look on their endeavor.   *Exeunt.*

4.11   *Enter Caesar and his army.*

CAESAR
But being charged, we will be still by land—   i

---

34 **raught** reached   35 **demurely** with subdued sound   37 **of note** of rank

4.10. Location: The field of battle.
3 **fire, air** (Comprising the four elements, along with earth and water
where Antony is already prepared.)   4 **foot** foot soldiers   6 **for sea** to
fight at sea   7 **forth** forth from   8 **appointment** disposition of forces,
equipment.   **discover** descry

4.11. Location: The field of battle.
1 **But being** unless we are.   **still** inactive

Which, as I take 't, we shall, for his best force   2
Is forth to man his galleys. To the vales,   3
And hold our best advantage.   *Exeunt.* 4

4.12   *Enter Antony and Scarus.*

ANTONY
Yet they are not joined. Where yond pine does stand
I shall discover all. I'll bring thee word
Straight how 'tis like to go.   *Exit.*
          Alarum afar off, as at a sea fight.
SCARUS   Swallows have built   3
In Cleopatra's sails their nests. The augurers   4
Say they know not, they cannot tell, look grimly,
And dare not speak their knowledge. Antony
Is valiant, and dejected, and by starts
His fretted fortunes give him hope and fear   8
Of what he has and has not.

     Enter Antony.

ANTONY   All is lost!
This foul Egyptian hath betrayèd me.
My fleet hath yielded to the foe, and yonder
They cast their caps up and carouse together
Like friends long lost. Triple-turned whore! 'Tis thou   13
Hast sold me to this novice, and my heart
Makes only wars on thee. Bid them all fly;   15
For when I am revenged upon my charm,   16
I have done all. Bid them all fly. Begone!
          [Exit Scarus.]
O sun, thy uprise shall I see no more.

---

2 we shall i.e., we will be left undisturbed   **3 Is forth** has gone forth.
vales valleys   **4 hold . . . advantage** take the most advantageous position

**4.12. Location: The field of battle at first, though by scene's end the
action appears to be located in Alexandria.**
3 Straight immediately.   **like** likely   **4 augurers** augurs, soothsayers
8 fretted worn away   **13 Triple-turned** three times faithless (to Julius
Caesar, Gnaeus Pompey, and now Antony)   **15 Makes . . . thee** wages
war on you alone   **16 charm** practicer of charms or spells

Fortune and Antony part here; even here
Do we shake hands. All come to this? The hearts   20
That spanieled me at heels, to whom I gave   21
Their wishes, do discandy, melt their sweets   22
On blossoming Caesar; and this pine is barked   23
That overtopped them all. Betrayed I am.
O this false soul of Egypt! This grave charm,   25
Whose eye becked forth my wars and called them home,   26
Whose bosom was my crownet, my chief end,   27
Like a right gypsy hath at fast and loose   28
Beguiled me to the very heart of loss.   29
What, Eros, Eros!

        Enter Cleopatra.

                    Ah, thou spell! Avaunt!   30
CLEOPATRA
Why is my lord enraged against his love?
ANTONY
Vanish, or I shall give thee thy deserving
And blemish Caesar's triumph. Let him take thee   33
And hoist thee up to the shouting plebeians!
Follow his chariot, like the greatest spot   35
Of all thy sex; most monsterlike be shown   36
For poor'st diminutives, for dolts, and let   37
Patient Octavia plow thy visage up
With her preparèd nails!   *Exit Cleopatra.*
                    'Tis well thou'rt gone,
If it be well to live; but better 'twere
Thou fell'st into my fury, for one death   41

20 hearts good fellows   **21 spanieled** fawned upon like a spaniel
22 Their wishes whatever they wished.   **discandy** melt, dissolve
23 this pine i.e., Antony.   **barked** stripped of its bark and thus killed
25 This grave charm i.e., this sorceress who has heavy or fatal spells
26 becked beckoned   **27 crownet** coronet.   **end** aim. (Cleopatra's love
was the crown of Antony's achievements and the reward of his la-
bors.)   **28 right** veritable.   **fast and loose** a cheating game in which the
victim bets that he can make fast a knot in an ingeniously coiled rope,
whereupon the knot is pulled loose   **29 loss** ruin   **30 spell** enchantment, spell maker (?)   **Avaunt** begone   **33 triumph** triumphal procession (in Rome)   **35 spot** blemish, disgrace   **36 shown** exhibited
37 diminutives undersized creatures, i.e., the populace   **41 Thou fell'st
into** you had fallen a victim to

Might have prevented many. Eros, ho!   42
The shirt of Nessus is upon me. Teach me,   43
Alcides, thou mine ancestor, thy rage.   44
Let me lodge Lichas on the horns o' the moon,   45
And with those hands that grasped the heaviest club
Subdue my worthiest self. The witch shall die.
To the young Roman boy she hath sold me, and I fall
Under this plot. She dies for 't. Eros, ho!   *Exit.*

❖

4.13   *Enter Cleopatra, Charmian, Iras, [and]*
           Mardian.

CLEOPATRA
Help me, my women! O, he's more mad
Than Telamon for his shield; the boar of Thessaly   2
Was never so embossed.
CHARMIAN   To the monument!   3
There lock yourself and send him word you are dead.
The soul and body rive not more in parting   5
Than greatness going off.
CLEOPATRA   To the monument!   6
Mardian, go tell him I have slain myself.
Say that the last I spoke was "Antony,"   8
And word it, prithee, piteously. Hence, Mardian,

---

42 many i.e., many shameful experiences (?), or many other killings
through Antony's rage (?)   **43–45 Nessus, Alcides, Lichas** (When Hercules
or *Alcides* had fatally wounded the centaur *Nessus* for trying to rape
Hercules' wife Deianira, Nessus vengefully gave his blood-soaked shirt to
Deianira as a supposed love-charm for her husband. The poison gave
Hercules such agony that he cast his page *Lichas* into the air.)

**4.13. Location: Alexandria. This scene appears to follow scene 12
closely. The sense of location is very fluid, and it is not clear where the
end of 12 takes place.**
2 Telamon Ajax Telamon, who after the capture of Troy went mad and
slew himself when he was not awarded the shield and armor of Achilles.   **boar of Thessaly** the boar sent by Diana or Artemis to ravage the
fields of Calydon, and slain by Meleager   **3 embossed** foaming at the
mouth from rage and exhaustion.   **monument** tomb built in anticipa-
tion of Cleopatra's death   **5 rive** split, sever   **6 going off** i.e., bidding
farewell to its glory   **8 last** last word

And bring me how he takes my death. To th'
  monument!   *Exeunt.*

❖

4.14   *Enter Antony and Eros.*

ANTONY
  Eros, thou yet behold'st me?
EROS   Ay, noble lord.
ANTONY
  Sometimes we see a cloud that's dragonish,   2
  A vapor sometimes like a bear or lion,
  A towered citadel, a pendant rock,   4
  A forkèd mountain, or blue promontory
  With trees upon 't that nod unto the world
  And mock our eyes with air. Thou hast seen these signs;
  They are black vesper's pageants.
EROS   Ay, my lord.   8
ANTONY
  That which is now a horse, even with a thought
  The rack dislimns and makes it indistinct   10
  As water is in water.
EROS   It does, my lord.
ANTONY
  My good knave Eros, now thy captain is   12
  Even such a body. Here I am Antony,
  Yet cannot hold this visible shape, my knave.
  I made these wars for Egypt, and the Queen,
  Whose heart I thought I had, for she had mine—
  Which whilst it was mine had annexed unto 't
  A million more, now lost—she, Eros, has
  Packed cards with Caesar and false-played my glory 19
  Unto an enemy's triumph.   20
  Nay, weep not, gentle Eros. There is left us
  Ourselves to end ourselves.

**4.14. Location: Alexandria. (See location of scene 13; again, the sense of
time is immediate and the place fluid.)**
2 dragonish shaped like a dragon   **4 pendant** overhanging   **8 black
vesper's pageants** i.e., shows heralding the approach of night   **10 rack**
floating vapor or cloud.   **dislimns** effaces   **12 knave** boy   **19 Packed
cards** i.e., stacked the deck.   **false-played** falsely played away
20 triumph (1) victory (2) trump card

Enter Mardian.

                                    O, thy vile lady!
She has robbed me of my sword.
MARDIAN   No, Antony,   23
My mistress loved thee, and her fortunes mingled
With thine entirely.
ANTONY   Hence, saucy eunuch, peace!   25
She hath betrayed me and shall die the death.   26
MARDIAN
Death of one person can be paid but once,   27
And that she has discharged. What thou wouldst do
Is done unto thy hand. The last she spake   29
Was, "Antony, most noble Antony!"
Then in the midst a tearing groan did break
The name of Antony; it was divided   32
Between her heart and lips. She rendered life,   33
Thy name so buried in her.
ANTONY   Dead, then?
MARDIAN   Dead.
ANTONY
Unarm, Eros. The long day's task is done,
And we must sleep. [*To Mardian.*] That thou depart'st
  hence safe
Does pay thy labor richly; go.   *Exit Mardian.*
                    Off, pluck off! [*Eros unarms him.*]
The sevenfold shield of Ajax cannot keep   38
The battery from my heart. O, cleave, my sides!   39
Heart, once be stronger than thy continent;   40
Crack thy frail case! Apace, Eros, apace.   41
No more a soldier. Bruisèd pieces, go;
You have been nobly borne.—From me awhile.   43
                                        Exit Eros.
I will o'ertake thee, Cleopatra, and
Weep for my pardon. So it must be, for now

23 **sword** i.e., prowess as a soldier, masculinity   25 **saucy** insolent
26 **die the death** be put to death   27 **of** by   29 **unto thy hand** for you
32–33 **it . . . lips** i.e., she half-groaned Antony's name and then her heart
groaned as she died as if saying the rest   33 **rendered** gave up to
38 **sevenfold** with seven thicknesses. (The shield of Ajax was of brass
reinforced with seven thicknesses of oxhide.)   39 **battery** battering,
bombardment.   **cleave** split   40 **thy continent** that which contains
you   41 **Apace** quickly   43 **From** go from

All length is torture; since the torch is out,   46
Lie down and stray no farther. Now all labor
Mars what it does; yea, very force entangles   48
Itself with strength. Seal then, and all is done.   49
Eros!—I come, my queen.—Eros!—Stay for me.
Where souls do couch on flowers, we'll hand in hand,   51
And with our sprightly port make the ghosts gaze.   52
Dido and her Aeneas shall want troops,   53
And all the haunt be ours.—Come, Eros, Eros!   54

    Enter Eros.

EROS
  What would my lord?
ANTONY   Since Cleopatra died   55
I have lived in such dishonor that the gods
Detest my baseness. I, that with my sword
Quartered the world, and o'er green Neptune's back   58
With ships made cities, condemn myself to lack   59
The courage of a woman—less noble mind
Than she which by her death our Caesar tells
"I am conqueror of myself." Thou art sworn, Eros,
That when the exigent should come which now   63
Is come indeed, when I should see behind me
Th' inevitable prosecution of   65
Disgrace and horror, that on my command
Thou then wouldst kill me. Do 't. The time is come.
Thou strik'st not me, 'tis Caesar thou defeat'st.
Put color in thy cheek.

46 length prolongation of life.   **the torch** i.e., the life of Cleopatra
48 very force any resolute action   **49 with strength** i.e., with its own
strength.   **Seal** finish the business (as in sealing a letter)   **51 couch** lie
(here, in the Elysian fields)   **52 sprightly** (1) high-spirited (2) spirit-like,
ghostly.   **port** bearing   **53 Dido . . . troops** i.e., Antony and Cleopatra
will be the most distinguished lovers in the Elysian fields, outshining
even the Queen of Carthage and her famous lover. (In the *Aeneid*,
Aeneas deserts Dido in order to found Rome, putting public good ahead
of private passion as Antony does not. Dido scorns Aeneas when they
meet in the underworld; Antony imagines them in the Elysian fields.)
want troops lack followers   **54 all . . . ours** i.e., we shall be the objects
of everyone's attention   **55 would my lord** does my lord desire
58 Quartered cut into quarters, divided and conquered.   **o'er . . . back**
i.e., on the sea   **59 With . . . cities** i.e., assembled flotillas as dense and
populous as cities.   **to lack** for lacking   **63 exigent** exigency, time of
compelling need   **65 prosecution** pursuit

EROS   The gods withhold me!   69
  Shall I do that which all the Parthian darts,
  Though enemy, lost aim and could not?
ANTONY   Eros,
  Wouldst thou be windowed in great Rome and see   72
  Thy master thus with pleached arms, bending down   73
  His corrigible neck, his face subdued   74
  To penetrative shame, whilst the wheeled seat   75
  Of fortunate Caesar, drawn before him, branded   76
  His baseness that ensued?
EROS   I would not see 't.   77
ANTONY
  Come, then, for with a wound I must be cured.
  Draw that thy honest sword, which thou hast worn
  Most useful for thy country.
EROS   O, sir, pardon me!
ANTONY
  When I did make thee free, swor'st thou not then
  To do this when I bade thee? Do it at once,
  Or thy precedent services are all   83
  But accidents unpurposed. Draw, and come.   84
EROS
  Turn from me then that noble countenance
  Wherein the worship of the whole world lies.   86
ANTONY   Lo thee!   [*He turns away.*]
EROS [*Drawing his sword*]
  My sword is drawn.
ANTONY   Then let it do at once
  That thing why thou hast drawn it.
EROS   My dear master,
  My captain, and my emperor, let me say,
  Before I strike this bloody stroke, farewell.
ANTONY   'Tis said, man, and farewell.
EROS
  Farewell, great chief. Shall I strike now?
ANTONY   Now, Eros.

69 The gods withhold me i.e., God forbid   **72 windowed** placed as in a
window   **73 pleached** folded or bound   **74 corrigible** submissive to
correction   **75 penetrative** penetrating.   **wheeled seat** i.e., chariot
76–77 branded . . . ensued stigmatized as by a brand the shame of him
that followed   **83 precedent** former   **84 accidents unpurposed** events
leading to no purpose   **86 worship** honor, worth

EROS *(Kills himself)*
  Why, there then! Thus I do escape the sorrow
  Of Antony's death.   *[He dies.]*
ANTONY   Thrice nobler than myself!
  Thou teachest me, O valiant Eros, what
  I should, and thou couldst not. My queen and Eros
  Have by their brave instruction got upon me   98
  A nobleness in record. But I will be   99
  A bridegroom in my death, and run into 't
  As to a lover's bed. Come, then, and Eros,
  Thy master dies thy scholar. To do thus
  I learned of thee.   *[He falls on his sword.]*
                  How, not dead? Not dead?
  The guard, ho! O, dispatch me!   104

        Enter [Dercetus and others of] a Guard.

FIRST GUARD   What's the noise?
ANTONY   I have done my work ill, friends.
  O, make an end of what I have begun!
SECOND GUARD   The star is fallen.
FIRST GUARD   And time is at his period.   109
ALL   Alas, and woe!
ANTONY   Let him that loves me strike me dead.
FIRST GUARD   Not I.
SECOND GUARD   Nor I.
THIRD GUARD   Nor anyone.   *Exeunt [Guard].*
DERCETUS
  Thy death and fortunes bid thy followers fly.
  This sword but shown to Caesar, with this tidings,
  Shall enter me with him.*[He takes up Antony's sword.]* 117

        Enter Diomedes.

DIOMEDES   Where's Antony?
DERCETUS   There, Diomed, there.
DIOMEDES
  Lives he? Wilt thou not answer, man? *[Exit Dercetus.]*
ANTONY
  Art thou there, Diomed? Draw thy sword and give me

98–99 got . . . record won a noble place in history before I have
104 dispatch finish   **109 his period** its end   **117 enter . . . him** admit
me to his service, put me in his good graces

Sufficing strokes for death.

DIOMEDES   Most absolute lord,   122
My mistress Cleopatra sent me to thee.

ANTONY
When did she send thee?

DIOMEDES   Now, my lord.

ANTONY   Where is she?

DIOMEDES
Locked in her monument. She had a prophesying fear
Of what hath come to pass. For when she saw—
Which never shall be found—you did suspect   127
She had disposed with Caesar, and that your rage   128
Would not be purged, she sent you word she was dead;
But, fearing since how it might work, hath sent
Me to proclaim the truth, and I am come,
I dread, too late.

ANTONY
Too late, good Diomed. Call my guard, I prithee.

DIOMEDES
What ho, the Emperor's guard! The guard, what ho!
Come, your lord calls.

Enter four or five of the Guard of Antony.

ANTONY
Bear me, good friends, where Cleopatra bides.   136
'Tis the last service that I shall command you.

FIRST GUARD
Woe, woe are we, sir, you may not live to wear   138
All your true followers out.

ALL   Most heavy day!   139

ANTONY
Nay, good my fellows, do not please sharp fate
To grace it with your sorrows. Bid that welcome   141
Which comes to punish us, and we punish it,
Seeming to bear it lightly. Take me up.
I have led you oft; carry me now, good friends,
And have my thanks for all.
                    Exeunt, bearing Antony [and Eros].

❧

122 **Sufficing** sufficient   127 **found** found true   128 **disposed with**
come to terms with   136 **bides** abides, dwells   138–139 **live . . . out** i.e.,
outlive those that serve you   141 **To grace** by gracing or honoring

4.15   *Enter Cleopatra, and her maids aloft, with Charmian and Iras.*

CLEOPATRA
  O Charmian, I will never go from hence.
CHARMIAN
  Be comforted, dear madam.
CLEOPATRA   No, I will not.
  All strange and terrible events are welcome,
  But comforts we despise. Our size of sorrow,
  Proportioned to our cause, must be as great
  As that which makes it.

    Enter [below] Diomedes.

                          How now? Is he dead?
DIOMEDES
  His death's upon him, but not dead.
  Look out o' th' other side your monument;
  His guard have brought him thither.

    *Enter [below] Antony, and the Guard
    [bearing him].*

CLEOPATRA   O sun,
  Burn the great sphere thou mov'st in; darkling stand   11
  The varying shore o' the world! O Antony,
  Antony, Antony! Help, Charmian, help, Iras, help!
  Help, friends below! Let's draw him hither.
ANTONY   Peace!
  Not Caesar's valor hath o'erthrown Antony,
  But Antony's hath triumphed on itself.
CLEOPATRA
  So it should be, that none but Antony
  Should conquer Antony, but woe 'tis so!
ANTONY
  I am dying, Egypt, dying. Only
  I here importune death awhile, until   20

4.15. Location: Alexandria. Cleopatra's monument.
s.d. aloft in the gallery above the main stage   **11 sphere** concentric
sphere in which, according to Ptolemaic astronomy, the sun moved
about the earth as did the planets and stars.   **darkling** in darkness
20 importune i.e., beg a delay of

Of many thousand kisses the poor last
I lay upon thy lips.

CLEOPATRA   I dare not, dear—   22
Dear my lord, pardon—I dare not,
Lest I be taken. Not th' imperious show   24
Of the full-fortuned Caesar ever shall
Be brooched with me. If knife, drugs, serpents, have   26
Edge, sting, or operation, I am safe.   27
Your wife Octavia, with her modest eyes
And still conclusion, shall acquire no honor   29
Demuring upon me. But come, come, Antony—   30
Help me, my women—we must draw thee up.
Assist, good friends.

ANTONY   O, quick, or I am gone.
                    [*They begin lifting.*]

CLEOPATRA
Here's sport indeed! How heavy weighs my lord!
Our strength is all gone into heaviness,   34
That makes the weight. Had I great Juno's power,
The strong-winged Mercury should fetch thee up
And set thee by Jove's side. Yet come a little;
Wishers were ever fools. O, come, come, come!   38
                    They heave Antony aloft to Cleopatra.
And welcome, welcome! Die when thou hast lived;
Quicken with kissing. Had my lips that power,   40
Thus would I wear them out.   [*She kisses him.*]

ALL   A heavy sight!   42

ANTONY   I am dying, Egypt, dying.
Give me some wine, and let me speak a little.

CLEOPATRA
No, let me speak, and let me rail so high
That the false huswife Fortune break her wheel,   46
Provoked by my offense.

ANTONY   One word, sweet Queen: 47
Of Caesar seek your honor, with your safety. O!   48

---

22 I dare not i.e., I dare not come down   **24 imperious show** imperial
triumphal procession   **26 brooched** adorned (as with a brooch)
27 operation power, efficacy   **29 still conclusion** silent aim or judgment
30 Demuring looking demurely   **34 heaviness** (1) sadness (2) weight
38 Wishers . . . fools i.e., we wish for unattainable things   **40 Quicken**
revive   **42 heavy** doleful   **46 false** treacherous.   **huswife** hussy, wanton
47 offense offensive speech   **48 Of** from

CLEOPATRA
They do not go together.

ANTONY   Gentle, hear me.
None about Caesar trust but Proculeius.

CLEOPATRA
My resolution and my hands I'll trust,
None about Caesar.

ANTONY
The miserable change now at my end
Lament nor sorrow at, but please your thoughts   54
In feeding them with those my former fortunes,
Wherein I lived the greatest prince o' the world,
The noblest; and do now not basely die,
Not cowardly put off my helmet to
My countryman—a Roman by a Roman
Valiantly vanquished. Now my spirit is going;
I can no more.

CLEOPATRA   Noblest of men, woo't die?   61
Hast thou no care of me? Shall I abide
In this dull world, which in thy absence is
No better than a sty? [*Antony dies.*] O, see, my women,
The crown o' th' earth doth melt. My lord!
O, withered is the garland of the war;
The soldier's pole is fall'n! Young boys and girls   67
Are level now with men. The odds is gone,   68
And there is nothing left remarkable
Beneath the visiting moon.   [*She faints.*]

CHARMIAN   O, quietness, lady!

IRAS   She's dead too, our sovereign.

CHARMIAN   Lady!

IRAS   Madam!

CHARMIAN   O madam, madam, madam!

IRAS   Royal Egypt, Empress!   [*Cleopatra stirs.*]

CHARMIAN   Peace, peace, Iras.

CLEOPATRA
No more but e'en a woman, and commanded
By such poor passion as the maid that milks
And does the meanest chares. It were for me   80

54 Lament i.e., neither lament   **61 woo't** wilt thou   **67 pole** polestar or
battle standard (with possible sexual suggestion)   **68 odds** distinctive
quality or measure, or perhaps the quality distinguishing one thing
from another   **80 chares** chores, drudgery.   **were** would be fitting

To throw my scepter at the injurious gods,
To tell them that this world did equal theirs
Till they had stolen our jewel. All's but naught;
Patience is sottish, and impatience does   84
Become a dog that's mad. Then is it sin   85
To rush into the secret house of death
Ere death dare come to us? How do you, women?
What, what, good cheer! Why, how now, Charmian?
My noble girls! Ah, women, women! Look,
Our lamp is spent, it's out. Good sirs, take heart.   90
We'll bury him; and then, what's brave, what's noble,
Let's do 't after the high Roman fashion
And make death proud to take us. Come, away.
This case of that huge spirit now is cold.
Ah, women, women! Come. We have no friend
But resolution and the briefest end.   96

>   *Exeunt, [those above] bearing
>   off Antony's body.*

❖

5.1   *Enter Caesar, Agrippa, Dolabella, Maecenas,*
   [Gallus, Proculeius,] with his council of war.

CAESAR
  Go to him, Dolabella, bid him yield;
  Being so frustrate, tell him, he mocks   2
  The pauses that he makes.
DOLABELLA   Caesar, I shall.   [*Exit.*] 3

   Enter Dercetus, with the sword of Antony.

CAESAR
  Wherefore is that? And what art thou that dar'st
  Appear thus to us?
DERCETUS   I am called Dercetus.
  Mark Antony I served, who best was worthy
  Best to be served. Whilst he stood up and spoke
  He was my master, and I wore my life
  To spend upon his haters. If thou please
  To take me to thee, as I was to him
  I'll be to Caesar; if thou pleasest not,
  I yield thee up my life.
CAESAR   What is 't thou sayst?
DERCETUS
  I say, O Caesar, Antony is dead.
CAESAR
  The breaking of so great a thing should make   14
  A greater crack. The round world   15
  Should have shook lions into civil streets   16
  And citizens to their dens. The death of Antony   17
  Is not a single doom; in the name lay   18
  A moiety of the world.
DERCETUS   He is dead, Caesar,   19
  Not by a public minister of justice,
  Nor by a hirèd knife; but that self hand   21
  Which writ his honor in the acts it did

5.1. Location: Alexandria. Caesar's camp.
2 **frustrate** helpless, baffled   **2–3 mocks . . . makes** makes himself
ridiculous by his delays (in yielding)   **14 breaking** (1) destruction
(2) disclosure   **15 crack** (1) cracking apart (2) loud report   **16 civil**
city   **17 their** i.e., the lions'; or else, the citizens scurry to safety indoors, in their own "dens." (In either case, nature is inverted.)   **18 Is
. . . doom** i.e., signifies the death and destruction of much more than a
single man   **19 moiety** half   **21 self** same

Hath, with the courage which the heart did lend it,
Splitted the heart. This is his sword.

                              [*He offers the sword.*]

I robbed his wound of it. Behold it stained
With his most noble blood.

CAESAR   Look you, sad friends,
The gods rebuke me, but it is tidings   27
To wash the eyes of kings.

AGRIPPA   And strange it is
That nature must compel us to lament
Our most persisted deeds.

MAECENAS   His taints and honors   30
Waged equal with him.

AGRIPPA   A rarer spirit never   31
Did steer humanity; but you gods will give us   32
Some faults to make us men. Caesar is touched.

MAECENAS
When such a spacious mirror's set before him,
He needs must see himself.

CAESAR   O Antony,
I have followed thee to this; but we do launch   36
Diseases in our bodies. I must perforce   37
Have shown to thee such a declining day,   38
Or look on thine; we could not stall together   39
In the whole world. But yet let me lament
With tears as sovereign as the blood of hearts   41
That thou, my brother, my competitor   42
In top of all design, my mate in empire,   43
Friend and companion in the front of war,   44

---

27 but it is if it be not   **30 persisted** persistently desired or pursued
31 Waged equal with battled equally in   **32 steer humanity** govern any
individual.   **will give** insist on giving   **36 followed** pursued   **36–37 but
. . . bodies** i.e., I pursued you as men seek to cure diseases for their
health's sake. (In introducing the extended medical metaphor of
ll. 36–46, *launch* means "lance.")   **37 perforce** necessarily   **38 shown
to thee** i.e., suffered myself at your hands   **39 stall** dwell   **41 as sovereign . . . hearts** as precious or efficacious as hearts' blood. (Caesar
weeps rather than using bleeding as a cure; bleeding suggests both a
medical remedy and death by the sword.)   **42 competitor** associate,
partner (and rival)   **43 In . . . design** at the head of every grand enter-
prise   **44 front** forehead, face

The arm of mine own body, and the heart   45
Where mine his thoughts did kindle—that our stars,   46
Unreconcilable, should divide   47
Our equalness to this. Hear me, good friends—   48

    Enter an Egyptian.

But I will tell you at some meeter season.   49
The business of this man looks out of him;   50
We'll hear him what he says.—Whence are you?   51

EGYPTIAN
A poor Egyptian yet. The Queen my mistress,   52
Confined in all she has, her monument,
Of thy intents desires instruction,
That she preparedly may frame herself   55
To th' way she's forced to.

CAESAR   Bid her have good heart.
She soon shall know of us, by some of ours,   57
How honorable and how kindly we
Determine for her; for Caesar cannot live
To be ungentle.

EGYPTIAN   So the gods preserve thee!   *Exit.*

CAESAR
Come hither, Proculeius. Go and say
We purpose her no shame. Give her what comforts   62
The quality of her passion shall require,   63
Lest, in her greatness, by some mortal stroke   64
She do defeat us; for her life in Rome   65
Would be eternal in our triumph. Go,   66
And with your speediest bring us what she says   67

45–46 the heart . . . kindle i.e., (Antony was) the brave heart where my
heart kindled its (*his*) thoughts of courage   **47–48 should . . . this**
should divide our equal partnership to this extreme   **49 meeter season**
more suitable time   **50 looks . . . him** reveals itself in his eyes
51 Whence are you where do you come from   **52 A . . . yet** i.e., (I come
from) Egyptian Cleopatra, still reduced in circumstance (and awaiting
your will); or, I am a poor Egyptian still, though subject to Rome's
authority   **55 frame herself** shape her course of action   **57 ours** my
people   **62 purpose** intend   **63 passion** grief   **64 greatness** greatness of
spirit   **65 life in Rome** presence in Rome alive   **66 eternal in our
triumph** an eternal glory in our triumphal procession   **67 with your
speediest** as quickly as you can

And how you find of her.
PROCULEIUS   Caesar, I shall.   68

                              Exit Proculeius.

CAESAR
Gallus, go you along. [*Exit Gallus.*] Where's Dolabella,
To second Proculeius?
ALL   Dolabella!
CAESAR
Let him alone, for I remember now   71
How he's employed. He shall in time be ready.
Go with me to my tent, where you shall see
How hardly I was drawn into this war,   74
How calm and gentle I proceeded still   75
In all my writings. Go with me and see   76
What I can show in this.   *Exeunt.*

✦

5.2   *Enter Cleopatra, Charmian, Iras, and Mardian.*

CLEOPATRA
My desolation does begin to make
A better life. 'Tis paltry to be Caesar;
Not being Fortune, he's but Fortune's knave,   3
A minister of her will. And it is great
To do that thing that ends all other deeds,   5
Which shackles accidents and bolts up change,   6
Which sleeps and never palates more the dung,   7
The beggar's nurse and Caesar's.   8

     Enter [to the gates of the monument] Proculeius.

PROCULEIUS
Caesar sends greeting to the Queen of Egypt,
And bids thee study on what fair demands   10
Thou mean'st to have him grant thee.

---

68 of concerning   **71 Let him alone** don't bother about him now
74 hardly reluctantly   **75 still** always   **76 writings** i.e., letters to Antony

5.2. Location: Alexandria. Cleopatra's monument.
3 knave servant   **5–8 To do . . . Caesar's** i.e., to commit suicide, which
subdues accident and change and by which we sleep in death, relishing
no more the dungy earth that sustains both Caesar and the beggar.
(*Bolts up* means "fetters" or "locks up.")   **10 study on** consider
carefully

CLEOPATRA   What's thy name?
PROCULEIUS
  My name is Proculeius.
CLEOPATRA   Antony
  Did tell me of you, bade me trust you; but
  I do not greatly care to be deceived,   14
  That have no use for trusting. If your master   15
  Would have a queen his beggar, you must tell him
  That majesty, to keep decorum, must
  No less beg than a kingdom. If he please
  To give me conquered Egypt for my son,
  He gives me so much of mine own as I   20
  Will kneel to him with thanks.
PROCULEIUS   Be of good cheer;
  You're fallen into a princely hand. Fear nothing.
  Make your full reference freely to my lord,   23
  Who is so full of grace that it flows over
  On all that need. Let me report to him
  Your sweet dependency, and you shall find   26
  A conqueror that will pray in aid for kindness   27
  Where he for grace is kneeled to.
CLEOPATRA   Pray you, tell him
  I am his fortune's vassal, and I send him   29
  The greatness he has got. I hourly learn   30
  A doctrine of obedience, and would gladly
  Look him i' the face.
PROCULEIUS   This I'll report, dear lady.
  Have comfort, for I know your plight is pitied
  Of him that caused it.   34
          [*Roman soldiers enter from behind and take*
                          Cleopatra prisoner.]
  You see how easily she may be surprised.
  [*To the soldiers.*] Guard her till Caesar come.
IRAS   Royal Queen!

---

14 to be deceived whether I am deceived or not　**15 That** since I　**20 as**
that　**23 Make . . . reference** refer your case　**26 dependency** submis-
siveness　**27 pray in aid** beg your assistance. (A legal term meaning "to
call in the assistance of an outside person.")　**for kindness** i.e., in
thinking of ways to be kind　**29–30 I send . . . got** i.e., I acknowledge his
superiority over all he has won, including myself　**34 Of** by　**s.d. Roman
soldiers** (Perhaps led by Gallus; see 5.1.69. Possibly some speech for him
has been omitted.)

CHARMIAN
  O Cleopatra! Thou art taken, Queen.
CLEOPATRA [*Drawing a dagger*]
  Quick, quick, good hands.
PROCULEIUS   Hold, worthy lady, hold!
                              [*He disarms her.*]
  Do not yourself such wrong, who are in this
  Relieved, but not betrayed.
CLEOPATRA   What, of death too,   40
  That rids our dogs of languish?
PROCULEIUS   Cleopatra,   41
  Do not abuse my master's bounty by   42
  Th' undoing of yourself. Let the world see
  His nobleness well acted, which your death   44
  Will never let come forth.
CLEOPATRA   Where art thou, Death?   45
  Come hither, come! Come, come, and take a queen
  Worth many babes and beggars!
PROCULEIUS   O, temperance, lady!   47
CLEOPATRA
  Sir, I will eat no meat, I'll not drink, sir;
  If idle talk will once be necessary,   49
  I'll not sleep neither. This mortal house I'll ruin,
  Do Caesar what he can. Know, sir, that I
  Will not wait pinioned at your master's court,   52
  Nor once be chastised with the sober eye
  Of dull Octavia. Shall they hoist me up
  And show me to the shouting varletry   55
  Of censuring Rome? Rather a ditch in Egypt
  Be gentle grave unto me! Rather on Nilus' mud
  Lay me stark naked and let the waterflies
  Blow me into abhorring! Rather make   59

40 Relieved rescued.   **of death too** i.e., (1) am I *relieved* or deprived even
of death (2) am I *betrayed* even of the right to die   **41 our dogs** even our
dogs.   **languish** lingering disease   **42 bounty** generosity   **44 acted**
accomplished   **45 let come forth** allow to be displayed   **47 babes and
beggars** i.e., those whom death takes easily and often, those to whom
"relief" is often given   **49 If . . . necessary** even if on occasion I must
resort to idle talk (to keep myself awake)   **52 wait** attend, as a slave.
pinioned like a bird with clipped wings, unable to fly   **55 varletry**
rabble   **59 Blow . . . abhorring** cause me to swell abhorrently with
maggots, or deposit their eggs on me until I become abhorrent

My country's high pyramides my gibbet   60
And hang me up in chains!
PROCULEIUS   You do extend
These thoughts of horror further than you shall
Find cause in Caesar.

Enter Dolabella.

DOLABELLA   Proculeius,
What thou hast done thy master Caesar knows,
And he hath sent for thee. For the Queen,   65
I'll take her to my guard.
PROCULEIUS   So, Dolabella,
It shall content me best. Be gentle to her.
[*To Cleopatra.*] To Caesar I will speak what you shall
    please,   68
If you'll employ me to him.
CLEOPATRA   Say I would die.
                                   Exit Proculeius.
DOLABELLA
Most noble Empress, you have heard of me?
CLEOPATRA
I cannot tell.
DOLABELLA   Assuredly you know me.
CLEOPATRA
No matter, sir, what I have heard or known.
You laugh when boys or women tell their dreams;
Is 't not your trick?
DOLABELLA   I understand not, madam.   74
CLEOPATRA
I dreamt there was an emperor Antony.
O, such another sleep, that I might see
But such another man!
DOLABELLA   If it might please ye—
CLEOPATRA
His face was as the heavens, and therein stuck   78
A sun and moon, which kept their course and lighted
The little O, th' earth.
DOLABELLA   Most sovereign creature—

60 gibbet gallows   **65 For** as for   **68 what** whatever   **74 trick** manner,
way   **78 stuck** were set

CLEOPATRA
   His legs bestrid the ocean; his reared arm   81
   Crested the world; his voice was propertied   82
   As all the tunèd spheres, and that to friends;   83
   But when he meant to quail and shake the orb,   84
   He was as rattling thunder. For his bounty,   85
   There was no winter in 't; an autumn it was
   That grew the more by reaping. His delights   87
   Were dolphinlike; they showed his back above   88
   The element they lived in. In his livery   89
   Walked crowns and crownets; realms and islands were 90
   As plates dropped from his pocket.
DOLABELLA   Cleopatra—   91
CLEOPATRA
   Think you there was or might be such a man
   As this I dreamt of?
DOLABELLA   Gentle madam, no.
CLEOPATRA
   You lie, up to the hearing of the gods.
   But if there be nor ever were one such,   95
   It's past the size of dreaming. Nature wants stuff   96
   To vie strange forms with fancy; yet t' imagine   97
   An Antony were nature's piece 'gainst fancy,   98
   Condemning shadows quite.
DOLABELLA   Hear me, good madam: 99
   Your loss is as yourself, great; and you bear it
   As answering to the weight. Would I might never   101
   O'ertake pursued success but I do feel,   102

81 bestrid straddled   **82 Crested** formed a crest for; surmounted (like a
raised arm in heraldry)   **82–83 propertied . . . friends** endowed with
qualities which, when he spoke to friends, recalled the harmony of the
heavenly bodies in their spheres   **84 quail** make quail, overawe.   **orb**
world   **85 For** as for   **87–89 His . . . in** i.e., his pleasures were both of
the ordinary and rising out of it, just as a dolphin rises out of the
element in which it lives, the sea   **89–90 In . . . crownets** i.e., among his
retainers (those who would wear his livery) were kings and princes
91 plates coins   **95 nor ever were** or if there never existed   **96 It's . . .
dreaming** no dream can come up to it, my image of him   **96–97 Nature
. . . fancy** nature lacks material to equal the remarkable forms produced
by fancy or imagination   **97–99 yet . . . quite** i.e., yet the very act of
imagining an Antony would itself be a work of nature, in fact would be
nature's masterpiece in the competition with fancy   **101 As . . . weight**
commensurate with the weightiness of the loss   **101–102 Would . . . do**
i.e., may I never succeed at what I desire if I do not

By the rebound of yours, a grief that smites   103
My very heart at root.
CLEOPATRA   I thank you, sir.
Know you what Caesar means to do with me?
DOLABELLA
I am loath to tell you what I would you knew.
CLEOPATRA
Nay, pray you, sir.
DOLABELLA   Though he be honorable—
CLEOPATRA   He'll lead me, then, in triumph.
DOLABELLA   Madam, he will, I know 't.   *Flourish.*

    Enter Proculeius, Caesar, Gallus, Maecenas, and
    others of his train.

ALL   Make way there! Caesar!
CAESAR   Which is the Queen of Egypt?
DOLABELLA   It is the Emperor, madam. *Cleopatra kneels.*
CAESAR
Arise, you shall not kneel. I pray you, rise.
Rise, Egypt.
CLEOPATRA [*Rising*]   Sir, the gods will have it thus;
My master and my lord I must obey.
CAESAR   Take to you no hard thoughts.
The record of what injuries you did us,
Though written in our flesh, we shall remember
As things but done by chance.
CLEOPATRA   Sole sir o' the world,   119
I cannot project mine own cause so well   120
To make it clear, but do confess I have   121
Been laden with like frailties which before
Have often shamed our sex.
CAESAR   Cleopatra, know
We will extenuate rather than enforce.   124
If you apply yourself to our intents,   125
Which towards you are most gentle, you shall find
A benefit in this change; but if you seek
To lay on me a cruelty by taking   128
Antony's course, you shall bereave yourself   129

103 rebound reflection   **119 sir** master   **120 project** set forth
121 clear free of blame   **124 enforce** lay stress upon and punish (the
faults)   **125 If . . . intents** if you comply with my plans   **128 lay . . .
cruelty** force me to be cruel   **129 bereave** rob

Of my good purposes and put your children
To that destruction which I'll guard them from
If thereon you rely. I'll take my leave.

CLEOPATRA
And may, through all the world! 'Tis yours, and we,   133
Your scutcheons and your signs of conquest, shall   134
Hang in what place you please. Here, my good lord.   135
               [*She gives him a scroll.*]

CAESAR
You shall advise me in all for Cleopatra.   136

CLEOPATRA
This is the brief of money, plate, and jewels   137
I am possessed of. 'Tis exactly valued,
Not petty things admitted. Where's Seleucus?   139

    [*Enter Seleucus.*]

SELEUCUS   Here, madam.

CLEOPATRA
This is my treasurer. Let him speak, my lord,
Upon his peril, that I have reserved
To myself nothing. Speak the truth, Seleucus.

SELEUCUS
Madam, I had rather seal my lips
Than to my peril speak that which is not.

CLEOPATRA   What have I kept back?

SELEUCUS
Enough to purchase what you have made known.

CAESAR
Nay, blush not, Cleopatra. I approve
Your wisdom in the deed.

CLEOPATRA   See, Caesar! O, behold
How pomp is followed! Mine will now be yours,   150
And, should we shift estates, yours would be mine.   151
The ingratitude of this Seleucus does

---

133 And may i.e., (1) you may leave when you choose (2) you may have
your will in anything   **134 scutcheons** shields showing armorial bear-
ings; hence, shields hung up as monuments of victory   **135 Hang** (1) be
hung up or displayed as your trophies (2) be hanged as your captives
136 in all for Cleopatra i.e., in all matters pertaining to yourself
137 brief list   **139 Not . . . admitted** petty things omitted   **150 pomp is
followed** noble and royal persons are served.   **Mine** my followers
151 shift estates reverse fortunes, exchange places

Even make me wild.—O slave, of no more trust
Than love that's hired! [*Seleucus retreats from her.*]
  What, goest thou back? Thou shalt   154
Go back, I warrant thee! But I'll catch thine eyes,
Though they had wings. Slave, soulless villain, dog!
O rarely base!

CAESAR   Good Queen, let us entreat you.   157

CLEOPATRA
O Caesar, what a wounding shame is this,
That thou vouchsafing here to visit me,   159
Doing the honor of thy lordliness
To one so meek, that mine own servant should
Parcel the sum of my disgraces by   162
Addition of his envy! Say, good Caesar,   163
That I some lady trifles have reserved,   164
Immoment toys, things of such dignity   165
As we greet modern friends withal, and say   166
Some nobler token I have kept apart
For Livia and Octavia, to induce   168
Their mediation; must I be unfolded   169
With one that I have bred? The gods! It smites me   170
Beneath the fall I have. [*To Seleucus.*] Prithee, go hence,
Or I shall show the cinders of my spirit   172
Through th' ashes of my chance. Wert thou a man,   173
Thou wouldst have mercy on me.

CAESAR   Forbear, Seleucus.   [*Exit Seleucus.*]   175

CLEOPATRA
Be it known that we, the greatest, are misthought   176
For things that others do; and when we fall
We answer others' merits in our name,   178
Are therefore to be pitied.

CAESAR   Cleopatra,
Not what you have reserved nor what acknowledged
Put we i' the roll of conquest. Still be 't yours;

---

154 **hired** paid for 157 **rarely** exceptionally 159 **vouchsafing** deigning to
come 162 **Parcel** particularize 163 **envy** malice 164 **lady** ladylike,
feminine 165 **Immoment toys** trifles of no moment or importance
166 **modern** common. **withal** with 168 **Livia** Octavius Caesar's wife
169–170 **unfolded With** exposed by 170 **one that I have bred** one of my
household 172 **cinders** smoldering hot coals 173 **chance** (fallen) fortune 175 **Forbear** withdraw 176 **misthought** misjudged 178 **We . . .
name** we are accountable for the misdeeds of others done in our name

Bestow it at your pleasure, and believe   182
Caesar's no merchant, to make prize with you   183
Of things that merchants sold. Therefore be cheered.
Make not your thoughts your prison. No, dear Queen,   185
For we intend so to dispose you as   186
Yourself shall give us counsel. Feed and sleep.
Our care and pity is so much upon you
That we remain your friend; and so adieu.

CLEOPATRA
My master, and my lord!

CAESAR   Not so. Adieu.
                Flourish. Exeunt Caesar and his train.

CLEOPATRA
He words me, girls, he words me, that I should not   191
Be noble to myself. But hark thee, Charmian.
                        [*She whispers to Charmian.*]

IRAS
Finish, good lady. The bright day is done,
And we are for the dark.

CLEOPATRA [*To Charmian*] Hie thee again.   194
I have spoke already, and it is provided;
Go put it to the haste.

CHARMIAN   Madam, I will.

        Enter Dolabella.

DOLABELLA
Where's the Queen?

CHARMIAN   Behold, sir.   [*Exit.*]

CLEOPATRA   Dolabella!

DOLABELLA
Madam, as thereto sworn by your command,
Which my love makes religion to obey,   199
I tell you this: Caesar through Syria
Intends his journey, and within three days
You with your children will he send before.
Make your best use of this. I have performed
Your pleasure and my promise.

---

182 Bestow use   **183 make prize** haggle   **185 Make . . . prison** i.e.,
don't imprison yourself in your thoughts by misconceiving of your
situation   **186 dispose** dispose of   **191 words** puts me off with mere
words   **194 Hie thee again** return quickly   **199 makes religion** i.e., absolutely binds me

CLEOPATRA   Dolabella,
  I shall remain your debtor.
DOLABELLA   I your servant.
  Adieu, good Queen. I must attend on Caesar.
CLEOPATRA
  Farewell, and thanks.   *Exit [Dolabella].*
                     Now, Iras, what think'st thou?
  Thou an Egyptian puppet shall be shown
  In Rome, as well as I. Mechanic slaves   209
  With greasy aprons, rules, and hammers shall 210
  Uplift us to the view. In their thick breaths,
  Rank of gross diet, shall we be enclouded   212
  And forced to drink their vapor.
IRAS   The gods forbid!   213
CLEOPATRA
  Nay, 'tis most certain, Iras. Saucy lictors   214
  Will catch at us like strumpets, and scald rhymers 215
  Ballad us out o' tune. The quick comedians   216
  Extemporally will stage us and present   217
  Our Alexandrian revels; Antony
  Shall be brought drunken forth, and I shall see
  Some squeaking Cleopatra boy my greatness   220
  I' the posture of a whore.
IRAS   O the good gods!
CLEOPATRA   Nay, that's certain.
IRAS
  I'll never see 't! For I am sure my nails
  Are stronger than mine eyes.
CLEOPATRA   Why, that's the way
  To fool their preparation and to conquer
  Their most absurd intents.

      Enter Charmian.

                     Now, Charmian!
  Show me, my women, like a queen. Go fetch   227

209 Mechanic slaves common laborers   **210 rules** straightedged measuring sticks   **212 Rank . . . diet** reeking of coarse food   **213 drink** drink in, breathe deeply   **214 lictors** minor officials in attendance on Roman magistrates   **215 scald** scurvy   **216 Ballad us** sing ballads about us.   **quick** quick-witted   **217 Extemporally** in improvised performance   **220 boy** (Allusion to the practice of having women's parts acted by boys on the Elizabethan stage.)   **227 Show** display

My best attires. I am again for Cydnus,
To meet Mark Antony. Sirrah Iras, go—
Now, noble Charmian, we'll dispatch indeed—   230
And when thou hast done this chare I'll give thee leave   231
To play till doomsday. Bring our crown and all.   232
                          [*Exit Iras.*] *A noise within.*
Wherefore's this noise?

          Enter a Guardsman.

GUARDSMAN   Here is a rural fellow
That will not be denied Your Highness' presence.
He brings you figs.

CLEOPATRA
Let him come in.   *Exit Guardsman.*
                    What poor an instrument   236
May do a noble deed! He brings me liberty.
My resolution's placed, and I have nothing   238
Of woman in me. Now from head to foot
I am marble-constant; now the fleeting moon   240
No planet is of mine.

          Enter Guardsman, and Clown [bringing in a
          basket].

GUARDSMAN   This is the man.   241
CLEOPATRA Avoid, and leave him.   *Exit Guardsman.*   242
Hast thou the pretty worm of Nilus there,   243
That kills and pains not?

CLOWN   Truly, I have him, but I would not be the party
    that should desire you to touch him, for his biting is
    immortal. Those that do die of it do seldom or never   247
    recover.

CLEOPATRA Remember'st thou any that have died on 't?

CLOWN   Very many, men and women too. I heard of   250
    one of them no longer than yesterday—a very honest
    woman, but something given to lie, as a woman   252

---

230 dispatch (1) finish (2) hasten   **231 chare** task, chore   **232 s.d. Exit Iras**
(It is possible that Charmian leaves too.)   **236 What** how   **238 placed**
fixed   **240 fleeting** inconstant, changing   **241 s.d. Clown** rustic   **242 Avoid**
withdraw   **243 worm** snake, serpent (but elsewhere in this scene with the
added connotation of "the male sexual organ" and "earthworm")
247 immortal (Blunder for *mortal.*)   **250 heard of** heard from   **252 to lie**
(with sexual second meaning hinted at also in *honest*, i.e., chaste, *die*, i.e.,
reach orgasm, and *worm*)

should not do but in the way of honesty—how she
died of the biting of it, what pain she felt. Truly, she
makes a very good report o' the worm. But he that will
believe all that they say shall never be saved by half
that they do. But this is most falliable, the worm's an   257
odd worm.

CLEOPATRA Get thee hence, farewell.

CLOWN I wish you all joy of the worm.

                              [*He sets down his basket.*]

CLEOPATRA Farewell.

CLOWN You must think this, look you, that the worm
will do his kind.   263

CLEOPATRA Ay, ay; farewell.

CLOWN Look you, the worm is not to be trusted but in
the keeping of wise people, for indeed there is no
goodness in the worm.

CLEOPATRA Take thou no care; it shall be heeded.   268

CLOWN Very good. Give it nothing, I pray you, for it is
not worth the feeding.

CLEOPATRA Will it eat me?

CLOWN You must not think I am so simple but I know
the devil himself will not eat a woman. I know that a
woman is a dish for the gods, if the devil dress her   274
not. But, truly, these same whoreson devils do the   275
gods great harm in their women, for in every ten that
they make, the devils mar five.

CLEOPATRA Well, get thee gone. Farewell.

CLOWN Yes, forsooth. I wish you joy o' the worm.

                                              Exit.

[*Enter Iras with royal attire.*]

CLEOPATRA
Give me my robe. Put on my crown. I have
Immortal longings in me. Now no more   281
The juice of Egypt's grape shall moist this lip.
                              [*The women dress her.*]
Yare, yare, good Iras, quick. Methinks I hear   283

---

257 falliable (Blunder for *infallible*.)   **263 his kind** its natural function
268 Take thou no care don't worry   **274 dress** prepare, as in cooking (with
a suggestion also of dressing in alluring clothes)   **275 whoreson** i.e.,
accursed. (A slang expression.)   **281 Immortal longings** longings for
immortality   **283 Yare** quick

Antony call; I see him rouse himself
To praise my noble act. I hear him mock
The luck of Caesar, which the gods give men
To excuse their after wrath. Husband, I come!   287
Now to that name my courage prove my title!
I am fire and air; my other elements   289
I give to baser life. So, have you done?
Come then, and take the last warmth of my lips.
Farewell, kind Charmian. Iras, long farewell.
          [*She kisses them. Iras falls and dies.*]
Have I the aspic in my lips? Dost fall?   293
If thou and nature can so gently part,
The stroke of death is as a lover's pinch,
Which hurts, and is desired. Dost thou lie still?
If thus thou vanishest, thou tell'st the world
It is not worth leave-taking.   298

CHARMIAN
Dissolve, thick cloud, and rain, that I may say
The gods themselves do weep!

CLEOPATRA   This proves me base.
If she first meet the curlèd Antony,   301
He'll make demand of her, and spend that kiss   302
Which is my heaven to have. [*To an asp.*] Come, thou
     mortal wretch,   303
With thy sharp teeth this knot intrinsicate   304
Of life at once untie. Poor venomous fool,
Be angry, and dispatch. O, couldst thou speak,
That I might hear thee call great Caesar ass
Unpolicied!

CHARMIAN   O eastern star!

CLEOPATRA   Peace, peace!   308
Dost thou not see my baby at my breast,
That sucks the nurse asleep?

CHARMIAN   O, break! O, break!

---

287 their after wrath i.e., the wrath of the gods visited on those who have
been fortunate   **289 other elements** i.e., earth and water, the heavier
elements   **293 aspic** asp   **298 is . . . leave-taking** does not deserve a cere-
monious farewell   **301 curlèd** with curled hair   **302 make demand** (1) ask
questions (2) ask pleasure.   **spend that kiss** expend his desire on her
303 mortal deadly.   **wretch** (An affectionate term of abuse.)
304 intrinsicate intricate   **308 Unpolicied** outwitted.   **eastern star** i.e.,
Venus, the morning star

CLEOPATRA
As sweet as balm, as soft as air, as gentle—
O Antony!—Nay, I will take thee too.
              [*Applying another asp to her arm.*]
What should I stay—   *Dies.* 313
CHARMIAN
In this wild world? So, fare thee well.   314
Now boast thee, Death, in thy possession lies
A lass unparalleled. Downy windows, close;   316
And golden Phoebus never be beheld
Of eyes again so royal! Your crown's awry;   318
I'll mend it, and then play—   319

    Enter the Guard, rustling in.

FIRST GUARD
Where's the Queen?
CHARMIAN   Speak softly. Wake her not.
FIRST GUARD
Caesar hath sent—
CHARMIAN   Too slow a messenger.
              [*She applies an asp to herself.*]
O, come apace, dispatch! I partly feel thee.
FIRST GUARD
Approach, ho! All's not well. Caesar's beguiled. 323
SECOND GUARD
There's Dolabella sent from Caesar. Call him.
FIRST GUARD
What work is here, Charmian? Is this well done?
CHARMIAN
It is well done, and fitting for a princess
Descended of so many royal kings.
Ah, soldier!   *Charmian dies.*

    Enter Dolabella.

DOLABELLA
How goes it here?
SECOND GUARD   All dead.
DOLABELLA   Caesar, thy thoughts

313 **What** why   314 **wild** savage. (Sometimes emended to *vild*, vile.)
316 **Downy windows** i.e., soft eyelids   318 **Of** by   319 **mend** fix,
straighten   323 **beguiled** cheated, tricked

Touch their effects in this. Thyself art coming   330
To see performed the dreaded act which thou
So sought'st to hinder.

Enter Caesar and all his train, marching.

ALL   A way there, a way for Caesar!   333
DOLABELLA
  O sir, you are too sure an augurer;
  That you did fear is done.
CAESAR   Bravest at the last,   335
  She leveled at our purposes and, being royal,   336
  Took her own way. The manner of their deaths?
  I do not see them bleed.
DOLABELLA   Who was last with them?
FIRST GUARD
  A simple countryman, that brought her figs.   339
  This was his basket.
CAESAR   - Poisoned, then.
FIRST GUARD   O Caesar,
  This Charmian lived but now; she stood and spake.
  I found her trimming up the diadem
  On her dead mistress; tremblingly she stood,
  And on the sudden dropped.
CAESAR   O, noble weakness!
  If they had swallowed poison, 'twould appear
  By external swelling; but she looks like sleep,
  As she would catch another Antony   347
  In her strong toil of grace.
DOLABELLA   Here on her breast   348
  There is a vent of blood, and something blown;   349
  The like is on her arm.
FIRST GUARD
  This is an aspic's trail, and these fig leaves
  Have slime upon them, such as th' aspic leaves
  Upon the caves of Nile.
CAESAR   Most probable
  That so she died; for her physician tells me

330 **Touch their effects** meet with realization   333 **A way** make a path
335 **That** that which   336 **leveled at** aimed at, guessed   339 **simple** humbly born   347 **As** as if   348 **toil** net   349 **vent** discharge. **blown** depos-
ited, or swollen

She hath pursued conclusions infinite   355
Of easy ways to die. Take up her bed,
And bear her women from the monument.
She shall be buried by her Antony.
No grave upon the earth shall clip in it   359
A pair so famous. High events as these
Strike those that make them; and their story is   361
No less in pity than his glory which   362
Brought them to be lamented. Our army shall
In solemn show attend this funeral,
And then to Rome. Come, Dolabella, see
High order in this great solemnity.   366
       Exeunt omnes, [*bearing the dead bodies*].

---

355 conclusions experiments   **359 clip** embrace, clasp   **361 Strike . . .
them** touch with sorrow those who brought about these acts   **362 his
glory which** is the glory of him who   **366 s.d. omnes** all

Date and Text

On May 20, 1608, Edward Blount entered on the Stationers' Register, the official record book of the London Company of Stationers (booksellers and printers), "A booke Called. Antony. and Cleopatra," along with "A booke called. The booke of Pericles prynce of Tyre." Blount was friendly with Shakespeare's company, and his entry may have been a "staying entry" designed to prevent some unscrupulous publisher from pirating these texts. If so, the tactic did not succeed with *Pericles*, issued in 1609 by another publisher, but it did succeed with *Antony and Cleopatra*. The play was first printed in the First Folio of 1623. It is a good text, set evidently from Shakespeare's own draft in a more finished state than most of his foul or working papers, though not yet prepared to be a promptbook.

The year 1608 is thus the latest possible date for *Antony and Cleopatra*. Evidently it was written in 1606–1607, however, for a "newly altered" edition in 1607 of Samuel Daniel's play *Cleopatra* seems to have been influenced by Shakespeare's play. Shakespeare himself had probably consulted the original edition of *Cleopatra*, published in 1594, or the slightly revised edition of 1599, but Daniel's more thorough revision in 1607 shows signs of his having seen Shakespeare's play in the interim. Also, a play by Barnabe Barnes called *The Devil's Charter* (1607) may contain a parody of Cleopatra's death by asps.

---

8 slents sarcasms   **9 throughly** thoroughly   **10 not so . . . of** not so surpassing as to be unmatchable by   **11 upon present view** on first sight   **12 pricked to the quick** dug in the spur deeply, i.e., wounded the heart   **13 made . . . herself** i.e., she answered them in their own languages

Textual Notes

These textual notes are not a historical collation, either of the early folios or of more recent editions; they are simply a record of departures in this edition from the copy text. The reading adopted in this edition appears in boldface, followed by the rejected reading from the copy text, i.e., the First Folio. Only major alterations in punctuation are noted. Changes in lineation are not indicated, nor are some minor and obvious typographical errors.

Abbreviations used:
F the First Folio
s.d. stage direction
s.p. speech prefix

Copy text: the First Folio.

1.1. 41 On One   **52 whose** who

1.2. 4 charge change   **41 fertile** foretell   **64 Alexas** [printed in F as s.p.]   **83 Saw** Saue   **93 s.p. [and through l. 118] First Messenger** Messen (*or* Mess)   **116 minds** windes   **120 s.p. Second Messenger** 1. Mes   **121 s.p. Third Messenger** 2. Mes   **124 s.p. Fourth Messenger** 3. Mes   **126 s.p. Fourth Messenger** Mes   **137 s.d. Enter Enobarbus** [after "hatch," l. 137, in F]   **144 occasion** an occasion   **186 leave** loue   **191 Hath** Haue

1.3. 2 who's Whose   **20 What, says** What sayes   **43 services** Seruicles   **63 vials** Violles   **82 by my** by

1.4. 3 Our One   **8 Vouchsafed** vouchsafe   **9 abstract** abstracts   **21 smell** smels   **34 s.p. First Messenger** Mes   **44 deared** fear'd   **46 lackeying** lacking   **48 s.p. Second Messenger** Mes   **57 wassails** Vassailes   **58 Modena** Medena   **59 Pansa** Pausa   **77 we** me

1.5. 35 s.d. Alexas Alexas from Caesar   **52 dumbed** dumbe   **53 he, sad or** he sad, or   **64 man** mans

2.1. 2 s.p. [and throughout scene] Menas Mene   **22 joined** ioyne   **39 ne'er** neere   **42 warred** wan'd

2.2. 77 Alexandria; you Alexandria you   **128 so** say   **129 reproof** proofe   **180 s.d. Exeunt** Exit omnes   **Manent** Manet   **204 lovesick . . . The** Louesicke. / With them the   **214 glow** gloue   **216 gentlewomen** Gentlewoman   **233 heard** hard

2.3. 23 afeard a feare   **31 away** alway   **32 [and elsewhere] Ventidius** Ventigius   **41 s.d. Enter Ventidius** [after "Ventigius," l. 41, in F]

2.4. 6 the Mount Mount   **9 s.p. Maecenas, Agrippa** Both

2.5. 2 s.p. All Omnes   **10 river. There** Riuer there   **11 off, I** off. I   **12 finned** fine   **23 s.d. Enter a Messenger** [after "Italy," l. 23, in F]   **44 is** 'tis   **85 s.d. Enter . . . again** [after "sir," l. 85, in F]

2.6. s.d. Agrippa Agrippa, Menas   **19 is** his   **39 s.p. Caesar, Antony, Lepidus** Omnes   **58 composition** composion   **67 meanings** meaning   **71 more of** more   **83 s.p. Caesar, Antony, Lepidus** All   **83 s.d. Manent** Manet

2.7. 1 their th' their   **4 colored** Conlord   **39 s.d. Whispers in 's ear** [at l. 41
in F]   **93 is** he is   **101 grows** grow   **113 bear** beate   **115 s.p. Boy** [not in F]
119 s.p. All [not in F]   **122 off** of   **126 Splits** Spleet's   **130 father's** Father
132 s.p. Menas [not in F]

3.1. 5 s.p. [and throughout scene] **Silius** Romaine   **8 whither** whether

3.2. 10 s.p. Agrippa Ant   **16 figures** Figure   **49 full** the full   **60 wept** weepe

3.3. 2 s.d. Enter . . . before [after "sir," l. 2, in F]   **19 lookedst** look'st

3.4. 8 them then   **9 took 't** look't   **24 yours** your   **30 Your** You   **38 has** he's

3.5. 13 world would   **hast** hadst   **15 grind the one** grind

3.6. 13 he there hither   **the kings** the King   **73 Adallas** Adullas
74 Manchus Mauchus   **76 Comagene** Comageat   **77 Lycaonia** Licoania

3.7. 4 it is it it   **19 s.d. Canidius** Camidias [also spelled "Camidius" in this
scene and elsewhere]   **23 Toryne** Troine   **29 s.p.** [and elsewhere] **Canidius**
Cam   **36 muleteers** Militers   **52 Actium** Action   **67 s.d. Exeunt** exit   **70 led**
leade   **73 s.p. Canidius** Ven

3.10. s.d. Enobarbus Enobarbus and Scarus   **14 June** Inne   **28 he** his

3.11. 6 s.p. All Omnes   **19 that** them   **46 seize** cease   **50 led** lead   **57 tow**
stowe   **58 Thy** The

3.12. 13 lessens Lessons

3.13. 55 Caesar Caesars   **74 deputation** disputation   **91 me. Of late,
when** me of late. When   **94 s.d. Enter a Servant** [after "him," l. 94, in F]
104 This the   **133 s.d. Enter . . . Thidias** [after "whipped," l. 133, in F]
140 whipped . . . Henceforth whipt. For following him, henceforth
165 smite smile   **168 discandying** discandering   **171 sits** sets   **202 on**
in   **204 s.d. Exit** Exeunt

4.2. 11 s.d. Enter . . . servitors [after l. 10 in F]   **20 s.p. All** Omnes

4.3. 9 s.p. [and throughout scene] **Fourth Soldier** 2   **12 s.p.** [and throughout
scene] **Third Soldier** 1   **17 s.p.** [and throughout scene] **Fifth Soldier** 3
18 s.p. Sixth Soldier 4   **25, 31 s.p. All** Omnes

4.4. 5 too too, Anthony   **6 s.p. Antony** [not in F, or mistakenly placed in l. 5
as part of Cleopatra's speech]   **8 s.p. Cleopatra** [not in F]   **24 s.p. Captain**
Alex   **32–33 compliment . . . Now** Complement, Ile leaue thee. / Now

4.5. 1, 3, 6 s.p. Soldier Eros

4.6. 37–38 do 't . . . I doo't. I feele I

4.7. 3 s.d. Exeunt exit

4.8. 2 gests guests   **18 My** Mine   **23 favoring** sauouring

4.12. 3 s.d. Alarum . . . fight [at 0. s.d. in F]   **4 augurers** Auguries
21 spanieled pannelled

4.13. 10 death. To death to'

4.14. 4 towered toward   **10 dislimns** dislimes   **19 Caesar** Caesars   **104 ho**
how   **119 s.p. Dercetus** Decre   **145 s.d. Exeunt** Exit

4.15. 56 lived the liued. The   **78 e'en** in   **96 s.d. off** of

5.1. s.d. Maecenas Menas   **3 s.d. Dercetus** Decretas   **5, 13, 19 s.p. Dercetus**
Dec   **26 you, sad** you sad   **28, 31 s.p. Agrippa** Dol.   **48 s.d.** [at l. 51 in F]
59 live leaue

5.2. 26 dependency dependacie   **35** [F repeats s.p. **Pro.**]   **55 varletry** Var-
lotarie   **80 O, th'** o' th'   **86 autumn** Anthony   **103 smites** suites   **172 spirit**
spirits   **185 prison** prisons   **207 s.d. Exit** [at l. 206 in F]   **216 Ballad** Ballads   **223 my** mine   **228 Cydnus** Cidrus   **318 awry** away   **319 s.d. in** in,
and Dolabella

Shakespeare's Sources

In writing *Antony and Cleopatra*, Shakespeare relied to an unusual extent on his chief source, "The Life of Marcus Antonius" in the first-century Greek biographer Plutarch's *The Lives of the Noble Grecians and Romans* (in an English version by Sir Thomas North, 1579). Perhaps the best-known example in all Shakespeare of his skillful use of source material is in Act 2, scene 2 (ll. 201–236), when Enobarbus describes the first meeting of Antony and Cleopatra on the river Cydnus. As can be seen from a comparison of Shakespeare's lines with North's translation in the selection that follows, Shakespeare retains virtually every detail describing Cleopatra's barge: the poop of gold, the sails of purple, the oars of silver, the flutes, the boys with fans, the gentlewomen like the Nereides, and so on. He borrows phrases and images virtually intact from North, as in the account of Cleopatra's own person, "laid under a pavilion of cloth of gold of tissue, appareled and attired like the goddess Venus commonly drawn in picture," and the "wonderful passing sweet savor of perfumes that perfumed the wharf's side" while Antony "was left post alone in the marketplace." Yet Shakespeare also transforms this scene by putting the description in the mouth of Enobarbus, a largely invented character. Enobarbus' sardonic view derived from military experience, his wry but genuine admiration for Cleopatra, and the prurient curiosity of his Roman listeners, all combine to produce the paradox of cloying appetite and insatiable hunger that helps to define the unforgettable greatness of Cleopatra as a character.

Shakespeare turns to Plutarch for the other fabulous stories as well: eight wild boars roasted whole for only twelve guests (2.2.189–190), Cleopatra teasing Antony by causing an old dried salt fish to be placed on his fishing line (2.5.15–18), Menas the pirate suggesting to Pompey that they cut the anchor cable with all their noble guests still aboard (2.7.62–85), Cleopatra's sudden changes from weeping to laughing, and her willingness to be flattered by those who tell her Antony has married Octavia solely out of necessity (3.3), Octavius' tenderness for his sister, the ill-omened nesting of swallows in Cleopatra's sails (4.12.4–5), Antony's disregarding the advice of a valiant captain not to fight at sea (3.7.62–71), Cleopatra's study of swift means of death (5.2.353–356), Antony's jealous reaction to the embassy of the young Thyreus, or Thidias (3.13.86–170), the suicide of Antony's servant Eros (4.14.85–97), Cleopatra's difficulty in lifting Antony up to her tomb or monument (4.15.30–38), his warning that she should trust none but Proculeius (4.15.50), Cleopatra's deception of Caesar through persuading him that she desires to live (5.2.110–190), the countryman with the basket of figs (5.2.233–235), Cleopatra's death "attired and arrayed in her royal robes" attended by Charmian and Iras, and much more.

Despite these extensive and detailed borrowings, Shakespeare partly turned elsewhere for his estimate of his main characters. To Plutarch, Antony is the tragic victim of infatuation. For all Cleopatra's cultivation and fascination—she knows several languages and rules her country with royal bearing—she is the source of Antony's downfall. Plutarch's attitude is, like Enobarbus', admiring but ironic. "In the end," he writes, "the horse of the mind, as Plato termeth it, that is so hard of rein (I mean the unreined lust of concupiscence) did put out of Antonius' head all honest and commendable thoughts." This "Roman" view is present in *Antony and Cleopatra*, to be sure, but is counterbalanced by the "Egyptian" view that finds greatness in Antony and Cleopatra's capacity for love. Shakespeare's play sets up a debate among conflicting traditions as found in various medieval and Renaissance treatments of this famous story. The moralistic perspective condemning vice was popular in medieval texts, such as *De Casibus Virorum Illustrium* and its continuation, John Lydgate's *The Fall of Princes*. The interpretation of Cleopatra as love's martyr was to be found in Geoffrey Chaucer's *The Legend of Good Women*. And finally, the view of Antony and Cleopatra as heroic protagonists rising above their guilt found expression in several neo-Senecan dramas of the later sixteenth century. Most important for Shakespeare were *The Tragedy of Antony*, translated from Robert Garnier's *Marc-Antoine* by Mary Herbert, Countess of Pembroke, in about 1590 (published 1592 and 1595), and *The Tragedy of Cleopatra* by Samuel

Daniel (1593), a companion play dealing mainly with the
end of Cleopatra's life. Garnier's play had been based on
Étienne Jodelle's *Cléopâtre Captive* (1552), the first regular
French tragedy. Shakespeare certainly gained from works
such as these a sense of tragic greatness in his protagonists.
Another influential work may have been the *Chronicle of
the Romans' Wars* by Appian of Alexandria (translated
1578).

The Lives of the Noble Grecians and
Romans Compared Together by . . . Plutarch
Translated by Thomas North

FROM THE LIFE OF MARCUS ANTONIUS

[A year after he and Octavius Caesar defeat Brutus and Cassius in 42 B.C. at Philippi, as shown in Act 5 of *Julius Caesar*,
Antony undertakes a military campaign in Asia. Plutarch describes his valor, his great generosity, his courtesy to all, and
his fame as "a worthy man."]

But besides all this, he had a noble presence, and showed a
countenance of one of a noble house. He had a goodly thick
beard, a broad forehead, crook-nosed, and there appeared
such a manly look in his countenance as is commonly seen in
Hercules' pictures stamped or graven in metal. Now it had
been a speech of old time that the family of the Antonii were
descended from one Anton, the son of Hercules, whereof the
family took name. This opinion did Antonius seek to confirm
in all his doings, not only resembling him in the likeness of
his body, as we have said before, but also in the wearing of
his garments. For when he would openly show himself
abroad before many people, he would always wear his cas-
sock girt down low upon his hips, with a great sword hanging
by his side, and upon that some ill-favored cloak. Furthermore, things that seem intolerable in other men, as to boast
commonly, to jest with one or other, to drink like a good fellow with everybody, to sit with the soldiers when they dine,
and to eat and drink with them soldierlike—it is incredible

what wonderful love it wan[1] him amongst them. And further-more, being given to love, that made him the more desired, and by that means he brought many to love him. For he would further every man's love and also would not be angry that men should merrily tell him of those he loved. But besides all this, that which most procured his rising and advancement was his liberality, who gave all to the soldiers and kept nothing for himself. And when he was grown to great credit, then was his authority and power also very great, the which notwithstanding himself did overthrow by a thousand other faults he had.

[Plutarch describes various events prior to the commencement of the action in *Antony and Cleopatra*, including Antony's buying Pompey's house when it is put up for sale, and his leaving his dissolute life to marry Fulvia, a widow, "a woman not so basely minded to spend her time in spinning and housewifery, and was not contented to master her husband at home but would also rule him in his office abroad." When Antony and Octavius Caesar become enemies after the assassination of Julius Caesar, Octavius sends Hirtius and Pansa, consuls, to drive Antony out of Italy, but he defeats and kills them at Modena. Antony shows remarkable stamina in adversity on this occasion: "It was a wonderful example to the soldiers to see Antonius, that was brought up in all fineness and superfluity, so easily to drink puddle water and to eat wild fruits and roots; and moreover it is reported that even as they passed the Alps they did eat the barks of trees and such beasts as never man tasted of their flesh before." Thereafter, Antony and Octavius make peace and agree to divide all the Roman Empire into three with Lepidus as the third partner.]

He had a noble mind, as well to punish offenders as to reward well-doers, and yet he did exceed more in giving than in punishing. Now for his outrageous manner of railing he commonly used, mocking and flouting of every man, that was remedied by itself; for a man might as boldly exchange a mock with him, and he was as well contented to be mocked

1 **wan** won

as to mock others. But yet it oftentimes marred all, for he thought that those which told him so plainly and truly in mirth would never flatter him in good earnest in any matter of weight. But thus he was easily abused by the praises they gave him, not finding how these flatterers mingled their flattery under this familiar and plain manner of speech unto him as a fine device to make difference of meats[2] with sharp and tart sauce, and also to keep him by this frank jesting and bourding[3] with him at the table, that their common flattery should not be troublesome unto him, as[4] men do easily mislike to have too much of one thing; and that they handled him finely thereby, when they would give him place in any matter of weight and follow his counsel that it might not appear to him they did it so much to please him but because they were ignorant and understood not so much as he did.

Antonius being thus inclined, the last and extremest mischief of all other—to wit, the love of Cleopatra—lighted on him, who did waken and stir up many vices yet hidden in him and were never seen to any; and if any spark of goodness or hope of rising were left him, Cleopatra quenched it straight and made it worse than before. The manner how he fell in love with her was this. Antonius, going to make war with the Parthians, sent to command Cleopatra to appear personally before him when he came into Cilicia[5] to answer unto such accusations as were laid against her, being this: that she had aided Cassius and Brutus in their war against him. The messenger sent unto Cleopatra to make this summons unto her was called Dellius, who, when he had throughly considered her beauty, the excellent grace and sweetness of her tongue, he nothing mistrusted[6] that Antonius would do any hurt to so noble a lady, but rather assured himself that within few days she should be in great favor with him. Thereupon he did her great honor and persuaded her to come into Cilicia as honorably furnished as she could possible, and bade her not to be afraid at all of Antonius, for he was a more courteous lord

---

2 make difference of meats i.e., vary the palate. (*Meats* means "foods.")
3 bourding joking, buffoonery   **4 as** since   **5 Cilicia** an eastern province of the Roman Empire in southern modern-day Turkey, on the Mediterranean near Cyprus. (The Cydnus River is in Cilicia. The *Parthians* are further east, southeast of the Caspian Sea.)   **6 nothing mistrusted** did not fear in the least

than any that she had ever seen. Cleopatra, on the other side, believing Dellius' words and guessing by the former access and credit she had with Julius Caesar and Gnaeus Pompey (the son of Pompey the Great) only for her beauty, she began to have good hope that she might more easily win Antonius. For Caesar and Pompey knew her when she was but a young thing and knew not then what the world meant; but now she went to Antonius at the age when a woman's beauty is at the prime and she also of best judgment. So she furnished herself with a world of gifts, store of gold and silver and of riches and other sumptuous ornaments as is credible enough she might bring from so great a house and from so wealthy and rich a realm as Egypt was. But yet she carried nothing with her wherein she trusted more than in herself and in the charms and enchantment of her passing[7] beauty and grace.

Therefore, when she was sent unto by divers letters, both from Antonius himself and also from his friends, she made so light of it and mocked Antonius so much that she disdained to set forward otherwise but to take her barge in the river of Cydnus, the poop whereof was of gold, the sails of purple, and the oars of silver, which kept stroke in rowing after the sound of the music of flutes, hautboys, citterns, viols, and such other instruments as they played upon in the barge. And now for the person of herself: she was laid under a pavilion of cloth of gold of tissue, appareled and attired like the goddess Venus commonly drawn in picture, and hard by her, on either hand of her, pretty fair boys appareled as painters do set forth god Cupid, with little fans in their hands with the which they fanned wind upon her. Her ladies and gentlewomen also, the fairest of them, were appareled like the nymphs Nereides (which are the mermaids of the waters) and like the Graces, some steering the helm, others tending the tackle and ropes of the barge, out of the which there came a wonderful passing sweet savor of perfumes that perfumed the wharf's side, pestered with innumerable multitudes of people. Some of them followed the barge all alongst the river's side; others also ran out of the city to see her coming in. So that in the end there ran such multitudes of people one

7 **passing** surpassing

after another to see her that Antonius was left post alone in the marketplace, in his imperial seat, to give audience; and there went a rumor in the people's mouths that the goddess Venus was come to play with the god Bacchus for the general good of all Asia.

When Cleopatra landed, Antonius sent to invite her to supper to him. But she sent him word again he should do better rather to come and sup with her. Antonius therefore, to show himself courteous unto her at her arrival, was contented to obey her and went to supper to her, where he found such passing sumptuous fare that no tongue can express it. But amongst all other things he most wondered at the infinite number of lights and torches hanged on the top of the house, giving light in every place, so artificially set and ordered by devices, some round, some square, that it was the rarest thing to behold that eye could discern or that ever books could mention. The next night Antonius, feasting her, contended to pass her in magnificence and fineness, but she overcame him in both. So that he himself began to scorn the gross service of his house, in respect of Cleopatra's sumptuousness and fineness. And when Cleopatra found Antonius' jests and slents[8] to be but gross and soldierlike, in plain manner, she gave it him finely and without fear taunted him throughly.[9]

Now her beauty (as it is reported) was not so passing as unmatchable of[10] other women, nor yet such as upon present view[11] did enamor men with her; but so sweet was her company and conversation that a man could not possibly but be taken. And besides her beauty, the good grace she had to talk and discourse, her courteous nature that tempered her words and deeds, was a spur that pricked to the quick.[12] Furthermore, besides all these, her voice and words were marvelous pleasant, for her tongue was an instrument of music to divers sports and pastimes, the which she easily turned to any language that pleased her. She spake unto few barbarous people by interpreter, but made them answer herself,[13] or at the least the most part of them: as the Ethiopians,

---

8 slents sarcasms   9 throughly thoroughly   10 not so . . . of not so surpassing as to be unmatchable by   11 upon present view on first sight   12 pricked to the quick dug in the spur deeply, i.e., wounded the heart   13 made . . . herself i.e., she answered them in their own languages

the Arabians, the Troglodytes, the Hebrews, the Syrians, the
Medes, and the Parthians, and to many others also whose
languages she had learned. Whereas divers of her progeni-
tors, the kings of Egypt, could scarce learn the Egyptian
tongue only, and many of them forgot to speak the Macedonian.[14]

Now Antonius was so ravished with the love of Cleopatra
that though his wife Fulvia had great wars and much ado
with Caesar for his affairs, and that the army of the Parthians (the which the King's lieutenants had given to the only
leading of Labienus)[15] was now assembled in Mesopotamia,
ready to invade Syria, yet, as though all this had nothing
touched him,[16] he yielded himself to go with Cleopatra unto
Alexandria, where he spent and lost in childish sports (as a
man might say) and idle pastimes the most precious thing a
man can spend (as Antiphon[17] saith), and that is, time. For
they made an order[18] between them which they called *Amimetobion*, as much to say, no life comparable and matchable
with it, one feasting each other by turns and in cost exceeding all measure and reason. And for proof hereof I have heard
my grandfather Lampryas report that one Philotas, a physician born in the city of Amphissa, told him that he was at
that present time in Alexandria and studied physic; and that
having acquaintance with one of Antonius' cooks, he took
him with him to Antonius' house (being a young man desirous to see things) to show him the wonderful sumptuous
charge[19] and preparation of one only supper.[20] When he
was in the kitchen and saw a world of diversities of meats,
and amongst others eight wild boars roasted whole, he began to wonder at it and said: "Sure you have a great number
of guests to supper." The cook fell a-laughing and answered

---

14 Egyptian . . . Macedonian (Like other members of the Egyptian royal
family at this time, Cleopatra is of Macedonian race.)   **15 Labienus**
Quintus Labienus, a Roman general formerly allied to Brutus and
Cassius and sent by them to Orodes, King of Parthia, to seek aid against
Antony and Octavius; under Labienus' leadership the Parthians enjoy
great success against Antony in the Middle East. (See 1.2.105–109 in
Antony and Cleopatra.)   **16 had nothing touched him** scarcely concerned him at all   **17 Antiphon** an orator and teacher of rhetoric in
Athens, c. 480–411 B.C.   **18 order** arrangement (governing their enter-
tainment of each other)   **19 charge** expense   **20 one only supper** one
supper alone

him: "No," quoth he, "not many guests, nor above twelve in
all; but yet all that is boiled or roasted must be served in
whole, or else it would be marred straight.[21] For Antonius
peradventure will sup presently,[22] or it may be a pretty while
hence, or likely enough he will defer it longer, for that[23] he
hath drunk well today, or else hath had some other great matters in hand: and therefore we do not dress[24] one supper only
but many suppers, because we are uncertain of the hour he
will sup in." Philotas the physician told my grandfather this
tale. . . .

But now again to Cleopatra. Plato writeth that there are
four kinds of flattery, but Cleopatra divided it into many
kinds. For she, were it in sport or in matter of earnest, still[25]
devised sundry new delights to have Antonius at commandment, never leaving him night nor day nor once letting him
go out of her sight. For she would play at dice with him,
drink with him, and hunt commonly with him, and also be
with him when he went to any exercise or activity of body.
And sometimes also, when he would go up and down the city
disguised like a slave in the night and would peer into poor
men's windows and their shops and scold and brawl with
them within the house, Cleopatra would be also in a cham-
bermaid's array and amble up and down the streets with
him, so that oftentimes Antonius bare[26] away both mocks and
blows. Now though most men misliked this manner, yet the
Alexandrians were commonly glad of this jollity and liked it
well, saying very gallantly and wisely that Antonius showed
them a comical face, to wit, a merry countenance, and the
Romans a tragical face, to say,[27] a grim look.

But to reckon up all the foolish sports they made, reveling
in this sort, it were too fond[28] a part of me, and therefore I
will only tell you one among the rest. On a time he went to
angle for fish, and when he could take none, he was as angry
as could be, because Cleopatra stood by.[29] Wherefore he secretly commanded the fishermen that, when he cast in his

---

21 it would . . . straight the occasion would be ruined immediately. (The
food must be served *whole* or intact, hot, and not overcooked whenever
Antony wants to eat.)   **22 presently** immediately   **23 for that** because
24 dress prepare   **25 still** continually   **26 bare** bore   **27 to say** that is
to say   **28 fond** foolish   **29 stood by** i.e., was a witness to his lack of
success

line, they should straight dive under the water and put a fish on his hook which they had taken before; and so snatched up his angling rod and brought up fish twice or thrice. Cleopatra found it straight,[30] yet she seemed not to see it, but wondered at his excellent fishing. But when she was alone by herself among her own people, she told them how it was and bade them the next morning to be on the water to see the fishing. A number of people came to the haven and got into the fisher boats to see this fishing. Antonius then threw in his line, and Cleopatra straight commanded one of her men to dive under water before Antonius' men and to put some old salt fish upon his bait, like unto those that are brought out of the country of Pont. When he had hung the fish on his hook, Antonius, thinking he had taken a fish indeed, snatched up his line presently. Then they all fell a-laughing. Cleopatra, laughing also, said unto him: "Leave us, my lord, Egyptians (which dwell in the country of Pharus and Canobus), your angling rod. This is not thy profession; thou must hunt after conquering of realms and countries."

Now Antonius delighting in these fond and childish pastimes, very ill news were brought him from two places. The first from Rome, that his brother Lucius and Fulvia his wife fell out first between themselves[31] and afterwards fell to open war with Caesar and had brought all to nought, that they were both driven to fly out of Italy. The second news, as bad as the first, that Labienus conquered all Asia with the army of the Parthians, from the river of Euphrates and from Syria unto the countries of Lydia and Ionia. Then began Antonius with much ado a little to rouse himself, as if he had been wakened out of a deep sleep and, as a man may say, coming out of a great drunkenness. So first of all he bent himself[32] against the Parthians and went as far as the country of Phoenicia, but there he received lamentable letters from his wife Fulvia. Whereupon he straight returned towards Italy with two hundred sail, and as he went took up his friends by the way that fled out of Italy to come to him. By them he was informed that his wife Fulvia was the only cause of this war,

30 found it straight i.e., saw what was happening right away   **31 his brother . . . themselves** (Antony's brother Lucius joined with Fulvia against the triumvirate but quarreled with her.)   **32 bent himself** turned his efforts

who, being of a peevish, crooked, and troublesome nature, had purposely raised this uproar in Italy in hope thereby to withdraw him from Cleopatra. But by good fortune his wife Fulvia, going to meet with Antonius, sickened by the way and died in the city of Sicyon; and therefore Octavius Caesar and he were the easier made friends together.

For when Antonius landed in Italy, and that men saw Caesar asked nothing of him, and that Antonius on the other side laid all the fault and burden on his wife Fulvia, the friends of both parties would not suffer them to unrip any old matters and to prove or defend who had the wrong or right and who was the first procurer of this war, fearing to make matters worse between them. But they made them friends together and divided the empire of Rome between them, making the Sea Ionium[33] the bounds of their division. For they gave all the provinces eastward unto Antonius, and the countries westward unto Caesar, and left Africk unto Lepidus, and made a law that they three, one after another, should make their friends consuls when they would not be themselves.

This seemed to be a sound counsel, but yet it was to be confirmed with a straiter bond, which fortune offered thus. There was Octavia, the eldest sister of Caesar—not by one mother, for she came of Ancharia and Caesar himself afterwards of Accia. It is reported that he dearly loved his sister Octavia, for indeed she was a noble lady, and left[34] the widow of her first husband Caius Marcellus, who died not long before; and it seemed also that Antonius had been widower ever since the death of his wife Fulvia. For he denied not that he kept Cleopatra, but so did he not confess that he had her as his wife; and so with reason he did defend the love he bare unto this Egyptian Cleopatra. Thereupon every man did set forward this marriage, hoping thereby that this lady Octavia, having an excellent grace, wisdom, and honesty joined unto so rare a beauty that when she were with Antonius (he loving her as so worthy a lady deserveth) she should be a good means to keep good love and amity betwixt her brother and him. So when Caesar and he had made the match between them, they both went to Rome about this marriage, although it was against the law that a widow should be married within ten months after her husband's death. Howbeit the Senate dispensed with the law, and so the marriage proceeded accordingly.

Sextus Pompeius at that time kept in Sicilia,[35] and so made many an inroad into Italy with a great number of pinnaces[36] and other pirates' ships, of the which were captains two notable pirates, Menas and Menecrates, who so scoured all the sea thereabouts that none durst peep out with a sail. Furthermore, Sextus Pompeius had dealt very friendly with Antonius, for he had courteously received his mother when she fled out of Italy with Fulvia, and therefore they[37] thought good to make peace with him. So they met all three together by the mount of Misena upon a hill that runneth far into the sea, Pompey having his ships riding hard by at anchor and Antonius and Caesar their armies upon the shore side directly over against[38] him. Now, after they had agreed that Sextus Pompeius should have Sicily and Sardinia, with this condition, that he should rid the sea of all thieves and pirates and make it safe for passengers, and withal[39] that he should send a certain[40] of wheat to Rome, one of them did feast another and drew cuts who should begin. It was Pompeius' chance to invite them first. Whereupon Antonius asked him: "And where shall we sup?" "There," said Pompey, and showed him his admiral galley which had six banks of oars. "That," said he, "is my father's house they have left me." He spake it to taunt Antonius, because he had his father's house, that was Pompey the Great.[41] So he cast anchors enough into the sea to make his galley fast[42] and then built a bridge of wood to convey them to his galley from the head of Mount Misena, and there he welcomed them and made them great cheer. Now in the midst of the feast, when they fell to be merry with[43] Antonius' love unto Cleopatra, Menas the pirate

35 kept in Sicilia used Sicily as his base of operations   **36 pinnaces** light, two-masted sailing ships   **37 they** i.e., the triumvirs   **38 over against** opposite   **39 withal** in addition   **40 a certain** a certain quantity   **41 because he had . . . Great** i.e., because Antony had purchased the house of Pompey's father, Pompey the Great, after it had been confiscated by the government, and then balked at payment and lived riotously in the house   **42 fast** secure   **43 fell to be merry with** fell into merry talk about

came to Pompey and, whispering in his ear, said unto him: "Shall I cut the cables of the anchors and make thee lord not only of Sicily and Sardinia but of the whole empire of Rome besides?" Pompey, having paused awhile upon it, at length answered him: "Thou shouldst have done it and never have told it me, but now we must content us with that[44] we have. As for myself, I was never taught to break my faith nor to be counted a traitor." The other two also did likewise feast him in their camp, and then he returned into Sicily.

Antonius, after this agreement made, sent Ventidius before into Asia to stay[45] the Parthians and to keep them they should come no further.[46] And he himself in the meantime, to gratify Caesar, was contented to be chosen Julius Caesar's priest and sacrificer, and so they jointly together dispatched all great matters concerning the state of the empire. But in all other manner of sports and exercises wherein they passed the time away the one with the other, Antonius was ever inferior unto Caesar and alway lost, which grieved him much. With Antonius there was a soothsayer or astronomer of Egypt that could cast a figure[47] and judge of men's nativities to tell them what should happen to them. He, either to please Cleopatra or else for that he found it so by his art, told Antonius plainly that his fortune, which of itself was excellent good and very great, was altogether blemished and obscured by Caesar's fortune, and therefore he counseled him utterly to leave his company and to get him as far from him as he could. "For thy demon," said he, "that is to say, the good angel and spirit that keepeth thee, is afraid of his and, being courageous and high when he is alone, becometh fearful and timorous when he cometh near unto the other." Howsoever it was, the events ensuing proved the Egyptian's words true. For it is said that as often as they two drew cuts for pastime who should have anything, or whether they played at dice, Antonius alway lost. Oftentimes when they were disposed to see cockfight, or quails that were taught to fight one with another, Caesar's cocks or quails did ever overcome. The which spited[48] Antonius in his mind, although he made no outward show of it; and therefore he believed the Egyptian

44 **that** what   45 **stay** halt   46 **keep . . . further** prevent them from coming any further (into the Roman Empire)   47 **cast a figure** calculate astrologically a horoscope   48 **spited** vexed

the better.[49] In fine,[50] he recommended the affairs of his house unto Caesar and went out of Italy with Octavia his wife, whom he carried into Greece after he had had a daughter by her.

So Antonius lying[51] all the winter at Athens, news came unto him of the victories of Ventidius, who had overcome the Parthians in battle, in the which also were slain Labienus and Pharnabates, the chiefest captain King Orodes had. For these good news he feasted all Athens and kept open house for all the Grecians, and many games of price were played at Athens of the which he himself would be judge. Wherefore leaving his guard, his axes,[52] and tokens of his empire at his house, he came into the showplace or lists, where these games were played, in a long gown and slippers after the Grecian fashion, and they carried tipstaves[53] before him, as marshals' men do carry before the judges, to make place;[54] and he himself in person was a stickler[55] to part the young men when they had fought enough. After that, preparing to go to the wars, he made him a garland of the holy olive and carried a vessel with him of the water of the fountain Clepsydra, because of an oracle he had received that so commanded him.

In the meantime Ventidius once again overcame Pacorus (Orodes' son, King of Parthia) in a battle fought in the country of Cyrrestica, he being come again with a great army to invade Syria, at which battle was slain a great number of the Parthians and among them Pacorus, the King's own son slain. This noble exploit, as famous as ever any was, was a full revenge to the Romans of the shame and loss they had received before by the death of Marcus Crassus;[56] and he made the Parthians fly and glad to keep themselves within the confines and territories of Mesopotamia and Media after they had thrice together been overcome in several battles. Howbeit Ventidius durst not undertake to follow them any further, fearing lest he should have gotten Antonius' displea-

---

49 the better all the more   **50 In fine** in conclusion   **51 lying** residing   **52 axes** fasces, a bundle of rods bound up with an ax in the middle and its blade projecting; one of the *tokens* of empire   **53 tipstaves** metal-tipped staffs or staves carried as emblems of office   **54 make place** get people to move back and make room   **55 stickler** umpire   **56 Marcus Crassus** Roman triumvir, provincial governor of Syria, defeated and executed by Orodes in 53 B.C.

sure by it. Notwithstanding, he led his army against them that
had rebelled and conquered them again, amongst whom he
besieged Antiochus, King of Commagena, who offered him to
give a thousand talents to be pardoned his rebellion and
promised ever after to be at Antonius' commandment. But
Ventidius made him answer that he should send unto Antonius, who was not far off, and would not suffer Ventidius to
make any peace with Antiochus, to the end that yet this little
exploit should pass in his name and that they should not
think he did anything but by his lieutenant Ventidius. The
siege grew very long, because they that were in the town, seeing they could not be received upon no reasonable composition,[57] determined valiantly to defend themselves to the last
man. Thus Antonius did nothing and yet received great
shame, repenting him much that he took not their first offer.
And yet at last he was glad to make truce with Antiochus
and to take three hundred talents for composition. Thus after
he had set order for the state and affairs of Syria, he returned again to Athens, and having given Ventidius such honors as he deserved, he sent him to Rome to triumph for the
Parthians. Ventidius was the only man that ever triumphed
of[58] the Parthians until this present day, a mean man born[59]
and of no noble house nor family, who only came to that[60]
he attained unto through Antonius' friendship, the which
delivered him happy occasion to achieve to great matters.
And yet to say truly, he did so well quit[61] himself in all his
enterprises that he confirmed that which was spoken of
Antonius and Caesar, to wit, that they were alway more fortunate when they made war by their lieutenants than
by themselves. For Sossius, one of Antonius' lieutenants in
Syria, did notable good service; and Canidius, whom he had
also left his lieutenant in the borders of Armenia, did conquer it all. So did he also overcome the kings of the Iberians
and Albanians and went on with his conquests unto Mount
Caucasus. By these conquests the fame of Antonius' power
increased more and more and grew dreadful unto all the
barbarous nations.

But Antonius, notwithstanding, grew to be marvelously
offended with Caesar upon certain reports that had been

57 composition terms of settlement   **58 of** over   **59 mean man born**
person born of low station   **60 that** that which   **61 quit** acquit

brought unto him, and so took sea to go towards Italy with three hundred sail. And because those of Brundusium would not receive his army into their haven, he went further unto Tarentum. There his wife Octavia, that came out of Greece with him, besought him to send her unto her brother, the which he did. Octavia at that time was great with child and moreover had a second daughter by him, and yet she put herself in journey and met with her brother Octavius Caesar by the way, who brought his two chief friends, Maecenas and Agrippa, with him. She took them aside and, with all the instance[62] she could possible, entreated them they would not suffer[63] her, that was the happiest woman of the world, to become now the most wretched and unfortunatest creature of all other. "For now," said she, "every man's eyes do gaze on me, that am the sister of one of the emperors and wife of the other. And if the worst counsel take place (which the gods forbid) and that they grow to wars, for yourselves it is uncertain to which of them two the gods have assigned victory or overthrow. But for me, on which side soever the victory fall, my state can be but most miserable still." These words of Octavia so softened Caesar's heart that he went quickly unto Tarentum. But it was a noble sight for them that were present to see so great an army by land not to stir and so many ships afloat in the road quietly and safe, and furthermore the meeting and kindness of friends lovingly embracing one another. First Antonius feasted Caesar, which he granted unto for his sister's sake. Afterwards they agreed together that Caesar should give Antonius two legions to go against the Parthians and that Antonius should let Caesar have a hundred galleys armed with brazen spurs at the prows. Besides all this, Octavia obtained of her husband twenty brigantines[64] for her brother, and of her brother, for her husband, a thousand armed men. After they had taken leave of each other, Caesar went immediately to make war with Sextus Pompeius, to get Sicilia into his hands. Antonius also, leaving his wife Octavia and little children begotten of her with Caesar, and his other children which he had by Fulvia, went directly into Asia.

Then began this pestilent plague and mischief of Cleopa-

---

62 instance urgent entreaty **63 suffer** permit **64 brigantines** small sailing and rowing vessels

tra's love (which had slept a long time and seemed to have
been utterly forgotten, and that Antonius had given place to
better counsel) again to kindle and to be in force so soon as
Antonius came near unto Syria. And in the end, the horse of
the mind, as Plato termeth it, that is so hard of rein (I mean
the unreined lust of concupiscence) did put out of Antonius'
head all honest and commendable thoughts. For he sent
Fonteius Capito to bring Cleopatra into Syria, unto whom, to
welcome her, he gave no trifling things, but unto that she had
already he added the provinces of Phoenicia, those of the
nethermost Syria, the isle of Cyprus, and a great part of Cilicia, and that country of Jewry where the true balm is,[65] and
that part of Arabia where the Nabathaeans do dwell, which
stretcheth out towards the ocean. These great gifts much misliked[66] the Romans. But now, though Antonius did easily give
away great seigniories, realms, and mighty nations unto
some private men, and that also he took from other kings
their lawful realms (as from Antigonus, King of the Jews,
whom he openly beheaded, where never king before had suffered like death), yet all this did not so much offend the Romans as the unmeasurable honors which he did unto
Cleopatra. But yet he did much more aggravate their malice
and ill will towards him because that, Cleopatra having
brought him two twins,[67] a son and a daughter, he named his
son Alexander and his daughter Cleopatra and gave them,
to[68] their surnames, the Sun to the one and the Moon to the
other.

[Antony sends Cleopatra back into Egypt and undertakes a
campaign into Arabia and Armenia, where he is devastated
by the Parthian army. He retreats in haste and makes his way
back to Cleopatra in Egypt, where he is "drowned with the
love of her." When Octavia hopes to rejoin Antony and reconcile him to Octavius, she is rebuffed, and all Rome is angry that
Antony "did unkindly use so noble a lady." Antony sharpens
the insult by his public display in Egypt, assembling all the
people in the showplace where young men do their exercise.
There, "upon a high tribunal silvered," set "in two chairs of
gold, the one for himself and the other for Cleopatra, and

65 where . . . is i.e., where Christ was crucified and resurrected
66 misliked displeased   67 two twins i.e., twins   68 to as

lower chairs for his children," Antony announces his estab-
lishment of Cleopatra as "Queen of Egypt, of Cyprus, of
Lydia, and of the lower Syria." Caesarion, supposed son of
Julius Caesar, is made king of the same realms, while Antony's son Alexander is given Armenia, Media, and Parthia,
and Ptolemy is given Phoenicia, Syria, and Cilicia. Antony
complains that Caesar has not given him his share of Sicily
taken away from Pompey, that Caesar has detained some
shipping Antony needed, and that Caesar retains more than
he deserves of Lepidus' share of the empire now that Lepidus
has been excluded. Caesar's answers do not heal the rift.

Antony attempts through a follower named Domitius to
persuade Cleopatra to return to Egypt, but she, fearing a new
alliance between Caesar and Antony, persuades Canidius to
be her spokesman with Antony and to urge that she be allowed to remain in the war now looming between Antony and
Octavius. Caesar openly taunts Antony that those who
conduct his war effort are chiefly "Mardian the eunuch,
Photinus, and Iras, a woman of Cleopatra's bedchamber that
frizzled her hair and dressed her head," and Charmian. An
unsettling omen reported at the time is that in the "admiral-
galley of Cleopatra," called the *Antoniad*, the swallows that
have bred under the poop are driven away by other birds that
pluck down their nests. Among the allies summoned to aid
Antony are "Bocchus, King of Libya; Tarcondemus, King of
high Cilicia; Archelaus, King of Cappadocia; Philadelphus,
King of Paphlagonia; Mithridates, King of Comagena; and
Adallas, King of Thracia." Absent in person but sending
forces are "Polemon, King of Pont; Manchus, King of Arabia;
Herodes, King of Jewry; and furthermore Amyntas, King of
Lycaonia and of the Galacians." The scene of confrontation
is the southern Adriatic, the so-called Ionian Sea, between
the lower boot of Italy and the northwestern coast of
modern-day Greece.]

Now Antonius was made so subject to a woman's will that,
though he was a great deal the stronger by land, yet for Cleopatra's sake he would needs have this battle tried by sea,
though he saw before his eyes that for lack of watermen his
captains did press[69] by force all sorts of men out of Greece

69 press conscript

that they could take up in the field, as travelers, muleteers,[70]
reapers, harvestmen, and young boys, and yet could they not
sufficiently furnish his galleys, so that the most part of them
were empty and could scant row because they lacked watermen enough. But on the contrary side, Caesar's ships were
not built for pomp, high and great only for a sight and bravery,[71] but they were light of yarage,[72] armed and furnished
with watermen as many as they needed, and had them all in
readiness in the havens of Tarentum and Brundusium.[73] So
Octavius Caesar sent unto Antonius to will him to delay no
more time but to come on with his army into Italy, and that
for his own part he would give him safe harbor to land without any trouble, and that he would withdraw his army from
the sea, as far as one horse could run, until he had put his
army ashore and had lodged his men. Antonius on the other
side bravely sent him word again and challenged the combat
of him, man for man, though he were the elder; and that if he
refused him so, he would then fight a battle with him in the
fields of Pharsalia, as Julius Caesar and Pompey had done
before.

Now whilst Antonius rode at anchor, lying idly in harbor at
the head[74] of Actium in the place where the city of Nicopolis
standeth at this present, Caesar had quicky passed the Sea
Ionium and taken a place called Toryne before Antonius understood that he had taken ship.[75] Then began his men to be
afraid, because his army by land was left behind. But Cleopatra making light of it: "And what danger, I pray you," said
she, "if Caesar keep at Toryne?"

The next morning by break of day, his enemies coming
with full force of oars in battle against him, Antonius was
afraid that if they came to join, they would take and carry
away his ships that had no men-of-war in them. So he armed
all his watermen and set them in order of battle upon the
forecastle of their ships and then lift[76] up all his ranks of oars
towards the element,[77] as well of the one side as[78] the

---

70 muleteers drivers of teams of mules   **71 bravery** splendor, show
72 light of yarage easily maneuvered at sea   **73 Tarentum and Brundusium** (In the heel of Italy.)   **74 head** head of land projecting out at
Actium (in modern-day northwest Greece)   **75 he had taken ship** i.e.,
Caesar had sailed   **76 lift** lifted   **77 element** sky   **78 as well of . . . as**
both on . . . and

other, with the prows against the enemies, at the entry and mouth of the gulf which beginneth at the point of Actium, and so kept them in order of battle as if they had been armed and furnished with watermen and soldiers. Thus Octavius Caesar, being finely deceived by this stratagem, retired presently, and therewithal Antonius very wisely and suddenly did cut him off from fresh water. For, understanding that the places where Octavius Caesar landed had very little store of water and yet very bad,[79] he shut them in with strong ditches and trenches he cast[80] to keep them from sailing out at their pleasure and so to go seek water further off.

Furthermore, he dealt very friendly and courteously with Domitius, and against Cleopatra's mind. For he being sick of an ague[81] when he went and took a little boat to go to Caesar's camp,[82] Antonius was very sorry for it, but yet he sent after him all his carriage, train,[83] and men; and the same Domitius, as though he gave him to understand[84] that he repented his open treason, he died immediately after. There were certain kings also that forsook him and turned on Caesar's side, as Amyntas and Deiotarus.

Furthermore, his fleet and navy, that was unfortunate in all things and unready for service, compelled him to change his mind and to hazard battle by land. And Canidius also, who had charge of his army by land, when time came to follow Antonius' determination, he turned him clean contrary[85] and counseled him to send Cleopatra back again and himself to retire into Macedon, to fight there on the mainland. And furthermore told him that Dicomes, King of the Getes, promised him to aid him with a great power, and that it should be no shame nor dishonor to him to let Caesar have the sea, because himself and his men both had been well practiced and exercised in battles by sea in the war of Sicilia against Sextus Pompeius; but rather that he should do against all reason,[86] he having so great skill and experience of battles by land as he had, if he should not employ the

---

79 bad ·i.e., inhospitable aspects or qualities   80 cast dug, threw up
81 ague fever   82 go . . . camp i.e., desert to Caesar's side   83 carriage,
train baggage, property, and followers   84 gave . . . understand wished
him to understand   85 turned . . . contrary i.e., entirely changed Antony's mind   86 should . . . reason would be acting wholly
unreasonably

force and valiantness of so many lusty[87] armed footmen as
he had ready, but would weaken his army by dividing them
into ships.

But now, notwithstanding all these good persuasions,
Cleopatra forced him to put all to the hazard of battle by sea,
considering with herself how she might fly and provide for
her safety, not to help him to win the victory but to fly more
easily after the battle lost. Betwixt Antonius' camp and his
fleet of ships there was a great high point of firm land that
ran a good way into the sea, the which Antonius often used
for a walk without mistrust of fear or danger. One of Caesar's men perceived it and told his master that he would
laugh if they could take up Antonius in the midst of his walk.
Thereupon Caesar sent some of his men to lie in ambush for
him, and they missed not much of taking of him (for they
took him that came before him) because they discovered[88]
too soon, and so Antonius scaped very hardly.[89] So when Antonius had determined to fight by sea, he set all the other
ships afire but threescore ships of Egypt and reserved only
the best and greatest galleys from three banks unto ten
banks of oars. Into them he put two-and-twenty thousand
fighting men, with two thousand darters[90] and slingers.

Now as he was setting his men in order of battle, there was
a captain, and a valiant man, that had served Antonius in
many battles and conflicts and had all his body hacked and
cut, who, as Antonius passed by him, cried out unto him and
said: "O noble emperor, how cometh it to pass that you trust
to these vile brittle ships? What, do you mistrust these
wounds of mine and this sword? Let the Egyptians and Phoenicians fight by sea, and set us on the mainland where we
use[91] to conquer or to be slain on our feet." Antonius passed
by him and said never a word, but only beckoned to him with
his hand and head, as though he willed him to be of good
courage, although indeed he had no great courage himself.

[Plutarch here describes the Battle of Actium, with Canidius
the general on Antony's side and Taurus on Caesar's.]

---

87 lusty vigorous, valiant   **88 discovered** revealed themselves   **89 scaped
very hardly** hardly escaped   **90 darters** spear throwers   **91 use** are
accustomed

Howbeit the battle was yet of even hand and the victory doubtful, being indifferent to both, when suddenly they saw the threescore ships of Cleopatra busy about their yard masts and hoising sail to fly. So they fled through the midst of them that were in fight, for they had been placed behind the great ships, and did marvelously disorder the other ships. For the enemies themselves wondered much to see them sail in that sort, with full sail, towards Peloponnesus. There Antonius showed plainly that he had not only lost the courage and heart of an emperor but also of a valiant man, and that he was not his own man (proving that true which an old man spake in mirth, that the soul of a lover lived in another body and not in his own), he was so carried away with the vain love of this woman as if he had been glued unto her and that she could not have removed[92] without moving of him also. For when he saw Cleopatra's ship under sail, he forgot, forsook, and betrayed them that fought for him and embarked upon a galley with five banks of oars to follow her that had already begun to overthrow him and would in the end be his utter destruction. When she knew his* galley afar off, she lift up a sign in the poop of her ship, and so Antonius, coming to it, was plucked up where Cleopatra was. Howbeit he saw her not at his first coming, nor she him, but went and sat down alone in the prow of his ship and said never a word, clapping his head between both his hands. In the meantime came certain light brigantines of Caesar's that followed him hard.

[Only when they get to Taenarus in southern Greece, after three days of speaking to absolutely no one, is Antony able to overcome his chagrin to the extent of supping and sleeping again with Cleopatra. He makes his way to Libya alone only to find it in the hands of his enemies and so eventually ends up in Egypt, once more with Cleopatra, but embittered and having been deserted by many followers including Canidius. Their life of dissipation and banqueting is governed now not by the rule of *Amimetobion,* "no life comparable," but *Synapothanumenon,* "the order and agreement of those that will die together."]

92 removed departed

Cleopatra in the meantime was very careful in gathering
all sorts of poisons together to destroy men. Now to make
proof of those poisons which made men die with least pain,
she tried it upon condemned men in prison. For when she
saw the poisons that were sudden and vehement and brought
speedy death with grievous torments, and in contrary manner that such as were more mild and gentle had not that
quick speed and force to make one die suddenly, she afterwards went about to prove[93] the stinging of snakes and ad-
ders, and made some to be applied unto men in her sight,
some in one sort and some in another. So when she had
daily made divers and sundry proofs, she found none of all
them she had proved so fit as the biting of an aspic,[94] the
which only causeth a heaviness of the head, without swoon-
ing or complaining, and bringeth a great desire also to
sleep, with a little sweat in the face, and so by little and
little taketh away the senses and vital powers, no living
creature perceiving that the patients feel any pain. For they
are so sorry when anybody waketh them and taketh them
up as those that being taken out of a sound sleep, are very
heavy and desirous to sleep.

This notwithstanding, they sent ambassadors unto Octavius Caesar in Asia, Cleopatra requesting the realm of
Egypt for her children and Antonius praying that he might
be suffered to live at Athens like a private man if Caesar
would not let him remain in Egypt. And because they had
no other men of estimation about them, for that[95] some
were fled and those that remained they did not greatly trust
them, they were enforced to send Euphronius, the schoolmaster of their children. For Alexas Laodicean, who was
brought into Antonius' house and favor by means of Tima-
genes and afterwards was in greater credit[96] with him than
any other Grecian (for that he had alway been one of Cleopatra's ministers to win Antonius and to overthrow all his
good determinations to use his wife Octavia well), him Antonius had sent unto Herodes, King of Jewry, hoping still to
keep him his friend that he should not revolt from him. But
he remained there and betrayed Antonius. For where[97] he
should have kept Herodes from revolting from him, he per-

---

93 prove test   **94 aspic** asp   **95 for that** because   **96 credit** estimation,
trust   **97 where** whereas

suaded him to turn to Caesar, and trusting King Herodes, he presumed to come in Caesar's presence. Howbeit Herodes did him no pleasure,[98] for he was presently taken prisoner and sent in chains to his own country and there by Caesar's commandment put to death. Thus was Alexas, in Antonius' lifetime, put to death for betraying of him.

Furthermore, Caesar would not grant unto Antonius' requests. But for Cleopatra, he made her answer that he would deny her nothing reasonable so that[99] she would either put Antonius to death or drive him out of her country. Therewithal he sent Thyreus, one of his men, unto her, a very wise and discreet man who, bringing letters of credit[100] from a young lord unto a noble lady, and that besides greatly liked[101] her beauty, might easily by his eloquence have persuaded her. He was longer in talk with her than any man else was, and the Queen herself also did him great honor, insomuch as he made Antonius jealous of him. Whereupon Antonius caused him to be taken and well-favoredly[102] whipped, and so sent him unto Caesar and bade him tell him that he made him angry with him because he showed himself proud and disdainful towards him, and now specially when he was easy to be angered by reason of his present misery. "To be short, if this mislike[103] thee," said he, "thou hast Hipparchus, one of my enfranchised bondmen, with thee. Hang him if thou wilt, or whip him at thy pleasure, that we may cry quittance."[104] From henceforth Cleopatra, to clear herself of the suspicion he had of her, she made more of him than ever she did. For first of all, where[105] she did solemnize the day of her birth very meanly and sparingly, fit for her present misfortune, she now in contrary manner did keep it with such solemnity[106] that she exceeded all measure of sumptuousness and magnificence, so that the guests that were bidden to the feasts and came poor went away rich.

Now things passing thus, Agrippa, by divers letters sent one after another unto Caesar, prayed him to return to Rome, because the affairs there did of necessity require his person

---

98 did him no pleasure i.e., provided him no protection or recommendation **99 so that** so long as, provided that **100 letters of credit** letters of introduction **101 liked** i.e., liked and admired **102 well-favoredly** handsomely, soundly **103 mislike** displease **104 quittance** quits **105 where** whereas formerly **106 solemnity** ceremonial splendor

and presence. Thereupon he did defer the war till the next year following. But when winter was done, he returned again through Syria by the coast of Africk to make wars against Antonius and his other captains. When the city of Pelusium was taken, there ran a rumor in the city that Seleucus, by Cleopatra's consent, had surrendered the same. But to clear herself that she did not, Cleopatra brought Seleucus' wife and children unto Antonius, to be revenged of them at his pleasure. Furthermore, Cleopatra had long before made many sumptuous tombs and monuments, as well for excellency of workmanship as for height and greatness of building, joining hard to[107] the temple of Isis. Thither she caused to be brought all the treasure and precious things she had of the ancient kings her predecessors: as gold, silver, emeralds, pearls, ebony, ivory, and cinnamon, and besides all that, a marvelous number of torches, faggots, and flax. So Octavius Caesar, being afraid to lose such a treasure and mass of riches, and that this woman for spite would set it afire and burn it every whit, he always sent someone or other unto her from him to put her in good comfort, whilst he in the meantime drew near the city with his army.

So Caesar came and pitched his camp hard by the city, in the place where they run and manage their horses. Antonius made a sally[108] upon him and fought very valiantly, so that he drave Caesar's horsemen back, fighting with his men even into their camp. Then he came again to the palace, greatly boasting of this victory, and sweetly kissed Cleopatra, armed as he was when he came from the fight, recommending one of his men-of-arms unto her that had valiantly fought in this skirmish. Cleopatra, to reward his manliness, gave him an armor and headpiece of clean gold. Howbeit the man-at-arms, when he had received this rich gift, stale away by night and went to Caesar.

Antonius sent again to challenge Caesar to fight with him hand to hand. Caesar answered him that he had many other ways to die than so. Then Antonius, seeing there was no way more honorable for him to die than fighting valiantly, he determined to set up his rest,[109] both by sea and land. So being

---

107 joining hard to adjoining hard by   **108 sally** attack   **109 set up his rest** stake everything he had. (A metaphor from primero, a gambling game.)

at supper (as it is reported) he commanded his officers and household servants that waited on him at his board[110] that they should fill his cups full and make as much of him as they could. "For," said he, "you know not whether you shall do so much for me tomorrow or not, or whether you shall serve another master; and it may be you shall see me no more, but a dead body." This notwithstanding, perceiving that his friends and men fell a-weeping to hear him say so, to salve that he had spoken he added this more unto it, that he would not lead them to battle where he thought not rather safely to return with victory than valiantly to die with honor.

Furthermore, the selfsame night, within little of midnight, when all the city was quiet, full of fear and sorrow, thinking what would be the issue and end of this war, it is said that suddenly they heard a marvelous sweet harmony of sundry sorts of instruments of music, with the cry of a multitude of people, as[111] they had been dancing and had sung as they use[112] in Bacchus' feasts, with movings and turnings after the manner of the Satyrs. And it seemed that this dance went through the city unto the gate that opened to the enemies, and that all the troop that made this noise they heard went out of the city at that gate. Now such as in reason[113] sought the depth of the interpretation of this wonder thought that it was the god unto whom Antonius bare[114] singular devotion to counterfeit and resemble him that did forsake them.

The next morning, by break of day, he went to set those few footmen he had in order upon the hills adjoining unto the city, and there he stood to behold his galleys which departed from the haven and rowed against the galleys of his enemies, and so stood still, looking what exploit his soldiers in them would do. But when by force of rowing they were come near unto them, they first saluted Caesar's men, and then Caesar's men resaluted them also, and of two armies made but one, and then did all together row toward the city.

When Antonius saw that his men did forsake him and yielded unto Caesar, and that his footmen were broken and overthrown, he then fled into the city, crying out that Cleo-

110 **board** table   111 **as** as if   112 **use** were accustomed to do   113 **in reason** understandably   114 **bare** bore

patra had betrayed him unto them with whom he had made
war for her sake. Then she, being afraid of his fury, fled into
the tomb which she had caused to be made, and there
locked the doors unto her and shut all the springs of the
locks with great bolts, and in the meantime sent unto Antonius to tell him that she was dead. Antonius, believing it, said
unto himself: "What doest thou look for further, Antonius,
sith[115] spiteful fortune hath taken from thee the only joy thou
hadst, for whom thou yet reservedst thy life?" When he had
said these words, he went into a chamber and unarmed himself and, being naked, said thus: "O Cleopatra, it grieveth me
not that I have lost thy company, for I will not be long from
thee, but I am sorry that, having been so great a captain and
emperor, I am indeed condemned to be judged of less courage and noble mind than a woman."

Now he had a man of his called Eros, whom he loved and
trusted much, and whom he had long before caused to swear
unto him that he should kill him when he did command him;
and then he willed him to keep his promise. His man, drawing his sword, lift[116] it up as though he had meant to have
stricken his master, but turning his head at one side, he
thrust his sword into himself and fell down dead at his master's foot. Then said Antonius: "O noble Eros, I thank thee
for this, and it is valiantly done of thee to show me what I
should do to myself which thou couldst not do for me."
Therewithal he took his sword and thrust it into his belly and
so fell down upon a little bed. The wound he had killed him
not presently,[117] for the blood stinted a little when he was
laid;[118] and when he came somewhat to himself again, he
prayed them that were about him to dispatch him. But they
all fled out of the chamber and left him crying out and tor-
menting himself, until at last there came a secretary unto
him called Diomedes, who was commanded to bring him
into the tomb or monument where Cleopatra was.

When he heard that she was alive, he very earnestly prayed
his men to carry his body thither, and so he was carried in
his men's arms into the entry of the monument. Notwithstanding, Cleopatra would not open the gates, but came to
the high windows and cast out certain chains and ropes, in

115 sith since   116 lift lifted   117 presently immediately
118 stinted . . . laid stopped flowing somewhat when he was stretched
out

the which Antonius was trussed; and Cleopatra her own self, with two women only which she had suffered to come with her into these monuments, triced[119] Antonius up. They that were present to behold it said they never saw so pitiful a sight. For they plucked up poor Antonius, all bloody as he was and drawing on with pangs of death,[120] who, holding up his hands to Cleopatra, raised up himself as well as he could. It was a hard thing for these women to do, to lift him up; but Cleopatra, stooping down with her head, putting to all her strength to her uttermost power, did lift him up with much ado and never let go her hold, with the help of the women beneath that bade her be of good courage and were as sorry to see her labor so as she herself.

So when she had gotten him in after that sort and laid him on a bed, she rent her garments upon him, clapping her breast and scratching her face and stomach. Then she dried up his blood that had berayed[121] his face, and called him her lord, her husband, and emperor, forgetting her own misery and calamity for the pity and compassion she took of him. Antonius made her cease her lamenting and called for wine, either because he was athirst or else for that he thought thereby to hasten his death. When he had drunk, he earnestly prayed her and persuaded her that she would seek to save her life if she could possible, without reproach and dishonor, and that chiefly she should trust Proculeius above any man else about Caesar. And as for himself, that she should not lament nor sorrow for the miserable change of his fortune at the end of his days, but rather that she should think him the more fortunate for the former triumphs and honors he had received, considering that while he lived he was the noblest and greatest prince of the world, and that now he was overcome not cowardly but valiantly—a Roman by another Roman.

As Antonius gave the last gasp, Proculeius came that was sent from Caesar. For after Antonius had thrust his sword in himself, as they carried him into the tombs and monuments of Cleopatra, one of his guard, called Dercetaeus, took his sword with which he had stricken himself and hid it; then he secretly stale[122] away and brought Octavius Caesar the first

119 **triced** hauled   120 **drawing . . . death** drawing painfully toward death   121 **berayed** befouled   122 **stale** stole

news of his death and showed him his sword that was blood-
ied. Caesar, hearing these news, straight withdrew himself
into a secret place of his tent and there burst out with tears,
lamenting his hard and miserable fortune that had been his
friend and brother-in-law, his equal in the empire and companion with him in sundry great exploits and battles. Then
he called for all his friends and showed them the letters Antonius had written to him and his answers also sent him again
during their quarrel and strife, and how fiercely and proudly
the other answered him to all just and reasonable matters he
wrote unto him.

After this he sent Proculeius and commanded him to do
what he could possible to get Cleopatra alive, fearing lest
otherwise all the treasure would be lost; and furthermore he
thought that if he could take Cleopatra and bring her alive to
Rome, she would marvelously beautify and set out his triumph.[123] But Cleopatra would never put herself into Proculeius' hands, although they spake together. For Proculeius
came to the gates, that were thick and strong and surely
barred, but yet there were some crannies through the which
her voice might be heard; and so they without[124] understood
that Cleopatra demanded[125] the kingdom of Egypt for her
sons, and that Proculeius answered her that she should be of
good cheer and not be afraid to refer all unto Caesar. After he
had viewed the place very well, he came and reported her
answer unto Caesar, who immediately sent Gallus to speak
once again with her, and bade him purposely hold her with
talk whilst Proculeius did set up a ladder against that high
window by the which Antonius was triced up, and came
down into the monument with two of his men hard by the
gate where Cleopatra stood to hear what Gallus said unto
her. One of her women which was shut up in her monuments with her saw Proculeius by chance as he came down,
and shrieked out, "O poor Cleopatra, thou art taken!" Then
when she saw Proculeius behind her as she came from the
gate, she thought to have stabbed[126] herself in with a short
dagger she ware of purpose[127] by her side. But Proculeius

---

123 triumph triumphal entry   **124 without** who were outside
125 demanded requested   **126 thought to have stabbed** intended to
stab, made an attempt to do so   **127 ware of purpose** wore for such a
purpose

came suddenly upon her and, taking her by both the hands, said unto her: "Cleopatra, first thou shalt do thyself great wrong, and secondly unto Caesar, to deprive him of the occasion and opportunity openly to show his bounty and mercy, and to give his enemies cause to accuse the most courteous and noble prince that ever was, and to appeach[128] him as though he were a cruel and merciless man that were not to be trusted." So even as he spake the word he took her dagger from her and shook her clothes for fear of any poison hidden about her.

Afterwards, Caesar sent one of his enfranchised men called Epaphroditus, whom he straitly[129] charged to look well unto her and to beware in any case that she made not herself away, and for the rest to use her with all the courtesy possible. And for himself, he in the meantime entered the city of Alexandria.

[Cleopatra refuses to yield Antony's body to Caesar; instead, she presides at his "honorable burial" with intense grief.]

Shortly after, Caesar came himself in person to see her and to comfort her. Cleopatra, being laid upon a little low bed in poor estate, when she saw Caesar come into her chamber she suddenly rose up, naked in her smock, and fell down at his feet marvelously disfigured, both for that[130] she had plucked her hair from her head as also for that she had martyred all her face with her nails; and besides, her voice was small and trembling, her eyes sunk into her head with continual blubbering; and moreover, they might see the most part of her stomach torn in sunder. To be short, her body was not much better than her mind; yet her good grace and comeliness and the force of her beauty was not altogether defaced. But notwithstanding this ugly and pitiful state of hers, yet she showed herself within by her outward looks and countenance.

When Caesar had made her lie down again and sat by her bed's side, Cleopatra began to clear and excuse herself for that she had done, laying all to the fear she had of Antonius. Caesar, in contrary manner, reproved[131] her in every point. Then

128 **appeach** accuse   129 **straitly** strictly   130 **for that** because
131 **reproved** contradicted

she suddenly altered her speech and prayed him to pardon her, as though she were afraid to die and desirous to live. At length, she gave him a brief and memorial[132] of all the ready money and treasure she had. But by chance there stood Seleucus by, one of her treasurers, who, to seem a good servant, came straight to Caesar to disprove Cleopatra, that she had not set in all[133] but kept many things back of purpose. Cleopatra was in such a rage with him that she flew upon him and took him by the hair of the head and boxed him well-favoredly.[134] Caesar fell a-laughing and parted the fray. "Alas," said she, "O Caesar! Is not this a great shame and reproach, that thou having vouchsafed to take the pains to come unto me and hast done me this honor, poor wretch and caitiff[135] creature brought into this pitiful and miserable state, and that mine own servants should come now to accuse me, though it may be I have reserved some jewels and trifles meet for women, but not for me (poor soul) to set out myself withal, but meaning to give some pretty presents and gifts unto Octavia and Livia, that they, making means and intercession for me to thee, thou mightest yet extend thy favor and mercy upon me?" Caesar was glad to hear her say so, persuading himself thereby that she had yet a desire to save her life. So he made her answer that he did not only give her that to dispose of at her pleasure which she had kept back but further promised to use her more honorably and bountifully than she would think for.[136] And so he took his leave of her, supposing he had deceived her, but indeed he was deceived himself.

There was a young gentleman, Cornelius Dolabella, that was one of Caesar's very great familiars, and besides did bear no ill will unto Cleopatra. He sent her word secretly, as she had requested him, that Caesar determined to take his journey through Syria and that within three days he would send her away before with her children. When this was told Cleopatra, she requested Caesar that it would please him to suffer her to offer the last oblations[137] of the dead unto the soul of Antonius. This being granted her, she was carried[138] to

---

132 memorial memorandum   **133 set in all** set forth all (her possessions in the memorandum)   **134 well-favoredly** handsomely, soundly
135 caitiff miserable   **136 would think for** i.e., could reasonably hope
137 oblations offerings   **138 carried** escorted

the place where his tomb was, and there, falling down on her knees, embracing the tomb with her women, the tears running down her cheeks, she began to speak in this sort: "O my dear lord Antonius, not long sithence I buried thee here, being a free woman, and now I offer unto thee the funeral sprinklings and oblations, being a captive and prisoner; and yet I am forbidden and kept from tearing and murdering this captive body of mine with blows, which they carefully guard and keep only to triumph of[139] thee. Look therefore henceforth for no other honors, offerings, nor sacrifices from me, for these are the last which Cleopatra can give thee, sith now they[140] carry her away. Whilst we lived together, nothing could sever our companies; but now, at our death, I fear me they will make us change our countries. For as thou, being a Roman, hast been buried in Egypt, even so, wretched creature, I, an Egyptian, shall be buried in Italy, which shall be all the good that I have received by thy country. If therefore the gods where thou art now have any power and authority, sith our gods here have forsaken us, suffer not thy true friend and lover to be carried away alive, that in me they triumph of thee,[141] but receive me with thee, and let me be buried in one self[142] tomb with thee. For though my griefs and miseries be infinite, yet none hath grieved me more, nor that I could less bear withal,[143] than this small time which I have been driven to live alone without thee."

Then having ended these doleful plaints and crowned the tomb with garlands and sundry nosegays[144] and marvelous lovingly embraced the same, she commanded they should prepare her bath; and when she had bathed and washed herself, she fell to her meat and was sumptuously served. Now whilst she was at dinner there came a countryman and brought her a basket. The soldiers that warded[145] at the gates asked him straight[146] what he had in his basket. He opened his basket and took out the leaves that covered the figs and showed them that they were figs he brought. They all of them marveled to see so goodly figs. The countryman laughed to hear them and bade them take some if they would. They be-

---

139 of over   **140 they** i.e., our enemies   **141 that . . . of thee** so that through me they, our enemies, triumph over you   **142 self** single, same   **143 bear withal** bear with, endure   **144 nosegays** bouquets   **145 warded** stood guard   **146 straight** at once

lieved he told them truly, and so bade him carry them in. After Cleopatra had dined, she sent a certain table[147] written and sealed unto Caesar and commanded them all to go out of the tombs where she was but the two women; then she shut the doors to her. Caesar, when he received this table and began to read her lamentation and petition requesting him that he would let her be buried with Antonius, found straight what she meant and thought to have gone thither himself; howbeit, he sent one before in all haste that might be to see what it was. Her death was very sudden, for those whom Caesar sent unto her ran thither in all haste possible and found the soldiers standing at the gate, mistrusting nothing nor understanding of her death. But when they had opened the doors, they found Cleopatra stark dead, laid upon a bed of gold, attired and arrayed in her royal robes, and one of her two women, which was called Iras, dead at her feet, and her other woman, called Charmian, half dead and trembling, trimming the diadem which Cleopatra ware upon her head. One of the soldiers, seeing her, angrily said unto her, "Is that well done, Charmian?" "Very well," said she again,[148] "and meet for a princess descended from the race of so many noble kings." She said no more, but fell down dead hard by the bed.

Some report that this aspic was brought unto her in the basket with figs and that she had commanded them to hide it under the fig leaves, that when she should think to take out the figs the aspic should bite her before she should see her; howbeit, that[149] when she would have taken away the leaves for the figs, she perceived it and said, "Art thou here, then?" And so, her arm being naked, she put it to the aspic to be bitten. Others say again[150] she kept it in a box and that she did prick and thrust it with a spindle of gold, so that the aspic, being angered withal, leaped out with great fury and bit her in the arm. Howbeit few can tell the truth. For they report also that she had hidden poison in a hollow razor which she carried in the hair of her head; and yet was there no mark seen of her body or any sign discerned that she was poisoned, neither also did they find this serpent in her tomb.

147 table tablet   148 again in return   149 that i.e., people report that
150 again on the other hand

But it was reported only that there were seen certain fresh steps or tracks where it had gone on the tomb side toward the sea and specially by the door side. Some say also that they found two little pretty bitings in her arm, scant to be discerned, the which it seemeth Caesar himself gave credit unto, because in his triumph he carried Cleopatra's image with an aspic biting of her arm. And thus goeth the report of her death. Now Caesar, though he was marvelous sorry for the death of Cleopatra, yet he wondered at her noble mind and courage, and therefore commanded she should be nobly buried and laid by Antonius, and willed also that her two women should have honorable burial.

Cleopatra died being eight-and-thirty year old, after she had reigned two-and-twenty years and governed above fourteen of them with Antonius.

Text based on *The Lives of the Noble Grecians and Romans Compared Together by That Grave, Learned Philosopher and Historiographer, Plutarch of Chaeronea. Translated out of Greek into French by James Amyot . . . and out of French into English by Thomas North. . . . Thomas Vautroullier . . . 1579.* Whether Shakespeare read this edition or one of the subsequent editions of 1595 and 1603 (the 1603 text was reprinted in 1612) is not certain, but the differences are minor.

In the following, the departure from the original text appears in boldface; the original reading is in roman.

p. 165 **his** this

Further Reading

Adelman, Janet. *The Common Liar: An Essay on "Antony and Cleopatra."* New Haven, Conn.: Yale Univ. Press, 1973. Adelman's rich and suggestive book explores uncertainty in the play: uncertainties of the audience when confronted with contradictions and conflicting judgments, uncertainties about the lovers inherent in the source material Shakespeare draws upon, and uncertainties experienced by the protagonists and their observers onstage. Adelman traces this emphasis as it becomes itself the informing principle of the play's organization, unifying its language, theme, and structure.

Barroll, J. Leeds. *Shakespearean Tragedy: Genre, Tradition, and Change in "Antony and Cleopatra."* Washington, D.C.: Folger Books, 1984. Believing that Shakespeare was "predisposed to approach the idea of 'tragedy' from traditional vantage points," Barroll first examines the philosophical and literary traditions that Shakespeare draws upon, especially Saint Augustine's "emotion-oriented theory of human psychology." Barroll's reading of *Antony and Cleopatra* then focuses on the psychological complexity of the title characters as well as the "moral structure" of the play, as part of a larger argument about the nature of tragedy itself.

Beckerman, Bernard. "Past the Size of Dreaming." In *Twentieth Century Interpretations of "Antony and Cleopatra,"* ed. Mark Rose. Englewood Cliffs, N.J.: Prentice-Hall, 1977. Beckerman explores how the theatrical organization of the play focuses our attention not primarily on its epic sweep and splendor but on the subtle movements and tenuous communication of the love that Shakespeare has designed his play to frame.

Bono, Barbara J. "The Shakespearean Synthesis: *Antony and Cleopatra.*" *Literary Transvaluation: From Vergilian Epic to Shakespearean Tragicomedy.* Berkeley, Los Angeles, and London: Univ. of California Press, 1984. Bono focuses on Shakespeare's transformation of his source material, especially Virgil, and argues that the playwright's act of creative revaluing is mirrored in the actions of Cleopatra, who imaginatively reforms a repressive Roman world. Throughout the play, Cleopatra challenges Roman social and sexual barriers, offering instead a synthesis of opposing values through her assertions of androgyny, intimacy, and creative love.

Bradley, A. C. "Shakespeare's *Antony and Cleopatra*." *Oxford Lectures on Poetry*, 1909. Rpt., New York: St. Martin's Press, 1959. Bradley probes the differences between *Antony and Cleopatra* and the four major tragedies, arguing that in this play Shakespeare strives for unique and extraordinary effects, reserving all tragic force for the final scenes. The play, according to Bradley, leaves us not with sorrow but with pleasure: as the lovers lose the world, they gain our sympathy and admiration.

Burke, Kenneth. "Shakespearean Persuasion: *Antony and Cleopatra*." *Language as Symbolic Action*. Berkeley, Calif.: Univ. of California Press, 1966. Burke is interested in the play's rhetoric of persuasion: how it manipulates an audience into sympathy with the lovers. He argues that Shakespeare begins by identifying and adorning love with the play's—and Elizabethan England's—imperial theme, and then reverses direction, denying the lovers' grandeur and domesticating their love. Burke uses his analysis of the patterns of identification achieved by the play to generate a suggestive psychology of tragic response.

Charney, Maurice. "The Imagery of *Antony and Cleopatra*." *Shakespeare's Roman Plays: The Function of Imagery in the Drama*. Cambridge: Harvard Univ. Press, 1961. Charney focuses on the dominant verbal and visual imagery that underscores the play's central concerns and conflicts. The hyperbolic rhetoric of cosmic images and imperial vocabulary establishes a frame of reference that is ultimately devalued as the lovers become greater than the world they lose. Charney also examines the contrasting rhetorical styles of Rome and Egypt as they organize and focus the moral choices of the play.

Coleridge, Samuel Taylor. "*Antony and Cleopatra*." *Coleridge's Writings on Shakespeare*, ed. Terence Hawkes. New York: G. P. Putnam's Sons, 1959. Coleridge's high praise of *Antony and Cleopatra* has been influential in raising

critical estimation of the play; indeed, he finds it the
equal of the four major tragedies. He admires its sus-
tained artistic strength, especially as it explores the
energy and depth of Cleopatra's passion.

Daiches, David. "Imagery and Meaning in *Antony and Cleopatra*." *English Studies* 43 (1962): 343–358. Rpt. in *More
Literary Essays*. Edinburgh: Oliver and Boyd; Chicago:
Univ. of Chicago Press, 1968. Daiches locates the moral
center of *Antony and Cleopatra* in the protagonists' confrontation with experience as they play various roles and
search for identity. The play is both a triumph and a tragedy, rising above limited conceptions of morality, as the
lovers achieve in death what eluded them in life.

Dollimore, Jonathan. "*Antony and Cleopatra* (c. 1607): *Vir-
tus* under Erasure." *Radical Tragedy: Religion, Ideology,
and Power in the Drama of Shakespeare and His Contem-
poraries*. Chicago: Univ. of Chicago Press, 1984. Rejecting
Romantic claims that the play celebrates a love that transcends power and the forces of history, Dollimore argues
instead that *Antony and Cleopatra* is preeminently concerned with exploring the structures of sexual, political,
and military power. He sees Antony's desire for Cleopatra
as a compensatory infatuation in the face of Antony's loss
of an identity that was founded on the very power structure he is willing to sacrifice for her.

Doran, Madeleine. " 'High Events as These': The Language
of Hyperbole in *Antony and Cleopatra*." *Shakespeare's
Dramatic Language*. Madison: Univ. of Wisconsin Press,
1976. Doran explores the language of hyperbole, first as
an Elizabethan rhetorical trope expressing the ideal of
excellence and then as the dominant rhetorical device in
Shakespeare's play. The effect of the play's hyperbole is
neither "to overwhelm our judgment" nor to "sharpen
our critical faculty"; rather it serves "to give us a sense of
pleasurable participation in a credible, but rare, experience."

Goldman, Michael. "*Antony and Cleopatra*: Action as Imaginative Command." *Acting and Action in Shakespearean
Tragedy*. Princeton, N.J.: Princeton Univ. Press, 1985. Goldman sees *Antony and Cleopatra* as a play about greatness—a radiant attribute possessed by the lovers that
enables them to command others' imaginations (though

not always their political loyalties). This greatness depends upon a charismatic power to charm, and, by extension, to transform, to make the morally questionable into the dramatically valuable.

Hibbard, G. R. "Feliciter audax: *Antony and Cleopatra* I.i. 1–24." In *Shakespeare's Styles: Essays in Honour of Kenneth Muir*, ed. Philip Edwards, Inga-Stina Ewbank, and G. K. Hunter. Cambridge and New York: Cambridge Univ. Press, 1980. Hibbard moves from a close and illuminating analysis of the opening lines of the play to a broader consideration of style in *Antony and Cleopatra*. The dominant features of its style—exemplified in Philo's speech—are a clarity and distinctiveness of imagery, and a remarkable mingling of the hyperbolic and the familiar.

Kaula, David. "The Time Sense of *Antony and Cleopatra*." *Shakespeare Quarterly* 15 (1964): 211–223. Rpt. in *Essays in Shakespearean Criticism*, ed. James L. Calderwood and Harold E. Toliver. Englewood Cliffs, N.J.: Prentice-Hall, 1970. Focusing on "the special importance of time in the play," Kaula argues that the major characters strive to create and preserve a stable sense of self in the face of the "turbulent flux of events" and the "instability of desire." Their efforts of self-fashioning are shaped by their sense of what aspect of time is most significant: for Caesar it "is the future; for Antony, the past; for Cleopatra, the present."

Mack, Maynard. "*Antony and Cleopatra:* The Stillness and the Dance." In *Shakespeare's Art: Seven Essays*, ed. Milton Crane. Chicago: Univ. of Chicago Press, 1973. For Mack, *Antony and Cleopatra* relentlessly generates multiple perspectives and unresolved polarities. Mack penetratingly explores these oppositions as they derive from the play's sources and as they are organized by the play. The "thrust of history," represented by Caesar's implacable power, and the timelessness and escape from mutability implied by the rhetoric of love, both find powerful voice in this play of "defiant pluralism."

Markels, Julian. *The Pillar of the World: "Antony and Cleopatra" in Shakespeare's Development*. Columbus, Ohio: Ohio State Univ. Press, 1968. Markels argues that *Antony and Cleopatra* marks a decisive moment in Shakespeare's dramatic exploration of the conflict of public responsibility and private desire. The play seeks a fusion of Roman ideals of honor and Egyptian conceptions of emotional fulfillment, resolving their opposition in a "vision of the immortal joining of public and private values."

Miola, Robert S. "*Antony and Cleopatra:* Rome and the World." *Shakespeare's Rome.* Cambridge: Cambridge Univ. Press, 1983. Within a broad consideration of Shakespeare's evolving concept of Rome and Roman values, Miola explores the presentation of that city in *Antony and Cleopatra* as both the locus of heroic value and as an arena for political infighting and self-interest. He argues that Antony's struggle to maintain his nobility in the face of contradictory pressures mirrors the struggle of Rome itself to remain true to its ideals.

Ornstein, Robert. "The Ethics of the Imagination: Love and Art in *Antony and Cleopatra.*" In *Later Shakespeare,* ed. John Russell Brown and Bernard Harris. Stratford-upon-Avon Studies 8. London: Edward Arnold; New York: St. Martin's Press, 1966. For Ornstein, *Antony and Cleopatra* celebrates the triumph of both love and art. The final scene proclaims the honesty of the imagination and the superiority of its truths to the paltry historical claim of conquering Caesar. As Cleopatra attains immortality in her final spectacle, so Shakespeare affirms the paradox that the artist's imagination embodies the most enduring reality.

Rackin, Phyllis. "Shakespeare's Boy Cleopatra, the Decorum of Nature, and the Golden World of Poetry." *PMLA* 87 (1972): 201–212. Rackin sees that the play dramatizes the tension between a rational, Roman calculus of value, which discounts "the seductions of rhetoric and the delusions of the senses," and an Egyptian delight in "theatricality." Shakespeare's representation of Cleopatra's suicide resolves the ambivalence; it signals the triumph of theatricality and art itself, as Cleopatra transcends the brazen world of history.

Stein, Arnold. "The Image of Antony: Lyric and Tragic Imagination." *Kenyon Review* 21 (1959): 586–606. Rpt. in *Essays in Shakespearean Criticism,* ed. James L. Calderwood and Harold E. Toliver. Englewood Cliffs, N.J.: Prentice-Hall, 1970. Stein explores the centrality of the lyric (the "expression of unapologetic imagination") in

Antony and Cleopatra, locating this impulse in the reality Antony creates through his magnanimous character and gestures. The lyric's "rightness of feeling," which demands our admiration, is necessarily overcome, though not extinguished, by the inevitable triumph of time and tragedy.

Waith, Eugene M. *The Herculean Hero in Marlowe, Chapman, Shakespeare, and Dryden*, pp. 113–121. New York: Columbia Univ. Press, 1962. Waith sees Antony as a type of the "Herculean hero," a tragic figure whose energy and intensity are uneasily contained within society. Antony follows this paradigm in his rage, his love, and his heroic determination that set him at odds with Roman values. Cleopatra "both accentuates and modifies" the Herculean pattern, as Antony finally commits himself not to Rome but to love.

Memorable Lines

You shall see in him
The triple pillar of the world transformed
Into a strumpet's fool.   (PHILO   1.1.11–13)

Let Rome in Tiber melt and the wide arch
Of the ranged empire fall! Here is my space.
Kingdoms are clay.   (ANTONY   1.1.35–37)

The nobleness of life
Is to do thus.   (ANTONY   1.1.38–39)

I love long life better than figs.   (CHARMIAN   1.2.34)

Eternity was in our lips and eyes,
Bliss in our brows' bent.   (CLEOPATRA   1.3.35–36)

O happy horse, to bear the weight of Antony!
                                            (CLEOPATRA   1.5.22)

"Where's my serpent of old Nile?"
                                (CLEOPATRA, quoting ANTONY   1.5.26)

My salad days,
When I was green in judgment.   (CLEOPATRA   1.5.76–77)

The barge she sat in, like a burnished throne,
Burnt on the water. The poop was beaten gold;
Purple the sails, and so perfumèd that
The winds were lovesick with them.
                                    (ENOBARBUS   2.2.201–204)

Age cannot wither her, nor custom stale
Her infinite variety.   (ENOBARBUS   2.2.245–246)

Celerity is never more admired
Than by the negligent.   (CLEOPATRA   3.7.24–25)

Let's have one other gaudy night.   (ANTONY   3.13.186)

Now he'll outstare the lightning. To be furious
Is to be frighted out of fear.   (ENOBARBUS   3.13.198–199)

Where souls do couch on flowers, we'll hand in hand,
And with our sprightly port make the ghosts gaze.
Dido and her Aeneas shall want troops,
And all the haunt be ours.   (ANTONY   4.14.51–54)

                     But I will be
A bridegroom in my death, and run into 't
As to a lover's bed.   (ANTONY   4.14.99–101)

O sun,
Burn the great sphere thou mov'st in; darkling stand
The varying shore o' the world!   (CLEOPATRA   4.15.10–12)

                  Shall I abide
In this dull world, which in thy absence is
No better than a sty?   (CLEOPATRA   4.15.62–64)

Let's do 't after the high Roman fashion
And make death proud to take us.   (CLEOPATRA   4.15.92–93)

His legs bestrid the ocean; his reared arm
Crested the world; his voice was propertied
As all the tunèd spheres, and that to friends;
But when he meant to quail and shake the orb,
He was as rattling thunder.   (CLEOPATRA   5.2.81–85)

                  For his bounty,
There was no winter in 't; an autumn it was
That grew the more by reaping.   (CLEOPATRA   5.2.85–87)

                  His delights
Were dolphinlike; they showed his back above
The element they lived in.   (CLEOPATRA   5.2.87–89)

. . . The bright day is done,
And we are for the dark.   (IRAS   5.2.193–194)

I shall see
Some squeaking Cleopatra boy my greatness
I' the posture of a whore.   (CLEOPATRA   5.2.219–221)

A woman is a dish for the gods, if the devil dress her not.
                                     (CLOWN   5.2.273–275)

I wish you joy o' the worm.   (CLOWN   5.2.279)

Give me my robe. Put on my crown. I have
Immortal longings in me.   (CLEOPATRA   5.2.280–281)

O, couldst thou speak,
That I might hear thee call great Caesar ass
Unpolicied!   (CLEOPATRA   5.2.306–308)

THE BANTAM SHAKESPEARE COLLECTION

The Complete Works in 28 Volumes

Edited with Introductions by David Bevington

Forewords by Joseph Papp

Ask for these books at your local bookstore or use this page to order.

Please send me the books I have checked above. I am enclosing $___ (add $2.50 to cover postage and handling). Send check or money order, no cash or C.O.D.'s, please.

Name _____

Address _____

City/State/Zip _____

Send order to: Bantam Books, Dept. SH 2, 2451 S. Wolf Rd., Des Plaines, IL 60018
Allow four to six weeks for delivery.
Prices and availability subject to change without notice.   SH 2 3/96

Contributors

DAVID BEVINGTON, Phyllis Fay Horton Professor of Humanities at the University of Chicago, is editor of *The Complete Works of Shakespeare* (Scott, Foresman, 1980) and of *Medieval Drama* (Houghton Mifflin, 1975). His latest critical study is *Action Is Eloquence: Shakespeare's Language of Gesture* (Harvard University Press, 1984).

DAVID SCOTT KASTAN, Professor of English and Comparative Literature at Columbia University, is the author of *Shakespeare and the Shapes of Time* (University Press of New England, 1982).

JAMES HAMMERSMITH, Associate Professor of English at Auburn University, has published essays on various facets of Renaissance drama, including literary criticism, textual criticism, and printing history.

ROBERT KEAN TURNER, Professor of English at the University of Wisconsin–Milwaukee, is a general editor of the New Variorum Shakespeare (Modern Language Association of America) and a contributing editor to *The Dramatic Works in the Beaumont and Fletcher Canon* (Cambridge University Press, 1966–).

JAMES SHAPIRO, who coedited the bibliographies with David Scott Kastan, is Assistant Professor of English at Columbia University.

✤

JOSEPH PAPP, one of the most important forces in theater today, is the founder and producer of the New York Shakespeare Festival, America's largest and most prolific theatrical institution. Since 1954 Mr. Papp has produced or directed all but one of Shakespeare's plays—in Central Park, in schools, off and on Broadway, and at the Festival's permanent home, The Public Theater. He has also produced such award-winning plays and musical works as *Hair*, *A Chorus Line*, *Plenty*, and *The Mystery of Edwin Drood*, among many others.